AFTERMATH

Keiah Ellis

I hope you enjoy the read, Shon! Stay blessed, my friend!

Keriah P Ellis

Special Thanks

To my Mom and Dad, Adrian and Vicki, for believing in me, and for, without hesitation, allowing me to pursue my dream. You two have always been there for me, and I am privileged to know you as parents, and as people. I am blessed to call you my friends, and I will love you both for all eternity. I thank my God at every remembrance of you both! I will always be your baby girl!

To all of the wonderful women that God has placed in my life, Melissa, Rose, Ashley, Nikia, Chrissy, Angel, and all my Friends of Faith, for your encouragement and support concerning this project. I couldn't ask for greater friends than you guys! I love you all, and can't wait for the next one!

To Jeanie and Steve Nichols, because without that week of refreshing, rejuvenation, and God-time in the cabin, this book may never have happened. You guys are such a blessing, and I love you both dearly!

And to everyone who showed such great enthusiasm when I told them about this venture. Here it is! Enjoy!

Ty sighed deeply as his grandmother lectured him for what seemed like the hundredth time that day. It wasn't that he didn't love his grandmother, or even value her opinion, but when she got going on her religious kick, he found himself tuning out.

"Ok, Grandma, I get it. But you have to understand. *I'm not going to college!*" Ty snapped fiercely. Guilt immediately set in and he regretted his tone. He didn't mean to snap at her, but his frustration from repeating himself over and over again, day after day, had just gotten the best of him.

"Baby, you are wasting your gift." The spirited old woman continued talking as though the young man had not said a word. "God gave you that artistic ability, and you ain't doing nothing with it. Do you know how many people would give life and limb to draw like this?"

Mrs. Casey held up the drawing she had found, examining it closely as Ty stood up to leave.

"Yeah, yeah, Gran. But what good has this 'gift' done me so far?" He took the picture gently from her wrinkled hands, and kissed her tenderly on her cheek. "I've got to go now, or I'm going to miss the game."

The thing with Ty was that he really was a good kid. He felt so bad leaving his grandmother there, shaking her head at his choices.

He never meant to hurt her or disappoint her. He wanted to make her proud. He would have given anything to just tell her that she was right and he was going to be the man she always pictured him to be—strong, wise, educated, loving. He wanted to be important and to make something of himself. He wanted his life to make a difference in the lives of others. But the circumstances of his present life had just knocked him down and sent him spinning in a direction he never intended to go.

He had never gotten into any real trouble. A bad report here and there was all he was guilty of. Considering what he had been through at such a young age, he had overcome a mountain of odds that were stacked against him. But lately, he was beginning to get more and more anxious. He couldn't put his finger on what it was, but something had begun to eat at him. He was feeling discontent with where his life was, but was unable to find direction or guidance to push him toward where he wanted to be. He was becoming increasingly bored at school and had begun to be disruptive and disrespectful to his teachers.

After getting several calls from his school, Mrs. Casey sat the sixteen year old down and laid down the rules. He knew that she was not joking, and that if he wanted to see the light of another day, he'd better straighten up. She was an old woman—74 years old to be exact—but Ernestine 'Teenie' Casey did not play around. Especially when it came to the life and future of her only grandson. He had already been through so much, and she refused to give up on him and let him fall by the wayside.

After abandoning his grandmother at the kitchen table, Ty headed straight for his bedroom. His grandmother believed he was preparing to go to the park and play some basketball, but his plans were entirely different. He was searching frantically for his stash of spray paint.

I've got twenty minutes before the train comes, he thought to himself. *I've got to get out of here! Where is my paint?*

As he continued to rummage around, a menacing darkness began to rise on the inside of and all around him, and he became more and more agitated. He felt a sudden surge of inner pressure as time ticked away. He knew he had to move fast if he was going to make it to his train on time. It seemed as though spray painting graffiti on trains was his only place of solace these days, and today felt particularly important—like something much deeper than just an urgency to get there on time.

I'd better get a move on.

~

Leisa Carson sat back and sighed happily, drinking in the beauty of nature that was all around her. *How can anyone experience a day like this and not believe there is a God? I know His doings when I see them, and this is definitely His handiwork!*

She had decided to take a "beauty break" from the monotony of daily chores. Whenever she had a long to-do list ahead of her, she would break the list down into groups of chores, and after each group was completed, she would stop for a few minutes and do something she considered meaningful. One of her favorite things to do was to take a glass of lemonade out to the hammock that hung between the two old trees in the backyard she shared with her husband. She would just lie there and enjoy the breezes that blew over her, or watch the clouds float slowly by above her head. She loved these times. She prayed and sang songs and just enjoyed all that God's creation had to offer her. It was her chance to stop and smell the wildflowers, both literally and figuratively. It helped to keep the mundane nature of things from driving her insane—or at least from dissolving her usual cheeriness into a flood of tears as she thought about how repetitive and ordinary her life seemed to have become.

Today's chores, however, didn't seem so bothersome. Today, she was preparing for the arrival of her twenty-two year old daughter, whom she hadn't seen in three months. This day was special, and nothing could stop her heart from singing for joy. The woman, born her daughter, who had now become one of her dearest friends, was on her way to town!

As she settled back into the hammock, eyes closing contentedly, peace flooded Leisa's soul. She could feel a sweet presence all around her, inviting her to come deeper. She heard a clear whisper, saying, "No matter what, I am here. Trust in me. Don't ever lose heart."

She quickly opened her eyes, hoping to catch a glimpse of the one to whom the whispering voice belonged, but no one was around. Still, she knew, *someone* was there.

~

"You were great—as usual." Mr. Grimly smacked his devilish lips. He zipped up his pants, and quickly gathered the rest of his clothes. He casually walked over to where she sat on the hotel bed, and roughly took her face in his hand. She struggled to pull away, but he held her with a fierce grip, forcing her to meet his gaze. He looked intently in her eyes, his own gleaming with lust and wicked pleasure. He smirked at her discomfort, pulling her closer to him. He leaned over, moving his lips slowly toward hers, as though he were going to kiss her, but just as their lips nearly met, he suddenly turned her head with a violent jerk. With his sickening breath hot on her face, he whispered in her ear, "Don't forget, sweetheart. This is our little secret. Tell anyone, and you're dead." He kissed her neck, and released her, as bitter, salty tears streamed down her face. She clutched the sheets tightly around her, counting silently the moments until he left the room. What he didn't know was that in her heart and mind, Raegan had already been dead for a long, long time.

~

"You're amazing. You know that?" Jason pulled Mya close to him and wrapped his strong arms around her.

She smiled up at him. "I've heard that a time or two. Is that why you love me so much?" She playfully wrapped her arms around his neck, and looked into his bright blue eyes.

He kissed her gently on her forehead, and took her face in his hands. "*Totally.* I've never met anyone else like you. You're the most incredible person I know. And I'm glad you're mine."

Mya giggled, feeling lightheaded and giddy. She had never experienced anything like this before, and she almost couldn't believe it was real. Who knew that she would find the man of her prayers at such a young age? They had already been through so much together, and she was beginning to believe this was love. She saw a bright future when she looked into his eyes.

Jason smirked as he watched his girlfriend drift off into her own little world of deep thought. She did that all the time. "Penny for your thoughts, pretty girl," he said, bringing her back to their present conversation as they stood in the park.

"I was just thinking that I'm glad you're mine too." This was the sappiest, and sweetest moment she had ever experienced—she could almost hear the romantic violin and piano music in the background swell to a climax, just like it would in a good chick flick, just as the guy gets the girl—and she drank in every intoxicating second of it. She felt like she was in a dream. This was the kind of moment she prayed she wouldn't wake up from. *The only thing that could make this moment absolutely perfect is if you were Jesus' too*, she thought. But that was a whole other topic for a whole other day.

~

"Mr. Hudson, Edward Carson is here to see you." D.T. Hudson's office intercom buzzed to life, startling him out of his afternoon daydream. He had been looking out the window, gazing at the beautiful city view he had from his high rise corner office. He pressed the button.

"Send him in, please. Thank you."

A few seconds later, the door of DT's office swung open. Behind it stood a grinning Edward Carson.

"Hey, there, Mr. Hudson!" he greeted his boss warmly.

"Ed, how are you? Come on in, and sit down. And quit calling me Mr. Hudson!" DT smiled as he walked from behind his desk and shook Edward's outstretched hand, shutting the door behind them.

The two men had been working together for the last ten years, and had become good friends. Edward loved to play around with the superior-subordinate dynamic, often calling his pal *Mr. Hudson* just to get a rise out of him. His Southern charm constantly drew chuckles out of DT, and the two greatly enjoyed one another's company.

"What's all the hoopla about, Ed? You seem to be in a great mood today! Most people would be mad to be at the job on a beautiful Saturday like today! I almost asked what have you been smoking, but I know you are much too holy for that!" The two laughed. Edward had spent the last few years trying to persuade DT to re-evaluate his life and turn to Christ. Edward was very proud of his walk of faith, and shared it whenever he was given the chance. DT admired him, and knew that there was a lot of truth to what he said, and he watched the way the Carson's lived their lives. To be honest, he was jealous, because even without all of the riches and honor that DT possessed, Edward Carson was living the life DT dreamed of.

"I do have a little extra bounce in my step, don't I? It must be because my Annie is coming home today! Finally! You know how much I love that girl! I have missed her, and she is finally coming to visit with her Daddy. It's been three whole months since I saw her last! This morning she boarded a train headed here."

DT *did* know how much Edward loved his daughter. He heard about her almost as much as he heard about Jesus, and had the pleasure of watching her grow up through her teenage and college years. She was a beautiful young woman, and she loved the Lord as much as she loved her parents. She was kind, and got along well with anyone she met. He'd always said that if he had a daughter, he would want her to be just like Annette Carson. She never went through that rebellious teen stage, and had excelled in college. She had been a journalism major, and moved to New York City to pursue a career in Christian magazine editing after she graduated. She was quite successful, and brought a great deal of pride and joy to her parents.

The amazing thing about Annette was that as close as she was to her father, she was just as close to her mother, and had a wonderful relationship with them both that transcended the biological bond of parents to children.

"Well, yeah, I guess that *would* put you in a good mood, now wouldn't it, Eddie? Maybe I can take you and your girls to dinner tonight. On me? Does that sound good?"

"Come on now, DT. You don't have to twist my arm! You know if you're treatin', I'm eatin'!" Edward exaggerated his natural Southern drawl to emphasize his enthusiasm in eating on his friend's dime. But all he really cared about was seeing his sweet little girl.

"Well, good! But I know you didn't come in here to hunt down a free meal, so what did you need?"

"Oh, yeah! I did almost forget what I came in here for! You said that you had pulled some resumes for the three openings you want me to fill. I came to get those. You got 'em handy?"

"Yeah. I gave them to Cheryl to run off copies for me. Hold on a second." DT reached over to the intercom button and tapped it. He asked his secretary to bring in the files he was looking for. She brought him a stack of folders. DT turned serious as he handed the folders over to Edward. "Here they are. I'm going to give you these and let you do your job as my human resources manager and sort them out. Now these are three of the most important positions we've ever had to fill. So, you'd better pick the right ones or…" he stopped speaking and used his finger to draw a line across his throat. "You got me?" He looked at his friend for a moment, straining to keep a straight face. When he couldn't hold it any longer, he let out a guffaw that nearly shook the walls. "Oh, man, Ed! You should have seen the look on your face. I always said you were pasty, but I think you went transparent right then! I really had you going there for a minute!"

His friend snatched the folders from his hands. "Mr. Hudson, that just ain't even right! You know my mind's not all here today! And then you're gonna go and pull something like that on me! Why, I oughta…!"

"Watch it now, or that offer for dinner will be taken off the table!"

"In *that* case, as you wish, sire!" Edward adopted a fake British accent to deliver his last verbal jabs. He managed a fake curtsy to match. "Shall we give you a ring later to iron out the details for dinner this evening, Your Majesty?"

DT laughed. "Now *that* sounds like a plan."

~

The train station was crowded that day. Many people stood around, lingering, listening, and watching for some sign that their wait had come to an end. Some waited to board a train to take them to a far away land, while others waited for the arrival of the ones they loved. Total strangers until now, they were knitted together by the common thread of waiting, if only for a moment.

Finally, off in the distance, the crowd heard the screech of the conductor's whistle, and began to gather their belongings in anticipation of the train's arrival. As people made their way to the platform, none could have foreseen what would come next. They all watched in stunned horror as the train, coming around the curved stretch of track toward them, seemed to jump its track, and smashed into the freight train that sat motionless on the track next to it. Several of the passenger cars derailed behind the engine car and turned over on their sides. The engine of the passenger train burst into flames, and billows of black smoke began to fill the crisp afternoon air.

Ty stood on a nearby hillside, paralyzed, disbelieving the events that were unfolding right before his eyes. He had dropped his backpack, and its contents now spilled out onto the ground in front of him. He held up his arm to shield his nose and mouth, as he began to choke on the smoke that was trying to fill his lungs. Had he been just minutes earlier, he would have been a part of the scene playing out below, not just a bystander. He would not know this side of heaven how close he'd come to being a casualty that day.

~

Meanwhile, in a scene taking place in a realm unseen by the naked eye, but more existent than the physical reality we know, the enemy of man's soul was thrashing about.

"Where is the incompetent idiot sent to take him out?" Satan's hatred for all oozed from the very core of his being. Holding nothing sacred, even his own legions were subject to his wrath. Every vile word he spoke dripped with the slime of his arrogance and sent shivers of vast emptiness and cold down the hearers' spines. He slithered about, scorn and disdain flashing in his darkly evil eyes, daring any to come forward and address him.

"Master?" the word had barely left the mouth of the blameworthy demon before Satan had his neck in an inescapable grip, his feet off the ground, dangling helplessly.

"You useless piece of garbage! Good-for-nothing, bumbling imbecile! What do I have to do to get anything done around here?

You couldn't complete the simple task of killing the boy!" The other demons crowded around, like wolves on a carcass, hissing and growling as they clamored for blood from one of their own. Hellburn squirmed and twisted, trying to release himself, but Satan had no intentions of letting him go that easily. He lifted him high above his head, and threw him hard and far across the chambers of his lair. Hellburn laid still for a moment, but was quickly re-energized and slithered back for more. The fear and wickedness present there worked as fuel for the occupants of the Godlessly dark and empty space.

Speaking to the reprimanded demon, he threatened, "I will give you one more chance at this. He already saw our masterpiece of a crash, and is now ready to be eliminated. This time, he is right on the edge. All you have to do is push…him…over."

Satan resumed his pacing, slinking to and fro, anxiety and frustration forbidding him to stop. The stench of dead, rotting, and burning flesh coupled with the indescribable sounds of torment, torture and regret calmed him temporarily, but the urgency of his short allotted time brought him back to his tirade.

"Do you misfits have any idea what we are up against? Our time is short! We must complete our task! This boy is danger to us, and we must stop him now! No more mistakes! *He must be eradicated*!" The words leaked from his mouth like bile from a decaying corpse. "And all these angels that are in our way must be *defeated*!" His last words were especially odious, as he remembered in his heart his former self. At his very core, he was a worshipper, a Light bearer, and the protector of the very presence of God. He had once stood as close to the throne as was possible. Yet, somehow his worship had turned to himself, and the same angels he had once been a leader of, he was now archenemy to, set to stop their work at any cost. He had lost his rightful place, and was now determined to steal that place from all others.

All he had to do was get Ty to the train tracks, he thought to himself. He looked out over the sea of evil minions before him. His voice trembled, seething with anger, disgust, and murderous hatred, "Listen here, you pathetic, worthless maggots, get out there and do what we do best. The crash, killing all those people, that was the easy part. Now comes the hard part—it's time to work on the living. Some of these people are just hanging on by a thread, so hit them where it hurts! Steal their joy, kill their families, destroy their lives! Tell them that they are worthless. Tell them that God hates them. Tell them that things will never get better. Tell them anything! I don't care what you tell them, just get it done! Hellburn, you know your job. Now *do it*."

Turning his back to the mass of demons who had taken that fateful fall from grace with him, he took little comfort in the murmurings of their praise. He had seen what this boy and the people of that sleepy little town were capable of if left untouched. This was bigger than what any of them knew, and Satan was scared.

~

High above the earth, in the glorious third heaven untouched by sin, the God of all creation watched the events below. The atmosphere surrounding Him was full of goodness and light unimaginable to the human heart. Ever present and aware of all, both inside and outside the realm of time, sadness filled His heart. But in the twinkling of an eye, righteous indignation set in and He called forth his angels.

"My faithful servants..." The host of them stood at attention, with Michael and Gabriel at the forefront. "You are always ready, and now the time has come." His voice, the sound of heralding trumpets and the rush of many waters, boomed across heaven's vast beauty. Pure unadulterated love wrapped every word like a gift, and strengthened the hearts of its hearers. "I promised My children that no weapon formed against them would prosper, and I keep My promises, even into eternity. The enemy has risen against them, and I have heard their cries. So now, my trusted and fearless warriors, I charge that as you mount guard around and about them, you also encourage them and remind them that I will never leave them nor forsake them. I have not forgotten them, nor turned My back on them. I am always with them, to the ends of the earth, and I know their ends from their beginnings. I have not abandoned them, and this is all in My plan. Tell them my love for them is everlasting, and in Me, they have nothing to fear."

The angels began to move about, positioning themselves for service. The Lord stepped over to the top of a stairway that led down into the earth realm. He stood firmly, watching and approving, as the angels went swiftly to and fro. Like a flood, the angels moved in one motion to obey the call of the Lord, and to minister to His people.

Chaos erupted in every direction. People shouted and scrambled to get close enough to see what was happening. For now, a haze of thick gray and black smoke restricted visibility.

"What happened?"

"Is everyone alright?"

"Can anyone see what happened?"

"Try to get down there and help!"

"Are they hurt?"

People began milling around helplessly, coughing and choking in the smoky air, eyes burning and watering, looking to one another to answer questions. Suddenly, the sound of sirens cut through the gathering darkness. Rescue workers barreled through the crowds, faces obstructed by masks meant to shield them from the smoke, shouting orders as they passed.

"We need everyone to back up! Everyone needs to get back! Get off the platform!" They began tossing luggage off to the side of the train platform. "People, please! Move! We have to make way to get these people to the emergency vehicles! Please, grab as much as you can, and help us clear a pathway! Quickly!"

People began frantically grabbing whatever items they could get their hands on in the semidarkness. No one cared whose bags were whose. They worked as a team to give the rescue workers as much room as they needed.

The sound of helicopter blades broke through the sound of the people clamoring about. The fast spinning motion drove away some of the smoke, allowing the witnesses to get a clearer view of the crash scene. People had begun to crawl out of the wreckage, and staggered around, disoriented and injured. The sound of yells and cries from deep within the twisted metal and mangled track began to filter up to the platform. The helicopter touched down on the side of the train station, and more emergency crew members jumped out and rushed to help. Dogs trained to sniff out and detect signs of life in crises were also brought to the scene.

Firefighters arrived in fire trucks, and began unloading their hoses. The fire had subsided slightly, but without acting quickly to put it out completely, the workers ran the risk of an explosion and more injuries and, possibly, fatalities.

~

Leisa watched in dismay as the television screen flashed aerial pictures of the rescue workers trying to reach injured people in the train wreckage. Coverage of the breaking news story had interrupted her afternoon lineup of home and garden shows, as she swept the kitchen floor. She dropped her broom, and grabbed the remote. She turned the volume up, and held her breath as she listened for more information.

She looked over at the clock and realized that it was very close to the time that her daughter's train was scheduled to arrive into town. *Oh, please, God, don't let that be Annie's train! PLEASE let her be alright!* she silently prayed.

She jumped as the phone rang loudly beside her. She picked it up quickly, hoping that it was her daughter saying that she was fine and had been nowhere near the train accident.

"Hello?" she said, anxiously.

"Leisa?"

"Eddie!" she was glad to hear her husband's voice, but concerned that it was not Annie on the line. "Eddie, where are you?"

"I'm still at work. Did you hear what happened?" He sounded out of breath.

"Yes, I'm watching right now. Have you heard from Annie?" She waited, wanting desperately to hear a *yes* from the other end.

"No! I was calling to see if you had heard from her!" Edward's voice rose, evidencing his rising panic.

Leisa's voice caught in her throat, as she tried to reassure her husband. "I'm sure she will be calling any minute. She probably can't get through with all the chaos at the station. We will just wait. But can you come home right now? Why don't you come home, and then we will wait for her call together, ok?"

Leisa heard herself speaking, but felt as though she were not the one doing the talking. Her voice was surprisingly calm, but her insides were a tangle of knots. She knew something was not right. Why wouldn't Annette have called yet? If she had arrived on time, and was at or near the train station when this accident occurred, she had to know that they were worried about her. And she always charged her cell phone, so she shouldn't be without battery power.

"Hello? Leisa? Did you hear me?" Ed had still been talking to his wife as she sat, nearly frozen in fear, lost in her own thoughts, and now waited for her response.

"I'm sorry, Eddie. What did you say?"

"I said that I will be home in a few minutes. Will you please call Annie's cell phone and see if you can reach her? I will see you in a bit."

"Alright. I will do that." She paused. "Eddie? I love you. It's going to be alright, ok?"

Ed distractedly answered, "I love you too. Please call Annette." The phone went dead.

As Leisa reached down to dial the phone number she had come to know by heart, she remembered her hammock experience earlier that day. It seemed like ages ago, but she remembered that peaceful calm that had settled over her when she heard that whisper.

Lord, that was you, wasn't it? What are you saying? What is happening?

Her hands trembled as she dialed, and her breath caught in her chest as she prayed that her daughter would pick up. The phone rang several times.

"Hi! This is Annette Piper! I can't come to the phone right now, but please leave me a message! I will definitely get back to you as soon as I can! Jesus loves you, and I hope you have a wonderful day! Bye!" Annette's cheerful voice on her answering machine was almost too much for Leisa to bear.

"Annie! It's Mom! Honey, please call me as soon as you get this message! Please!" Leisa quickly hung up, not wanting the sounds of her sobs to be caught on the recording. Her heart felt like lead in her chest, and she could not control the tears that welled and burned in her eyes. She sank to her knees in the middle of the kitchen floor and a foreboding sense of distress flooded her soul as the tears fell into her lap.

Leisa knew that all was not well. If she could help it, Annie always answered her phone, especially when one of her parents called. Something had to be very wrong.

Lord! Leisa's heart cried out from deep within her. *I'm scared! Please help me!*

Fear clutched Leisa's heart with a grip that she had never felt before, threatening to consume her where she sat. Gasping, she tried to calm herself down. She knew that if she was going to come out of this thing with her sanity and faith intact, she could not let fear overcome her.

"Father", she whispered weakly, "please help me!"

~

Teenie shook her head in disbelief as she listened to the continuing coverage of the train wreck that had occurred earlier that afternoon.

"Oh, Father, I know this must break Your heart. I know You are there with those people. Holy Spirit, do Your work and send Your comfort and peace to everyone involved. Let them know that Your plan is still at work here." Teenie stood up from the couch she had been reclining on and began to pace the floor of her tidy little living room, praying as she moved.

"We may not understand it down here, but, Lord, I know that Your hand is in everything that happens in this world. Your eyes are on us at all times. You are not the author of chaos or disaster, but You can turn any tragedy for our good. Please do that, Heavenly Father.

Show up and show out in this situation. You are a good God, and I love you, Lord! In Jesus' mighty and precious name, amen."

The old woman began humming quietly, still listening to the reporters discuss the accident. She looked at the clock on the fireplace mantle, glad that her own grandson was safely across town, out of harm's way. He probably had not heard about the wreck yet, since he was on the basketball court, away from televisions and radios. She knew he would be home by the time the sun went down, and she hoped that they could pray together for the victims when he got back.

The reporter on the news station solemnly looked into the camera. "We're told the death toll has just risen to twenty one people," she said. "There are many more injured, and the authorities fear that the number of dead will rise as night falls."

"Oh, Jesus! Be with the families tonight, Lord. Let them feel you tonight stronger than they ever have. They need to know you are always there with them."

Just then, Teenie felt the strongest urge to call Leisa Carson. Knowing the nudge of the Holy Spirit when she felt it, Teenie rushed over to her telephone. She didn't know why she was calling or what she was to say, but Teenie had lived long enough and walked with the Lord far enough to know that He would instruct her as she obeyed. She prayed as she dialed the Carson's house phone.

"Lord, guide me. Give me the words to say in due season."

Suddenly, Leisa's hopeful voice answered. "Annie?"

"No, baby, this is Teenie. Are you alright?"

"Oh, Teenie!" Leisa's voice cracked, and Teenie could hear her tears through the phone.

"Leisa, what is it?"

"It's Annie! I haven't heard from her. She was on a train on her way here and I can't get in touch with her! Teenie, I'm scared! What if she was on that train? What if she is hurt? What am I going to do?"

"Leisa! Listen to me! You start praying *right now*! I am coming over!" Teenie hung up the phone and grabbed her purse. She stopped for a moment to scribble a quick note to her grandson telling him where she was going, should he get home before she returned. She then rushed out the front door, slamming it behind her, and slid into her car.

"Oh, Lord. I don't know what is going on, but I trust You. Please guide me! Please help me to know what to do and say. Whatever is going on here, use me for Your good. I surrender myself to You right now."

Teenie was grateful that the roads were relatively clear and that the Carsons did not live more than ten minutes away from her. She pulled into their driveway just as Edward Carson turned in behind her. She got out of the car as quickly as she could, and hurried over to hug him as he got out of his car. The two headed toward the house.

"I heard what happened! Edward, don't you worry about anything! It's going to be alright." She stopped walking and turned the man to face her. She looked him squarely in his eyes and asked sternly, "Did you hear me? We trust the Lord in all circumstances. Don't you let the enemy get to you, ok? You've got to stay strong right now!"

Tears glistened in the corner of Ed's eyes as he nodded his agreement to Mrs. Casey. "Yes, ma'am."

The two resumed their quick pace toward the house. Leisa had seen them pull into the driveway and she now stood at the front door. She threw her arms around her husband and her friend when they reached her. She began sobbing again, and her husband lost control of his tears and began weeping. The old woman pulled away from the couple.

"Come on," she said softly, leading the two inside the house. She closed the door quietly behind them, and took each by the hand. She led them, like young children, over to the couch, and sat down between them, pulling them close to her.

Neither seemed to be able to stop crying, and she did not try to make them. She just rocked them tenderly, and began humming her song from earlier that afternoon.

"My sweet Annie Pie!" Leisa cried out the nickname for her daughter that she hadn't used in many years.

"Hush, hush now, Love," Teenie quieted the younger woman down. "Just relax. We can't get all worked up about what we don't know, baby. We just need to trust in the Lord and wait. Don't give up. It's gonna be alright."

When the couple's tears finally subsided, both stayed in the comfort of the old woman's arms. The three sat quietly for a few moments. Finally, Teenie broke the silence and spoke.

"Now, you all have cried and worried over what you think has happened. But are y'all ready to pray?"

Leisa and Edward sat up slowly and looked at one another. Both nodded.

"Let's show the devil that no matter what, God's gonna get the glory! I don't know what has happened, or if Annie is coming home or not, but any way it goes, the Lord is worthy of our praise. We've got to put our faith on this! We don't know what the Lord is doing, and our fear will only stop His mighty hand! Whether she's here or there, I know in my heart of hearts that Annette is just fine. We've got to exercise our faith and praise the Lord through this storm. Ok? We can't just sit here, worrying ourselves into a tizzy about what we don't even know for sure. But we do know for sure that God hears us when we call. So let's pray." While she spoke, Teenie slid forward on the couch and slowly stood up. She reached out her hands and helped Leisa and Edward to their feet as well.

She hugged each one of them tightly, and lifted her eyes up toward the ceiling.

"Heavenly Father, hear our humble cry this afternoon. If ever we've needed You, Lord, we need You right now." Teenie began to pray, taking the hands of Leisa and Edward in her own.

Leisa began whispering words of adoration and supplication to the Lord. "I love you, Lord. And I know that your ways are higher than mine and your thoughts are higher than mine. Please help me through what is happening. I don't want to lose my baby. She's my best friend. Lord, help me. I need you. Give me your peace. Fear is trying to grip me, and Lord, I am not strong enough to fight it on my own. Please!" Her voice trailed off as the tears began to flow anew. But this time, mixed with the concern and sadness, was a renewed sense of calm. It was as though Leisa could feel the hand of God holding her up.

Edward's head hung low as he searched his heart for words to say. He was so racked with raw emotion that his voice had no sound when he tried to speak. He wanted so badly to open his mouth and cry out words of faith, but he only felt emptiness inside.

My baby girl is gone. I just know it, he thought to himself. It was all he could do not to scream at the top of his lungs. Not knowing for certain was eating him from the inside out.

"Oh, God! Why hasn't she called?" Edward startled himself and the women in the room with his sudden outburst. He hadn't realized that he was speaking aloud. He looked over at Teenie. She and Leisa had both stopped praying and stared back at him. He dropped Teenie's hand and slowly backed away from the two women.

"I'm sorry. I just…I'm just not…I can't." Edward struggled to find the right words to express how he felt. When none would come, he turned away and walked toward the master bedroom at the back of the house.

Leisa started after him, but Teenie shook her head. "It's alright, sweetheart. Let him go for now."

~

Raegan lay back against the pillows in the bed. She closed her eyes and took a deep breath.

I wonder if death hurts.

She thought about dying often. It seemed as though no one would care one way or the other if she were alive or not. Everyone had their own thing going. Mya was her very best friend in the world, but it seemed like even they didn't have much in common these days. Mya was so caught up in her church stuff and her boyfriend, Jason, that Raegan always felt like a last minute obligation or a charity case that Mya felt like she needed to fix.

And it wasn't even that she didn't like Jason. She actually really did. He wasn't as fanatical about religion as Mya was. He was more like Raegan in that area. They didn't mind that Mya was into it, but it wasn't necessarily for them. But lately, even Jason was getting more involved in the church. So, that left Raegan out, too.

Mya had always been a Christian, but it seemed like, after last summer, she had taken it to another level. She was constantly talking to Raegan about Jesus and the Bible, and trying to get Raegan to fully commit her life to Christ and to begin attending church regularly. Raegan didn't mind, and had even considered doing it for a while. She was just concerned because she had been hiding this disgusting secret from Mya, and felt that if Mya knew the truth, she would stop being her friend for sure. And certainly with all the mess that was going on in her life, this Jesus man would not want her to contaminate his church members.

Sundays were some of the hardest days for Raegan. One of her teachers at school, Mrs. Carson, was very good friends with Mya. They belonged to the same church and had become especially close over the past year. Mrs. Carson started having special Sunday evening dinners at her house, and would invite Mya and a few others from their church over, and Mya often invited Raegan to come too. She loved the idea of it but hated going, all at the same time. Going there, to that beautiful house, with those cheerful people, talking and laughing and eating together like a family, reminded Raegan of everything she was not.

They were such a wonderful group. Mr. and Mrs. Carson were very active in their church community and had made many dear friends along the way. Mrs. Carson was a wonderful cook, and hospitality seemed to run in her veins. She and Mr. Carson had an "open kitchen" policy and loved the extra company whenever people came over. Each Sunday they invited Mya, who in turn invited Jason and Raegan, and Mrs. Teenie Casey, who usually brought her grandson, Ty.

Raegan's heart fluttered a little when she thought of Ty. From the day that they met, officially, at one of those dinners, she had felt a strange connection with him. It wasn't only that she was physically attracted to him. There was something more—something deeper—that drew her to him. Not usually shy, Raegan found herself unable to look directly at him, and smiling timidly every time he caught her eye. It was as if she were afraid that if he got a good look, he would see all the things that she was trying to hide. Sometimes she felt as if he could read everything that was going on with her, even in the depths of her soul.

She quickly tried to push thoughts of him out of her mind. *A guy like him would never want a girl like me,* she thought. *I'm used goods. And I don't have anything worthwhile to offer him anyway.*

It was an ideal October afternoon in Faries, Georgia. Mya smiled as she walked hand in hand with Jason along the pathway beside the park's duck pond. It had been a beautiful day, and it was turning into a gorgeous evening. Brisk breezes blew over them, and Mya snuggled a little deeper into her cardigan.

"Are you getting cold?" Jason noticed Mya's shiver.

"A little, but it's ok. I love this kind of weather!"

"Yeah, me too. It gives me an excuse to hold you a little tighter!" Jason tugged gently on Mya's hand, drawing her against his side, and wrapped his arm around her.

Mya sighed contentedly, and leaned against Jason as they walked. She felt so safe with him, and seemed to fit flawlessly beside him. But things hadn't always been so wonderful for the two of them. They'd had a rocky start, and several times Mya had wondered if they would survive as a couple. The thing was, it wasn't Jason and Mya who had the issues. It was people's reactions *to* them being together that gave them the most heartache.

Jason Charles Harrington was the all-American boy, sweet, and easy going. He had always been tall for his age, and was now already a few inches over six feet at age seventeen. He'd gotten his height and his athletic build and ability from his father. His thick, dark hair, bright blue eyes and toothy smile were from his mother. He kept a tan most of the year, as he was an avid outdoorsman and loved to be in the sunshine whenever he could, often traveling to fun and sunny places for school functions and family vacations. From the time he was young, people told him all the time what a good-looking guy he was, but it never seemed to go to his head. He was well liked by his classmates, teachers and friends, and could never be called shy. He loved to laugh and was constantly cracking jokes.

Mya Lafleur was the only child of two devoutly Christian parents. They had been high school sweethearts and got married shortly after they both graduated college. After four years of marriage, the Lafleurs decided they were ready to have children and prayed for a little girl. They tried for several months, but failed to conceive. They were unable to get any answers from the doctors to explain their difficulties. Finally, after another year of praying and trying, Mya was born. Her mother joyfully named her Mya Symone, which meant "my God is listening," because, after such a long battle, the Lafleurs prayers were answered and they at last held their daughter in their arms.

Mya was an undeniably beautiful girl. She was what many called an "old soul", reflecting the elegant style and grace of women of the early decades of the twentieth century. But her mother was careful to constantly reinforce Mya's inner beauty, not just her physical beauty, and Mya grew confident in her own sense of being very early on. She was a striking young woman, with smooth, milk chocolate colored skin, big, round dark brown eyes, and beautiful, soft black hair. She loved to change her hairstyles often. Sometimes she wore it natural, her tight curls held back with headbands and scarves. Other times she straightened it and wore it in a short pixie haircut. Sometimes she corn-rowed it into elegant ponytails at the nape of her neck. She viewed her hair as an accessory to be changed and transformed to match her attitude or outfit. She was tall and leggy, and she loved to dress to accentuate her features. She was regarded as the fashionista among her friends, and was often looked to for advice and ideas.

But despite her physical appeal, people were even more drawn to Mya's sweet spirit. She was definitely a pretty young woman on the outside, but anyone who met her agreed that her true allure came from somewhere deep inside. She was raised in church, and had loved and served the Lord from an early age. She was loved by her peers and was considered a role model by the adults in her life. She was kind and respectful, and humble despite her good looks, and always did her best to make everyone feel valued. Her parents often told her not to seek the love and approval of the "popular" crowd, but to look for the people who are on the outskirts—they usually ended up being the better friends. Mya took that message to heart, and made it a habit to be inclusive rather than exclusive in every-thing she was a part of.

She and Jason met the summer after their eighth grade school year. Jason's family had just moved to Faries from Burney, Pennsylvania, and his parents put him into sports camp over the summer to try to help him make some new friends before he started his freshman year in high school that fall. When his parents first told him of their planned move to Georgia, Jason had had mixed emotions about it. On the one hand, he had been a little sad because he really liked the city he was leaving, but, on the other, he loved meeting new people. He would be going into high school that next year and knew that things would be different anyway, but still wasn't sure that a move to a whole new state was really what he wanted.

He had also heard a lot of negative remarks and comments about the "South" and the people who lived there. They were not like his family and friends in Pennsylvania. Some words he'd heard quite often were "racism" and "prejudice." In his hometown, everyone was friendly, and got along with everyone else. There was not a lot of concern with differences among the people. Many of them had grown up together in the town and were like family, with relationships and connections dating back several generations. But even so, Jason's parents had diligently taught him to be open and good to everyone, including people who looked or acted or dressed or spoke differently than he did. He couldn't honestly say that he had met many people who were so drastically different from him and his family, but after he moved to Georgia, the value of those lessons proved to run quite deep. He just couldn't have predicted how soon he'd find that out.

That summer, Mya was participating in the same sports camp as a cheerleader. She was friendly and kindhearted, and got along with everyone there. She was very popular among the campers, and was voted "Most Spirited" at the end of the summer. By the end of camp, her name was known by everyone who participated, including Jason.

Mya had been very excited about cheerleading camp that summer. She loved spending time with other cheerleaders, and it would be her first year as team captain. She was relatively athletic but, for a cheerleader, and just about everything else in the rest of her life, she did not fit the typical mold. She was much taller than most of the girls, standing 5'7 compared to their 5'4 and shorter frames, but her peppy personality and inviting magnetism had made her the natural choice for captain. She had a "ready for anything" attitude that was contagious. But as she packed her bags that fateful summer, finding the love of her life had been the last thing she was prepared for.

Jason excelled at most sports, so he fit right in at the camp, becoming one of the most highly spoken of athletes of the entire group of campers. His chosen sport of that summer was baseball, and Mya had quickly taken notice of his natural athleticism. She liked to watch him practice swinging and catching with the other guys, and she often told her friends how handsome she thought he was. After a few weeks, she was asked to help organize a camp social, and had made plans to introduce herself formally to him.

Mya's charm had not been lost on Jason either. He heard about her constantly from the other campers and coaches, and often saw her around, always smiling and trying to help everyone. She was happy and bubbly, and loved what she was doing. No one seemed to have anything bad to say about her, and Jason hoped that he would get to know her personally. She seemed like the kind of girl he had always had his heart set on.

For as long as he could remember, most of the girls in Jason's life wanted to be his girlfriend, and he often found himself at the center of their affections, with each girl desperately vying for his attention. He didn't mind it, and enjoyed spending time with some of the girls, but he hadn't been in a serious relationship, and didn't feel as though any of those girls who liked him were the one he wanted to be with for the long term.

He didn't consider himself especially picky, but he was developing a stronger sense of what he was looking for. He had always been an active person, and he could not stand when girls were clingy and whiny when he couldn't be with them 24/7. He loved to hunt and fish, and he was very involved in sports, and that left little time for dating and relationship drama. His family and friends were always quick to advise him that he was too young for all that anyway. But when he met Mya Lafluer that summer, everything he thought he believed began to change.

~

DT gathered his briefcase and a stack of important papers from his cluttered desk. He figured he was the last one to leave the office that day, so, feeling no real need to rush, he moved slowly as he prepared to call it quits. He had an early flight out the next day, and he was not so thrilled about it. His business trips always seemed to end with him doing something he regretted and wished he hadn't.

Concern for the Carson's also rose up inside him. Edward had come rushing back to his office a little while ago, saying something about a train wreck and needing to get home. Of course, DT sent him home immediately. He hoped that Annette wasn't one of the people affected by the accident, but he wasn't entirely sure of what was even happening. He made a mental note to call Edward once he got into his car. He also reminded himself to call Raegan Nottaway to see if she would water his plants while he was away for the next couple of weeks.

Raegan was a lovely young lady that he had hired to take care of his plants and basic house maintenance while he was away on business trips. Her father was an employee of DT's oil company, and he knew the family pretty well. DT felt as though there were many secrets within the Nottaway household, but with all the things about himself he was trying to keep a tight lid on, he was not going to touch that subject with a ten foot pole.

Raegan seemed like a nice girl, but he could tell that she lacked self esteem. That was hard to understand, because she was one of the single most attractive young women he had ever laid eyes on. She could easily have been a model. She and her best friend Mya made quite an exquisite team, each possessing a beauty that could not be ignored. Raegan had a creamy complexion, the color of rich caramel, and big loose curls that framed her beautifully featured face. She was medium height, with an hourglass figure that was undoubtedly the envy of women twice her age. Her face was flawless. She had the loveliest mouth, with straight white teeth and naturally pouty lips. Her nose was perfectly symmetrical on her face, not too big and not too small. And she had the most piercing gray eyes. But they were sad. Whenever DT saw her, those sad gray eyes were the thing he always noticed. There was an anguish that lay deep inside her, and when he looked into her eyes, he couldn't help but feel that pain. DT was not sure what hurt she tried to hide with her pretty smile, but he knew that everything was not alright with her.

He dared not question her about it. He had no children of his own, or real experience with them to help him with the situation he faced with Raegan. And although he desperately wanted to do something to help her, he felt so powerless around her, because even if she did let him in on what was wrong, what could he do? He knew from experience that all the money in the world was not going to help if your soul was not well. And what else besides money could he offer her? His own life was in such shambles that it would be hypocritical of him to try to tell someone else how to fix her life.

DT shook his head, trying to snap himself out of his wandering thoughts. Now was not the time to get caught up in outside drama.

He had plenty of his own issues to deal with, and now he didn't have much time before he was supposed to be somewhere.

He quickened his pace and finished gathering the last of his of belongings. He used his remote control to close the blinds of his office and turn out the lights. He then left his office and locked the door behind him. As he walked down the hall and rounded the corner beside the elevator, he nearly dropped the armload of papers and his briefcase when he bumped into someone coming toward him from the other direction.

"Marcus! You scared me! What are you doing here? I thought I was here alone."

The young man smiled at him and said, "I'm sorry, sir. I didn't mean to frighten you. I just came by to get some paperwork. You're heading out of town tomorrow, right?" Marcus looked intently into DT's eyes.

"Um, yes. I've got a few meetings I have to attend out in south Louisiana, in New Orleans. It's just boring business stuff, but it shouldn't be too bad." DT stammered on. "Are those my financials for the month you're looking at?"

Marcus nodded. "Yes, sir. Nothing on them is going to change while you're gone, is it?"

DT felt as though this were not even really a question, but more of a command. He smiled sheepishly at the man. "No, Marcus. It won't."

Marcus held DT's gaze for a second longer. "Alright. Well, have a good trip. We can discuss things when you get back." He reached over and shook DT's hand with a firm grip. He then turned and walked back toward the row of office doors down the hallway. DT readjusted the papers and things in his hands, and then looked back toward where Marcus had headed, but the young man was nowhere to be seen.

Terrified, Ty could hardly catch his breath, and the smoke surrounding him threatened to burn a hole in his lungs. He stooped down and scooped up his spray paints and shoved them back into his backpack. He hoisted the pack onto his shoulder and turned around to head away from the mayhem taking place before him. He coughed a few times, and started jogging quickly to try to get out of the smoke's pathway.

As he moved, he wondered whether he should head straight home or go somewhere else first. His grandmother thought he was going to play basketball and wouldn't be expecting him for at least a few hours. The basketball courts were on the other side of town from the train tracks, so if he showed up now and told her what had happened, she would want to know why he was at the tracks and not on the courts like he told her he would. So unless he wanted to go back, admit that he had lied to his grandmother about where he was going, and never leave his house as a free man again, going home right then was out of the question.

"Well then, where do I go?" he wheezed aloud, still gasping. He had finally gotten far enough away from the train station that he was no longer under the cloud of smoke pouring from the wreckage, and could feel a gentle breeze blow past him and the sun was warmer on his face, but he still felt like his lungs were on fire. He paused for a few moments, taking the backpack off his shoulder, and gulped down a few deep breaths of fresh air. Then he walked slowly on for a few more minutes, dragging his pack behind him, before he finally collapsed onto the ground.

His mind reeled as he lay back on the grassy slope. When he closed his eyes, he could still see the train seemingly hiccup and bounce off the track, slamming into the freight train beside it. He could hear the roar of fire as the engine ignited. He could still smell the smoke that poured from the twisted and mangled metal. He could hardly believe what he had just seen, but his labored breathing and watery eyes told him it was no dream. He had not made that scene up in his own mind, and he knew that what had just happened would have devastating effects on the people involved.

Realizing that he almost *was* one of those people really shook Ty up. He had been so determined to be right there beside those train tracks so that he could tag the train and be gone before anyone even knew he was there. Had he gotten to the place he wanted when he intended to, he would have been right in the spot where the first car derailed. He would no doubt have been burned badly or killed by the explosion.

Suddenly, Ty remembered the feelings he'd had when he was searching for his paints in his room earlier that morning. Now that he thought about it, his paints had been exactly where he thought he had left them, yet he couldn't find them when he looked. It was as though they were hidden in plain sight. He also remembered how whatever else had been with him in his room that morning had pushed him so strongly to get to the train tracks at that exact moment. He recalled what sounded like an evil hiss, and the cold chill that had run down his spine while he rummaged around. He shuddered and tried to rub down the goose bumps that had just arisen on his arms.

He then thought about his grandmother. She was always telling him that the hand of the Lord was on him and that he had a great destiny in front of him. She always told him that the devil and his demons were after him and if he didn't fearlessly stand up and accept Christ, he ran the real risk of being out from under God's hedge of protection and an open target to be taken out by the devil. She also told him of the angels that were surrounding him, protecting him and looking out for him. She told him how these angels and demons were involved in his everyday life, whether he recognized it or not.

She was always telling him things like that. She talked about all the wonderful things she believed the Lord had in store for him, and how important he was. There were demons sent just for him, because he had a purpose and they wanted to stop him. But there were even more angels that knew his name and did everything they could to stop the plans of those demons, and who were sent specifically to help him get to where he was supposed to be. She seemed to know that Ty was headed for greatness, but Ty couldn't see that for himself. He loved his grandmother so much. But she seemed to know God in a way that he never would. It was like she talked to God and He talked back to her. Very often, she would know something that was going on with Ty that he hadn't shared with anyone. When he asked her how she figured stuff out, she would smile and say, "The Holy Ghost don't keep no secrets!"

Ty knew that God existed. And he believed that God loved him. What he didn't understand was if God were so great, and Jesus died for everyone's sins and all, why didn't God stop bad things from happening to His people?

Ty's thoughts drifted to his mother. She had been a kind, but troubled young woman. She was very intelligent, but had gotten mixed up in the wrong sphere of people. She had gotten hooked on drugs and alcohol in her early twenties, but had stopped using briefly when she found out she was pregnant with Ty. She tried to stay clean and sober after Ty was born, but the pull of her addictions proved to be too great. When Ty was twelve years old, she brought him to live with Teenie, his maternal grandmother.

At first, Ty's mother had tried to keep in regular contact with him, but after a few months, her calls and visits dwindled to nothing. Ty knew that she loved him, but she was just not able to break the stronghold of dependence on drugs that had a death grip on her soul. For a while, Ty kept on believing that his mother would get herself clean and come back to be a real part of his life. He would constantly wait for phone calls and knocks at the front door, hoping against hope that it would be her on the other end. It very rarely was.

Teenie had done her best to raise her grandson in a healthy, Godly environment. She consistently talked to him about the Lord, and made sure that he attended church with her. She knew that the moment her daughter walked away from her relationship with the Lord was the moment her troubles began. She was determined not to have that happen with her only grandson. She spoke words of faith to Ty about his mother and about his future. She frequently told him what a great man of God he was, and how he had the potential to change the world for Christ if he would accept and live for Him. She showed him a positive outlook on everything they faced, and prayed without ceasing. Often, she invited him to pray with her. Together, they would pray that the Lord would bring Ty's mother back to her right mind and that she would abandon the drugs and return to their lives. They had prayed for her protection and her safety, and her health. Ty had begun to sincerely consider accepting Jesus as his savior, and was steadily making changes toward living a life for the Lord.

And then they had gotten a call. There was a woman in the hospital, and her identification information had led authorities to Teenie. The woman had overdosed on what appeared to be a heroin and vodka binge, and was on a respirator. She was clinically brain dead, but the hospital did not want to make any decisions before at least trying to contact the woman's family. They asked Teenie to come to the hospital and verify if the woman was indeed her daughter.

In her heart, Teenie had known it was. She drove up to the hospital that fateful evening, nearly three years ago, and talked with the doctors. She signed all of the necessary documents, and asked for a few moments alone with her daughter before they turned the life support machines off. Ty had refused to come to the hospital with her, and she hadn't felt led to make him come see his mother one last time. She entered the hospital room, and the tears began to flow down her cheeks. She had done her best to never imagine the picture that was now a reality in front of her. She never wanted to see her precious daughter like that, thin and frail from the drugs, with tubes and wires attached to nearly every surface of her body. Teenie walked over and took her daughter's limp hand.

"Lord, I know my baby strayed from You. I know that she walked away from the truth she knew. But Your Word says that nothing can separate us from the love of Jesus Christ. I believe that, Lord. And I know that she believed in Jesus as the Son of the Most High God, who died for her sins. You said that made her saved. You said that she would have eternal life if she believed that and confessed it with her mouth. Lord, just give me peace in the midst of this. Help me to stand strong for my dear Tyler. Help him, Jesus. This is going to be hard for him. This isn't something a child should ever have to go through. But You said that You would be with us through the valley of the shadow of death and You would never leave us, nor forsake us. Please, Lord, show us Your mighty hand in this awful situation. Don't let me lose Tyler. Be with us, precious Lord."

Teenie leaned over and kissed her daughter's forehead. "Mama loves you, sweet girl," she whispered. She softly put the woman's hand back onto the hospital bed and turned to leave the room. Sadness gripped her heart, and the tears continued to stream down her face. But in her heart, she knew that things were going to be alright. An unearthly tranquility had enveloped her as she moved toward the door. As she walked out of the hospital room, a pretty nurse stepped in front of her, startling her slightly.

"Excuse me, ma'am. I don't mean to frighten you," she began. Teenie looked at the woman. Something seemed vaguely familiar about her. "I don't know if you remember me. Your name is Ernestine Casey, right? Teenie?"

Teenie nodded. She searched her brain, trying to recall the woman. There was something so comforting about the woman's face and voice, but Teenie could not figure out why. She had an air of gentleness about her, but there was a glow of resolute strength in her eyes as she looked at Teenie.

"My name is Adabel. You may not remember me, but I was one of your husband's nurses." The pieces fell together for Teenie as the woman spoke. She remembered that this was the nurse that had sat in the hospital with her into the wee hours of the morning during her husband's illness a few years earlier. They had prayed together and sang songs of praise together. The woman had been a source of strength and comfort to Teenie during one of the most difficult periods of her life. She had been with Teenie the day she saw her husband for the last time. And then, there she appeared, at her side again as she said goodbye to her daughter.

"Adabel!" Teenie threw her arms around the woman in a solid embrace. It was as though she were seeing a dear old friend after years of being apart. All of the emotions of seeing her daughter and knowing that it would be the last time she'd see her alive, mixed with the joy of seeing Adabel again, all came rushing out. She began to weep again, and Adabel tightened her grip on the older woman.

The two had stood there for a long time. Finally, Teenie stepped back and dried her eyes. She smiled sheepishly at Adabel. "Seems like I am always blubbering like a baby when I get around you!"

Adabel chuckled. "I've got two sturdy shoulders made just for you to cry on!" she said. Then she paused. "It's good to see you, Teenie. I hate that it's for a reason like this." Both women looked toward the door of Teenie's daughter's room.

"Yes, me too," Teenie agreed quietly.

"Teenie, I know this is hard for you. But you have to listen to me. I have an important message for you." There was a sharp urgency in Adabel's voice that had made Teenie quickly look back at her. Adabel looked deep into Teenie's eyes as she spoke. "You can not stop praying. I know that you believed for your husband to recover from the cancer that took his life. And I know you believed and prayed for your daughter to be delivered from her addictions. And I know that it's hurtful and confusing to see that it looks like your prayers weren't answered. But you have to keep on believing!"

Teenie stood incredulous. It was as though Adabel had been reading her mind at that very second. She had just been thinking how she had truly been standing on God's Word for her husband and daughter, and how she didn't understand why they were allowed to die. Her faith was taking a beating, and she wondered if she could handle it. She had been a child of God for over half a century, but at that very moment, with her daughter lying practically dead in the next room, and her husband gone and unable to stand with her, she felt alone and helpless like a newborn baby, cast away by its mother, unable to fend for herself. She hadn't wanted to say any of it aloud, but in her spirit, she was embroiled in a battle that she felt like she was losing. She was in complete turmoil.

"This is just a test of your faith. The Lord will never give you more than you can handle. He has not forgotten you or cast you away. You don't have to defend yourself. The Lord is your defense! You are not forgotten, and you are not alone. He knows exactly what's going on here, and if He didn't know that you were going to come out of this thing as more than a conqueror, He would not have allowed the enemy to step in. If there was not a plan in motion here, He wouldn't let these things go on. This is so much bigger than you understand. But you have to keep praying. Keep praying for Tyler. Keep standing strong before him. He needs to see your faith in action. Your prayers and the Word that you speak sends forth angels to work on your behalf. That's where your power lies. And Tyler needs to know that even though life doesn't always go the way we planned, God is still on the throne, and His plan is always at work. He needs to see that you don't just serve the Lord when things are going well. He needs to realize that there is a real enemy out there, who seeks to destroy, but greater is He that is in you than he that is in the world! This is such a critical time in Tyler's life. He needs you to stand in the gap for him, Teenie."

Adabel's sincerity had touched Teenie to her core. She couldn't remember telling the woman about Ty, but she figured she must have at some point during her husband's hospital stay. There had been so much going on at that time that she hardly remembered any of it. But Adabel's words that evening had pierced her soul. And what she spoke weren't just words of consolation or encouragement. They had come like a command directly from the throne of God.

Teenie knew in her heart that the woman was right. She could not, with clear conscience, take that attack from the enemy sitting down. She felt a surge of renewed authority swell up on her inside. That situation was no longer about what she had lost. She was not alone in this life or this fight. She still had a grandson who needed to see her live her words before him. In her mind's eye, she saw his face before her. She could picture his soft curly black hair, his creamy brown skin, and his sad brown eyes, dark as night, with the smallest glimmer of starlight left in them. He needed her. She didn't have the ability to help her husband or daughter anymore, but she determined that night that she would never let the enemy steal the life or the light from Tyler Andrew Casey.

"You are right, Adabel. Thank *you* for standing in the gap for *me* and for my grandson! I'm committing to the Lord right now to pray for that boy every single day for the rest of my life. As long as I am able, I will intercede on his behalf! That old devil ain't gonna take him from me or from Jesus! He will call upon the name of the Lord and he *will* be saved!"

Adabel smiled brightly. "Amen!"

Ty was fourteen years old at that time. The scene that night had taken place nearly three years ago, and Ty didn't even know about his grandmother's conversation with the nurse, but the pain he had felt that day was still fresh every time he thought about his mother. Since that day, his grandmother, however, seemed even more passionate about him accepting Jesus and getting saved. It seemed to Ty that the more bad things that happened to her, the more adamant she became. He admired her strength, but he just wasn't sure all that religious stuff was for him. Deep inside, he was afraid that it wouldn't work.

Besides that, he had become bitter with God after his mother died. He had refused to go to the hospital to see her when they got the call that she might be the woman they had found. He hadn't wanted to accept that she could be dead. When Teenie came home that night and told him it was indeed his mother, and that she was gone, his heart had broken, but he did not cry. He just stopped going to church as often with his grandmother, and found himself tuning her out more and more. Things in the rest of his life quickly started heading south as well. He lost interest in everything except spray painting graffiti, and today, on those ill-fated train tracks he just left, that had nearly cost him his life.

J ason pulled into Mya's driveway just as it was starting to get dark. She leaned over and kissed him on the cheek.

"I had a great time today, Chaz. Be careful driving home. I love you!" Even though their first "l-word" exchange was long gone, saying those words still gave Mya a rush. She smiled as Jason got out and walked around to the passenger side and opened her door.

"I love you too, babe. I will call you later." Jason smiled back at Mya as she took his outstretched hand and hopped down out of his truck. He hugged her and watched as she walked up to her front door. She found her keys, unlocked the door and turned to wave goodbye to him as she went inside.

Jason got back into his truck and headed toward his house. He expected his parents to be there when he got home. They had taken a short trip back to Burney to visit a few friends, and were taking the train back to Faries that afternoon. Jason wasn't sure what time they were scheduled to arrive, but he knew they should be back by now.

His house was still dark when he pulled in, but he figured that his parents may have gone out for dinner when they saw he was not at home. He parked his truck in the driveway outside the garage and went inside. He turned on the television on his way to check the answering machine for messages and the refrigerator for food. The machine light flashed, signaling new messages. He pressed play and opened the refrigerator.

"Jason Harrington, this is police Sgt. Williams. I have an urgent message and I need you to call me as soon as you get this message." The man's voice sounded troubled as he left his telephone number. "Please call me as soon as you get this message, son. This is very important."

Jason wondered what a police sergeant was calling him for. He waited, expecting to hear a message from his parents, but nothing else was recorded. He looked at the notepad beside the phone. His parents had written the phone number of the people they would be staying with, as well as the name and schedule of the train they would be coming back home on. The note said *Railway Express 1029 arriving at Faries train station at 2:30 pm.* At the bottom of the page was a note in his mother's swirly handwriting, *Jase, have a great weekend. We love you and will see you when we get back. Be good! Love, Mom and Dad*

Jason smiled as he read the note, and went back into the living room with a cold soda and a couple slices of cold pizza. He plopped down on the couch in front of the television. He picked up the remote control and flipped a few channels. All the stations seemed to have the same breaking story flashing. He turned up the volume to hear what they were talking about.

The reporter shuffled through the papers in her hands. "The train that crashed was a Railway Express passenger train. It was number 1-0-2-9, set for arrival here in Faries at 2:30 this afternoon. The death toll still stands at 21 people." The camera shot switched to an aerial view of the crash site, which was now a smoldering pile of tangled metal and ashes. The sky had darkened, and the bright lights of the train station platform now lit the site.

Jason sat straight up on the couch. He stared at the screen for a few more moments, but had stopped listening to what was being said. He jumped up from the couch and raced back to the kitchen. He punched play on the answering machine and grabbed a pen and the notepad he had just been reading from. He quickly skipped through the old messages that hadn't been deleted until he got to the message from Sgt. Williams.

Oh, God, he thought. *Is this what he is calling me about? Where are my mom and dad?* He scribbled down the number, and grabbed the phone from the cradle. He dialed the number and waited for an answer.

"Sgt. Williams."

"Um, yeah, this is Jason Harrington. You called me earlier and told me to call you back. I just got home and I saw the news about the train wreck. Is this about my mom and dad? Do you know where they are? They weren't here when I got home." Jason's voice turned husky, as he choked back tears.

"Jason, I need you to get to the police station as quick as you can. Alright? Can you do that? You're seventeen, right? You have your own vehicle?"

"Yes, sir."

"Well, come on over here now. We need to talk to you."

Jason hung up the phone and grabbed his keys and cell phone. He ran out the door and didn't even bother to lock it behind him. He jumped into his truck and slammed the door. He stuck the key in the ignition and the truck roared to life. He backed quickly out of the driveway. His hand shook as he reached for his cell phone and pressed the speed dial key.

"Hey, Chaz! You miss me already? It's only been twenty minutes! I wasn't expecting you to call me this soon," Mya's cheerful voice chirped playfully into the phone.

"Mya! I'm on my way to the police station." Jason interrupted her banter.

"Why? Baby, what's wrong?" she turned serious.

"I'm not sure! My parents aren't home and then I heard their train crashed and the policeman said they need to talk to me! Mya, I'm scared!" Jason sounded frantic.

"It's going to be alright. Just calm down and relax, okay? I want you to hang up and just drive carefully, alright? I will meet you there."

Jason hung up the phone and swallowed hard. He had never felt like this before. He didn't know what to do or what to think. Would the police want to talk to him if his parents were ok? Wouldn't they have said so if that was the case? Had he even heard everything right? Could he just be panicking and making something out of nothing?

Jason's mind raced, but he rode in silence the rest of the drive across town to the police station. Once he got there, he pulled into a parking space and jumped out of his truck. He looked around for Mya's car, but didn't see it, so he continued on into the station. He saw a man standing just inside the door, and went over to him.

"Sgt. Williams?" he asked hesitantly.

"Yes. Jason Harrington?" Jason nodded. "Hi. Can you follow me, please, son?"

The man led Jason into a conference room. There were two other officers in the room, a male and a female. They both had looks of concern on their faces. Sgt. Williams rolled a chair out from under the table and motioned for Jason to sit down. Jason sat down and looked around the room. He wondered if they could hear his heart pounding in his chest.

Sgt. Williams cleared his throat loudly. He paced slowly in front of Jason for a moment. After what seemed like an eternity to Jason, he stopped beside him and looked over at the other two officers. The woman nodded slightly. He looked back down at Jason, and began speaking slowly, as if choosing his words very deliberately. "Jason, as you know, there was a train wreck this afternoon. We won't have all of the details for some time, but it was very serious, and a lot of people were injured." He went silent for a few moments. "We have been looking for survivors since the crash occurred, but it looks like everyone in the first two train cars died. We have reason to believe that your mom and dad were in the first car. Son, we are really sorry, but your parents did not survive the crash this afternoon."

As Sgt. Williams spoke, tears welled up and burned in the corners of Jason's eyes. When he stopped talking, the tears spilled over and ran down Jason's cheeks. Just then, Mya burst through the front door and looked around the station. She saw Jason and the officers in the room, and ran over and opened the door. When she saw Jason's tear-streaked face and wet, red eyes, she knew that the news was bad.

"Chaz!" She ran over to him and spun his chair around until he was facing her. She knelt down in front of him and looked into his eyes. "Chaz? What is it?"

"They're dead," he said quietly, the tears still streaming down his face.

Mya's jaw dropped open and tears began to sting her eyes. "Oh, Chaz! Chaz! I'm so sorry! Come here!" She pulled the young man up to stand, and put her arms around him. He laid his head on her shoulder and wept. He didn't make much noise, but she could feel his entire body shudder with every sob.

"Mya, my parents are dead," he said into her shoulder. "They're never coming back. What am I going to do?"

"I don't know. But I'm right here. It's going to be alright. I don't know how, but God's gonna make this alright."

~

Leisa Carson was sitting on pins and needles waiting for news about Annette. By seven o'clock that evening, she felt as if she was going to crawl out of her skin, still having not heard anything. She sat quietly in her living room, not really knowing what to do or say, while Teenie moved about in the kitchen, cooking and cleaning up. Teenie hummed softly as she worked.

Then the doorbell rang.

Leisa gingerly sat down the mug of hot tea that Teenie had made for her. She stood up, just as Teenie shuffled past her to answer the door. Teenie looked at her, shook her head slightly, and motioned for Leisa to sit back down. Teenie reached the door and looked out the peephole. She unlocked the door and stepped back as she pulled it open.

There stood two female police officers. Teenie quietly invited them to come inside. They nodded and came in, and Teenie shut the door behind them. She led them into the living room where Leisa sat anxiously. She stood up and shook the women's hands.

"Ma'am, we'd like to speak with you and your husband," one of the officers said.

Teenie spoke up. "Her husband is not feeling up to all of this just yet. Please, go ahead and talk to us. We can relay the message when the time comes."

Leisa couldn't speak around the lump in her throat, so she just nodded her head. She moved over to stand closer to Teenie, who wrapped her arm around her.

"Well, as I'm sure you are aware, there was a serious train collision this afternoon. None of the passengers on the first two cars of the Railway train survived. Mrs. Carson, I'm afraid your daughter Annette was one of those victims, according to our records. Please accept our deepest sympathies and sincerest apologies for your loss." The young officer took a deep breath, and looked sadly at Leisa and Teenie.

"Annie Pie," Leisa moaned softly, as she slumped to her knees. Teenie kept her grip on Leisa as she lowered herself to the floor with her. Leisa began to weep, her whole body shaking uncontrollably.

The officers turned to leave the house. "We will show ourselves out. Again, we are truly sorry about your daughter, Mrs. Carson."

Teenie nodded her acknowledgement to them as they left, while she rocked and tried to comfort Leisa. She looked up when she heard noise coming from the direction of the master bedroom. Edward walked slowly out into the living room where Leisa and Teenie knelt.

"She's dead, isn't she? She was on that train. I know it, Teenie. Just say it!" Edward lashed out in his grief. "Faith and prayer aren't going to bring her back now, are they? She is supposed to be here with me, visiting her daddy! Why is this happening? *Why does it have to be* my *baby girl?*" His quivering voice rose to a shout.

Fresh tears welled up in all their eyes. "Edward!" Teenie spoke sharply.

With moist, bloodshot eyes, Edward looked from Teenie to Leisa. He shook his head as he slowly backed away from them. Suddenly, he turned and ran out the door leading into the garage. He got into his car and started it up. By the time Teenie stood up and made her way outside, all she saw were his tail lights as he turned the corner at the end of the street.

"Lord, he's hurting. Please keep him safe, wherever he goes," she whispered.

Before Mya left her house to go to the police station, she had filled her parents in on what little Jason had told her. They had prayed with her, and told her to call when she had more information. She'd prayed the whole drive over, and was devastated by the news she received once she arrived.

And now, standing there with Jason, crying sympathetically with him, Mya felt so helpless. She wanted to do or say something that would ease his pain, but at that moment, no words seemed strong enough. So she just held him and let him cry.

Finally, his tears subsided. He straightened up and wiped his nose and eyes with the cuff of his long sleeved button down. "My mom hates when I do that," he said, with a sad smile. He turned and looked for the chair he'd previously been sitting in, and sat back down. He leaned forward with his elbows resting on his knees and his head in his hands. He ran his fingers through his dark brown hair, and sighed deeply.

The female officer walked over and squatted down beside his chair. She began talking softly to him, and he nodded every once in a while. Silent tears began sliding down his face once again. The other officer and Sgt. Williams looked at Mya, who stood over Jason and the woman, and motioned for her to come outside the room. She turned quietly and followed them out.

"Hello, there. I'm Sgt. Williams. This is Officer Green."

"Hi. I'm Mya Lafleur. I'm Jason's girlfriend."

The officers shook Mya's hand. "We are sorry to have to be the bearers of such bad news. We're glad that Jason had someone to come and be with him during all this. How old are you, Ms. Lafleur?"

"I'm seventeen too."

"Oh, ok. Do you know if Jason has any family he can call tonight to come and get him? We think it would be best if he went with family or friends instead of going home alone."

Mya shook her head. "No, sir. All of his family lives back in Burney, Pennsylvania. That's where his parents were coming back from today." She stopped, and tried to choke back the sob that had risen in her chest. "But my parents said to call them as soon as I get some more information. I'm sure he can come stay with us tonight. They love Jason too. He's part of our family."

Sgt. Williams nodded. "Do you have a cell phone, or do you need to use one of our office phones?" He stopped and quietly chuckled. "That's a silly question, isn't it? Everyone seems to have a cell phone these days." Mya smiled too, and reached into her purse. She pulled out a purple phone and held it up. "If you will dial the number and call your parents, I will fill them in on what is going on and ask them about Jason staying with you all tonight, okay?"

Mya nodded as she flipped open her phone and hit the speed dial button that called her house. She handed the phone to Sgt. Williams. While he spoke to her parents, she turned and looked back into the room at Jason and the officer.

Oh, Lord, she prayed silently. *What can I do? How can I help him? He was so close to turning to You. Please don't let this turn him away. I don't want to lose him now. I* can't *lose him now.*

"Mya?" Sgt. Williams called her name. She turned back to him. "Here is your phone. You're a very lucky girl. You have some really great parents from what I can tell. They were very kind and said that Jason is more than welcome to stay with you all tonight. They said to have you to drive him there. He can leave his truck here, and your dad said that he will arrange to have it picked up tomorrow."

Mya smiled at Sgt. Williams. "Ok. Thanks. And I'm not lucky— I'm blessed." She recognized that now more than ever before. She was so grateful to have such wonderful parents who were safe and sound and waiting for her back at home. Sgt. Williams nodded and looked toward the room where Jason was. He walked over and opened the door. He walked in, and closed it behind him. Jason looked up at him, and nodded as he spoke. Then Jason stood up and the female officer led him to the door and out to where Mya stood. Sgt. Williams came out behind them.

"Again, young man, we are so sorry for your loss. But you have some people waiting who really love you, and we hope that everything works out for you. Please give us a call if you need any help in the future." Sgt. Williams came over and hugged Jason tightly.

Mya had never seen Jason look so small before. When it was just him and her, she always felt like the tiny one, protected by Jason's towering height and masculine strength. But standing there beside the muscular sergeant, he suddenly looked like a sad little boy who needed protecting. He hugged the sergeant back, and then turned and hugged the female officer. "Thank you," he whispered to them. He walked over to Mya and hugged her again. Mya looked over Jason's shoulder to Sgt. Williams and mouthed her thanks to him as well. Sgt. Williams nodded and walked with the female officer back into the conference room. Mya took Jason's hand and walked with him outside to her car, where she opened the passenger side door and he got in.

What a change, she thought. *Just a few hours ago, things were blissful and Jason was opening the door for me. I can't believe all this is really happening.*

Jason was silent on the ride back to Mya's house. Mya wasn't surprised. What could he say in a situation like this?

When they finally reached Mya's house, Jason moved slowly as he got out of the car and headed up the walkway. Mya walked behind him. When they reached the front door, Mya's mother was waiting for them. She gathered Jason in a warm embrace. He began crying again, and received her hug appreciatively. Mya's father stood behind them, and waited until they separated. He then hugged Jason too. Then they all went into the living room.

"Jason, we are so sorry to hear about your mom and dad. They were wonderful people and we know this is going to be tough to get through. But we love you and are here for you. We would like to pray for you right now, if that's alright." Mya's mother spoke tenderly. She was sitting beside Jason on the couch, and placed her hand on his back. Mya knelt down in front of him and took both his hands in hers. Her father sat on the other side of Jason and placed one of his hands on top of his wife's and the other on top of Mya's. Together, as a family, the Lafleurs prayed over Jason.

"Lord, we can not begin to understand the pain that Jason is facing right now. We don't know how to sympathize with him from a place of personal experience. We don't know what he is going through. But You do, Lord. You know exactly how he feels. You felt the same type of loss when You sent Your only Son Jesus to die on the cross for our sin. And You feel the loss every time something bad happens to one of Your people on earth. So Lord, right now we ask for the comfort of the Holy Spirit to overwhelm Jason. Allow Him to feel Your presence like he never has before. Open his eyes and his heart to see Your goodness, even in the midst of this tragedy. Lord, give us the words to say. Help us to know how to help him. Give us wisdom and sensitivity to his needs. Thank you, Lord for bringing him into our lives. Thank you for the blessing that he is to our family." Mya's father prayed earnestly and sincerely from his heart. He spoke words of love and affirmation over Jason. He ended his prayer with these words, "Lord, we plead the blood of Jesus over Jason. We ask that You would cover him and shield him from the darts of the enemy that are sure to come against his mind. May he become a son of God, with abundant and eternal life as his inheritance. In Jesus' name, amen."

The four of them sat for a moment, absorbing the words that Mya's father had just spoken. Then Mya's mother spoke. "Jason, it really is going to be alright. I know you don't see how right now, but this thing is going to work out. The Lord wouldn't have allowed this to happen if he didn't have some plan for a good outcome. Please don't be discouraged. Trust that all things are going to work together for your good as you love the Lord and seek to find His purpose." Jason nodded halfheartedly.

Mya released Jason's hands and stood up. Her parents straightened up on the couch. Jason leaned back with his head resting on the back of the couch. He closed his eyes. "What do I do now?" he asked quietly, clearly not only referring to just that moment, but also to the rest of his life.

Mrs. Lafleur patted his leg. "Just rest for a bit, honey. This is going to be a long road, but we are here for you. We will take care of some things in the morning. You just need to relax and get some sleep. Let your heart and your mind recover. There are some of Mr. Lafleur's clothes in the guest room. Just a t-shirt and some shorts. Go on in there and wash your face and change clothes. I put fresh sheets on the bed for you, so just make yourself comfortable, ok? We will talk to you in the morning." She gently pulled him to her, and kissed him tenderly on his temple. He lingered at her side for a moment and then stood up. He turned around and leaned down to hug Mr. Lafleur. He then turned and stepped over to Mya. He hugged her tightly, and whispered, "Thanks for being here, Mya. I love you!" She returned his squeeze, and whispered her love back to him.

"Thank you, guys," he said, as he turned and walked back into the guest room down the hall. He quietly shut the door behind him.

Mya's parents stood up and hugged her. "This is going to be hard for him, Mya. Probably harder than we realize. But you have to stand in prayer for him. That is the best thing you can do. Listen to him, be there for him and pray. The Lord is doing something here. We just have to stay vigilant, and keep standing." Her father spoke softly but firmly.

Her mother nodded her agreement. "Yes, honey, pray for him. He's not saved yet, and you know the enemy is going to bombard his mind with all kinds of lies in this season of sadness. There are going to be some vicious spiritual attacks on him now because of his vulnerable mental and emotional condition. That is just how the enemy works. He finds our weakest spots, in our weakest moments, and aims straight for them. We just have to believe that this situation will lead Jason *to* the arms of Jesus and not turn him away. That must be our constant prayer for him. Our prayers will dispatch angels on his behalf to combat the assaults of the enemy. And the enemy is going to hate us all the more for it. So this will be a difficult time for you too. You have to be prepared for a battle. But just know that we are standing for you as well. We are always praying for you, and we are here any time you need us." Mrs. Lafleur tenderly swept her finger along her daughter's cheek, noting the worry that was etched on her face. "You have had a long day too, sweetie. Why don't you go on to bed? I will come get you in the morning and we will fix Jason some breakfast. If he is up to it, he can go to church with us. If not, we will let him sleep in, and then start making some arrangements after service." She hugged Mya tightly, then lovingly turned her toward her bedroom, and patted her lightly on her backside. "Good night, Mya. We will see you in the morning."

"I know you guys are right. I just feel so weak and confused right now. I just want to do what's best for Chaz. I love him so much, and I know this has got to be agony for him. I just wish I could do something to make it better for him. I guess praying is the best thing I can do right now." Her voice trailed off as she started walking to her bedroom. She turned and smiled sadly at her parents as they watched her leave. "Good night, y'all. I love you both very much. Thanks for letting Chaz stay with us." She touched the door of the guest room as she passed by. No light shone under the door and all was quiet. She guessed Jason was already in the bed. She felt another tinge of sorrow as she thought about what he must have been feeling right then. She continued on to her room, and shut the door after she walked in. She sat down on her bed and inhaled deeply. It felt like she had been awake for days on end. She could only imagine how the people who were receiving news of the death of their loved ones must be feeling. She was so mentally and physically exhausted that she didn't think she could even change her clothes or turn down her bed. She just laid back on top of her comforter, fully dressed, except her shoes, which she had kicked off before they prayed for Jason.

Call Leisa Carson. The unexpected urge to call her teacher nearly overwhelmed Mya. It was not just a feeling or a thought to call her. It was a push that Mya felt from her gut. *Call Leisa Carson!* Mya suddenly felt a fresh burst of energy and reached over to the phone on her nightstand. She quickly dialed the Carson's house number. The phone rang three times.

"Hello?"

"Teenie? Is that you?" Mya was surprised to hear the old woman's voice on the other end of the phone.

"Yes, it is. Is this Mya?" Teenie recognized the young woman's voice immediately.

"Yes, ma'am. I called to speak to Mrs. Leisa. I have some awful news. I'm sure you heard about that train wreck this afternoon, right? Well, Jason's parents were on the train and they were both killed. We just found out a little while ago. He's here at my house, and I wanted to call Mrs. Leisa and tell her about it and ask her to pray and tell her that we won't be at dinner tomorrow night. Is she there?" Mya finally paused, waiting for Teenie to speak.

"Yes, baby, I heard about the wreck. That's actually why I am here. Annette was on that train too. She didn't make it either. We just got the official word a little bit ago."

"Oh, Teenie, no! Annie's gone too? Where is Mrs. Leisa? How is Mr. Edward? Oh, God, they must be devastated!"

"They are. But they need you to pray. They are gonna be alright, but we've gotta pray for them. All of them. I hate to hear that sweet Jason is sufferin' too. Jesus knows there is too much tragedy in this world. It must break His heart when this stuff happens. But we just gotta trust Him and keep praying and walking by faith. I will tell Leisa you called and what happened with Jason's parents. You just stand strong for him and the Carson's. It's gonna be alright, baby."

"Yes, ma'am. Thank you, Teenie. Please tell Mrs. Leisa and Mr. Edward that I love them and will definitely be praying for them."

"I will, baby. Good night."

"Good night, Teenie."

Mya hung up the phone. *Lord, why? Annie too? Why is this happening to Jason and the Carson's? I just don't understand this, Lord. Please help me to be strong for my friends.* She stood up and slowly walked over to her dresser. Dejected by this fresh batch of bad news, the fatigue and sorrow she'd felt just moments ago returned and weighed her down once again. She reached into her drawer and pulled out a pair of pajamas. She changed her clothes and slid under the covers into her bed. She closed her eyes, trying to quiet her racing mind, and eventually drifted off to sleep.

"Who was that on the phone, Teenie?" Leisa Carson felt weak and as if she didn't have another tear left in her body. "Was it Edward? Did he call to say where he was?" She was hopeful that her husband had realized how selfish he was being by walking out on her after they received confirmation about Annette, and had called to apologize and say he was on his way back home. She had cried her heart out with Teenie, but she desperately wanted to be in the arms of her husband in the midst of all this turbulence.

"No, baby, it wasn't Edward." Teenie did not want to cause Leisa any more anguish, so she tried to change the subject. But Leisa was persistent.

"Well, who was it? What did they want?" Leisa looked expectantly at her old friend, waiting for her to say who she'd just spoken with.

"It was Mya Lafleur." Teenie stopped.

"And she said…?" Leisa needed something to take her mind off her grief, so she seized the opportunity to focus on someone else.

"She was calling to ask you to pray for Jason." Teenie paused again, hating to bring up the subject of the wreck and death to Leisa all over again. "His parents were both killed in the accident this afternoon. They just found out."

"No!" Leisa cried out bitterly. She had been friends with the Harringtons for some time after they moved to Faries. The company Edward worked for sponsored most of the school activities in the community, and he was often sent out to school functions as the company representative. He himself was an avid sportsman, and often brought Leisa along to the games to watch and support the students. The couple had bonded with Jason's parents while watching Jason and his teammates participate in the sports activities.

Leisa was well known and loved by all the students and the other teachers at the school. She worked diligently to prove to all of them that her affection for them was genuine and not just superficial, or by obligation as a teacher or colleague. She spent a good amount of her free time mentoring, tutoring and helping students, even those outside of her own classes, as well as helping the other teachers wherever she could. She even kept up with previous students of hers, maintaining contact with them through their college experiences and beyond. She stayed abreast of potential students who were not yet ready for her class but would be in the near future, communicating with them and trying to spark their interest early. She also made sure to keep the parents of her students involved and updated on things that went on within the school. She was a confidante and friend, both inside and outside the classroom. Because of her unwavering commitment to her job and to the students of her school, by the time the kids actually came into her English class, she had already developed quite a bond with each one of them. This was certainly the case this year with her newest set of students, including Mya, whom she had grown close to over the last few years, and Jason, especially as his relationship with Mya grew.

For the last seven or eight months, Jason had been coming to Leisa's house with Mya on Sunday evenings for dinner, and Leisa's fondness for him steadily grew as she really got to interact with and know him. He was one of those extraordinary people who only came along every once in a while, and the more time she spent with him, the more she developed a special place in her heart for him. He was not a Christian yet, but he was one of the most sincere and well-mannered young men she knew. And she could see how much he and Mya liked each other.

Jason was a really sweet and solid guy, and it was easy to see where he had gotten it from. His parents, although not saved either, were such kind and wonderful people. Leisa especially liked the way they treated Mya. There had been a lot of negative attention and backlash thrown their way when Mya and Jason began dating, because many people in Faries were still dealing with old issues of narrow-mindedness and bigotry and were not used to seeing a mixed couple. But Jason's parents seemed to truly like Mya, and they never treated her with anything less than respect and genuine affection. They didn't just tolerate her. They embraced her and welcomed her into their family. That had really gone over well with Leisa.

She and Mya often discussed Jason and Mya's relationship. They regularly prayed together for Jason and his family's salvation and for strength for Mya's commitment to sexual purity within their relationship. They also discussed Mya's frustration and hurt with what she had to deal with because she and Jason were not the same skin color and had chosen to be together anyway. Leisa tried to sympathize with Mya when she opened up to her about it, but racism and prejudice were things that Leisa really couldn't understand on a personal level. Even so, she and Mya bonded over these discussions, and discovered how very much alike the two of them were. They had both grown up in Christian households, where they were taught that people were not their skin color and that their outside did not make them who they were. These conversations and times together were the beginning of a beautiful, strong, godly relationship between Mya and Leisa, much like what Leisa had had with her own daughter, Annette, when she was Mya's age. And while Mya was extremely close to her own parents, she and Leisa talked constantly, Leisa sometimes standing in like a second mother, always doing her best to encourage Mya to trust and follow the Lord in every situation, no matter how hard things seemed to get. This special connection they shared made it all the more difficult when Mya came to her, and Leisa had to witness how severely Mya suffered for dating Jason, because some people in their community could not accept a dark-eyed, brown-skinned girl dating a blue-eyed white boy, and threw harsh and hateful remarks toward them when they were out together. Leisa's heart ached for Mya and the completely unnecessary battle she was forced to fight.

Now, there was no mistaking that Mya and Jason's affection for one another was solid, but their youth and inexperience sometimes allowed the words of others to infiltrate their own thoughts and feelings, clouding their judgment and making them question their commitment to making things work. On several occasions, Mya had come to her parents, Leisa and a few others of her trusted church members for wisdom and counsel. She wanted to do what was right in the sight of the Lord, and she didn't want to sacrifice a good relationship just because people on the outside couldn't handle something new, but she also wasn't sure if she was strong enough to stand up to so many people who were against her. It was during these times that people within their church family, especially their pastor Chris James, rallied around Mya in prayer and encouraged her to seek the will of the Lord and not allow others' ignorance and hatred to stop her from following her heart to wherever the Lord was leading her.

As the months passed on, and the relationship between Leisa and Mya continued to blossom, Mya came to Leisa when she realized that her "liking" Jason had changed and become something much deeper, and wanted to pray about what she should do. She understood that the Lord had commanded her not to yoke herself unequally to a non-believer, and Jason had not yet accepted Christ as his Lord and Savior, but Mya did not want to abandon him and walk away from the relationship they had fought so hard to build. She believed the relationship was worth saving. One particular evening, she asked Leisa for her advice on what she thought she should do. They prayed together that vey night and asked the Lord for wisdom.

After that prayer, something was ignited within Mya. She became like a woman on a mission who was very proactive in seeking the answers to her prayers. She began to invite Jason to church, and talked to him daily about salvation. Leisa did the same, and encouraged Mya to invite Jason to the Sunday dinners at her house. Over the following year or so, as she sought after direction and His will, Mya's relationship with the Lord began to take on a whole new dimension and her zeal became evident to everyone. She really began to walk a path of righteousness and refused to compromise in any area. She became more vigilant of her attitude and actions, and did her best to show the love of God wherever she went. She began to invite Jason and her best friend Raegan into a new relationship with the Lord and pleaded constantly with them to accept Jesus as

Savior. Leisa proudly watched the change in Mya, and was thrilled when she began to notice a change in Jason as well. He was now coming to every church service with Mya. He was attentive and Leisa even saw him lift his hands in worship at times. She believed he was growing spiritually and continued to intercede on his behalf even though he still had not walked down the aisle to accept Christ or to follow Him in water baptism. Nevertheless, they could sense that every week he was one step closer.

And now this train collision has claimed the life of his parents.

Leisa knew what a devastating blow this would be to Jason. She cringed at the thought of what lengths the enemy was willing to go to, to try to stop someone from stepping from darkness into light. The pain she felt in her own heart was agonizing, despite knowing that her child was in the arms of Jesus at that very moment. She couldn't even imagine what Jason must have been going through, not knowing what death meant for his parents.

"Teenie, this is all just too much! Why did this happen?" Leisa felt as if she were in some hellish nightmare. She hurt for herself, but her heart nearly shattered when she pictured the young man across town. She felt the tears welling up on the inside of her again. She buried her face in her hands.

"No, no, child! This is not the time to start trying to figure things out. We don't know what the Lord's plan is in all of this! And the moment we start trying to fathom the thoughts of an unfathomable God, that's when we really lose our grip. This is the time we prove ourselves. Are we serving God just because things are working out well in our lives? Or do we serve Him out of love, in spite of our circumstances, knowing that He loved us first, even in our sinful state? That's what this time is about. It's easy to say the right Christian words and go through all the right motions when everything's going right for you. But what are you going to do now, when it feels like you're in a living hell? I'm not telling you something I don't know for myself. Don't forget, baby, I know *exactly* how you feel. I lost my little girl too. This ain't gonna be an easy road, but I know it's a road that you *can* travel. The Lord is too good to just leave you in this mess."

Being with Leisa to receive the news of Annette's death took Teenie back in her mind to the evening in the hospital when her own daughter passed away. She could still remember the smells and sounds that had permeated the hospital corridor as she'd said her final words to her precious little girl. It had been the second hardest night in her life, trumped only slightly by the night she bid farewell to her beloved husband of 43 glorious years.

She remembered both those nights so vividly, as if they had just happened. And she remembered a common thread that ran through each event—a little nurse named Adabel. She had just shown up one evening and seemed to never leave Teenie's side during the course of her husband's cancer battle and subsequent hospital stay. This little woman was a firecracker in the kingdom of God and kept Teenie's sprits lifted throughout her husband's whole ordeal. And then after he passed and she had made sure Teenie was settled into her new life without her husband, Adabel seemed to just quietly disappear.

That is, until the night Teenie got the call about her daughter. She had gone into the hospital room to spend a few minutes with her daughter for the last time on this side of heaven and was preparing to leave, when that little nurse walked back up to her. It was as if she had appeared out of thin air, again, right when Teenie needed someone most. Adabel had hugged her and loved on her and supported her once again. She had reminded Teenie who she was in Christ and that she was responsible to continue praying for the soul salvation of her grandson. She had essentially shaken Teenie out of her grief and brought her back to reality as the one still living.

But something else had happened that night that no one else knew about. Adabel had given her more than just a pep talk.

"Teenie, I have a message for you." Adabel's tone went serious once again. She had looked around and pulled Teenie to a corner where they could not be overheard by others in the hospital hallway. "I have a letter that your daughter wanted you to have. It's very important that you read it soon. No one knows I'm giving it to you, but she wanted me to make sure you got it. It's got some important information in it." She reached into the pocket of her scrubs and pulled out a tattered envelope. She handed it to Teenie. "I've got to go now, but please remember what I told you. And read that letter as soon as you can. I pray that the Lord would open your eyes to what you need to see. Stay strong, Teenie. God's got it under control." She winked at Teenie, and walked away.

Teenie looked down at the stained and ragged envelope in her hands. She then looked up to thank Adabel and tell her goodbye, but the nurse had vanished as quickly as she appeared. Teenie had looked all around the corridor for her, but she was nowhere to be seen. She wondered what Adabel meant by "open her eyes." She turned the letter over in her hands and examined it closer. She decided to find a quiet place and read the letter before she headed home. She was in no real hurry to have to go home and tell her grandson that his mother was dead.

She walked slowly down the hallway, past the commotion of the nurse's station and open waiting and hospital rooms. She kept going until she came upon a small, empty waiting area, just inside the glass doors that led outside. She looked around and made sure no one was heading her direction and sat down in one of the chairs.

She opened the envelope and pulled out the letter that was inside. She took a deep breath and unfolded it slowly. Now, thinking back on that moment, she remembered smiling faintly at her daughter's scrawling handwriting and reading the letter silently.

Dear Mama,

I hope you are not too sad as you read this. I know I have disappointed you with the way I have chosen to live my life, and I really hope you can forgive me. I never wanted things to be like this. I don't really know how it all happened. I wish I had more answers. It wasn't for a lack of your love or bad parenting on your part. I couldn't have asked for a better set of parents or a better childhood to have grown up in. But somewhere along the way, I lost my sure footing, and became disconnected from the Source. I was introduced to some things that ended up taking my life hostage. Once I was in their grip, I just couldn't find my way out.

There are a few things I need you to know about. I kept some things from you, but if you are reading this letter, it means that I am gone and the secrets have no reason to stay hidden. So here goes:

David Tyler Hudson III is Ty's father.

Teenie had stopped reading when she got to this part. She was extremely surprised at her daughter's admission. "Lord, how did I not know that?" she had said aloud. She shook her head in disbelief, and looked back to the letter.

I know you are probably surprised to hear that. I never gave you the details, but he and I had a very real and very strong relationship for quite some time. Please don't be angry with him for not being around. He has no idea that Ty is his son. I told him that I had cheated on him with someone else and gotten pregnant. That is why we broke up. He was a wonderful man. He treated me so well. Even after we ended our relationship, he came often to check on me. He sent me money and helped me out with doctor visit costs.

I think on some level he felt guilty though. He introduced me to an extravagant lifestyle that included exclusive clubs and bars and parties. He was never hard core into the drugs and alcohol, but through some people he introduced me to, I got a taste and became hooked. But it was my call. When DT asked me to get help, and even offered to pay for my treatment and Ty's childcare, it was my choice to turn it down. I didn't want to stop. I was enjoying myself, and nothing else really mattered. Now I think of my beautiful son and what I have put him through, and I am so sorry, Mama. I was a terrible mother to him, and I was a terrible daughter to you and Daddy. And then when Daddy died, it just ripped my heart out and sent me deeper into my addiction. I didn't want to face the fact that we were all getting older and death was a real possibility for each of us. But I should have gotten clean and come clean a long time ago.

In telling you all of this, I am asking you to please wait until Ty asks about the identity of his father before you say anything to him or to DT. Perhaps he will be grown up by the time you read this, but if not, please wait. You've been so good to him thus far, and I don't want this to shake all that up if it doesn't have to. And DT has his own issues that he is working out. I don't want to burden him with more because of my lies.

Tyler already may never get over all that I have done to him, and I don't want to add any more heartache to his life while he is still so young. And when you do tell DT that Ty is his son, please let him know that he is not obligated to adopt the "Daddy" role with him, since he has not been much in his life up to this point. Give him the option of deciding how to handle it. But however it all works out, Mama, just take care of my little boy, my sweet Tyler Andrew. Do for him what you did for me and what I couldn't do myself.

Again, Mama, I'm so sorry for all that I put you all through. I pray you forgive me and I pray the Lord forgive me. I love you so much.

Always,
Your baby girl, Mali Chandelle

The letter had had a date scrawled at the bottom of the page. It was dated about a year and a half earlier, shortly after Teenie's husband had passed away. She'd wondered when and how Adabel had gotten the letter from her daughter, but was so grateful that she had. Teenie was shocked to read all that her daughter had said, but was glad to have some insight into what she had been going through. She picked up the envelope again and noticed writing on the back that she hadn't seen before. She remembered turning the letter over in her hands, but didn't recall any writing on it's outside. But just then, when she reexamined the pages in her hands, there was a tiny note in the corner of the envelope's back.

"I really *am* getting old," she had chuckled to herself. She squinted and looked closely at the envelope to read the writing.

I was there with her right at the end. We prayed together, she repented and rededicated herself to Jesus Christ as Lord. She's in heaven with Him!

It was signed "*Adabel.*"

Ty lay for a few more minutes in the grass before he decided to risk getting in a great deal of trouble with his grandmother and headed on home. He began walking in the direction of his house and decided to at least call before he showed up. Maybe he could give her some excuse as to why he was coming back so early, and she wouldn't ask too many questions when he got home. He found a payphone along his route and dialed their home number. The phone rang six or seven times and finally the answering machine picked up.

Lucky break, he thought. *She must have left the house right after I did.*

Even so, Ty took his time walking back home. He really was in no hurry anyway. It was Saturday and Leisa Carson, his English teacher and Teenie's friend, would be bringing them dinner tonight. She did that every Saturday, and somehow her visit always turned into a prayer meeting centered on Ty and his salvation. But his issue wasn't that he *didn't* like Mrs. Carson. It was quite the opposite, in fact. She was one of the nicest people he knew, and he sometimes wished his own mother had been more like her. It was just that when she came around, his grandmother got even more persistent and the two of them spent hours on end talking to him and praying over him and singing. It made him extremely uncomfortable. He worried that he couldn't live up to this person that his grandmother and her friend seemed to expect him to become, no matter how much he wanted to or how much he tried.

On top of that, Teenie seemed to like Mrs. Carson a whole lot too. Maybe a little *too* much, in Ty's opinion. She treated her like a daughter. They were constantly together, laughing and talking, singing and praying. They seemed to share everything about their lives with each other. His discomfort with their blossoming relationship could explain some of his reluctance to get involved in all that religion stuff they were so into. He found himself sometimes being short or harsh when he spoke to his grandmother and Mrs. Carson, particularly during their Saturday night episodes. He almost always felt bad afterwards, but he couldn't really seem to help himself. Watching them interact with one another just made something awful go off inside him. He didn't like to see what looked like his grandmother trying to replace his mom with Mrs. Carson. Even though she had been dead for a few years, Ty still loved his mother dearly and did not want anyone, especially his grandmother, to forget about her.

But the same time, he also loved the way Mrs. Carson treated him. She treated him like he was her son, always doting on him and speaking kind words to him. Her love and compassion toward him stirred up so many different emotions in him that he often felt guilty about how much he really did like her. He didn't want to tarnish his mother's memory by moving on and letting some other woman become a mother figure to him. But even when he was a jerk to her or his grandmother, Mrs. Carson always just carried on and acted as though he were an angel or something. She never raised her voice at him or acted disappointed with him. Nothing he did seemed to ruffle her feathers. He was extremely conflicted on the whole situation and how exactly he felt.

In the mean time, Saturdays had become "get Ty saved" days, and Sundays seemed to be "show Ty what he's missing out on because he's *not* saved" days. Going to church with his grandmother got harder as he got older. That was part of the reason he stopped going as often. He knew that his not going really disappointed his grandmother, but she was trying to let him begin to make his own decisions. She hadn't stopped talking to him or praying for him, on Saturdays, Sundays or any other day. But she didn't force him to come with her to services anymore. She knew that there were a number of issues that Ty was dealing with, and she prayed that in his own time he would come to the conclusion that he was in need of a savior.

A whole other concern that made going to church hard for Ty was that he didn't want to open himself up that much, to the people in the church or to God. Every time someone gave a testimony of how God had healed them or brought someone back to Christ out of a life of sin, Ty was reminded of what he had lost. He wondered why God would do for all these other people, but *his* grandfather and *his* mother died. When he saw all the smiling faces and heard the singing voices, he felt resentment rise up within him. He didn't have anything to smile or sing about. His life seemed to be falling apart. But everyone kept telling him what a great plan God had for him and what an awesome testimony he had. He just couldn't see it for himself. He felt so hopeless at times. And then going to Sunday evening dinners at the Carson's house didn't help matters much. He felt like an outsider on some episode of Leave it to Beaver or the Cosby Show, where everyone was smiling and everyone was happy—everyone, except him.

Glad to be interrupted from his thoughts, Ty finally made it back home. He went inside and plopped down in the recliner in the living room. Although he was enjoying the alone time, without his grandmother or anyone else bothering him, he wondered where his grandmother was, and when she would be back. His lungs finally felt back to normal, and he could breathe without trouble, but he feared he smelled like smoke. That would be a dead giveaway—should his grandmother decide to show up soon—of his recent whereabouts and that he had not been where he said he would be, so he decided to take a shower and get cleaned up before she got back. He longed to wash out the images of the train wreck from his mind too, but he knew that was just wishful thinking. He grabbed his backpack and trudged to his bedroom.

He got a change of clothes from his dresser drawers and headed into the bathroom. He turned the water on and waited for a little while to let the water heat up. Once he got under the steady stream, he let his mind wander. It quickly landed on Raegan Nottaway, the cute girl he'd been eyeing for quite some time now. She was a classmate of his, and he'd had a few classes with her over the last few years, but they had never really spoken to one another.

But a few months ago, at one of the Carson's Sunday night dinners, she had come with Mya Lafleur and Jason Harrington. Ty and his grandmother had been at the house for several hours before the dinner, helping Mrs. Carson clean up and prepare the meal. When the doorbell rang, Teenie and Mrs. Carson instructed him to go answer it. He did, and nearly fainted when he opened the door and Raegan stood awkwardly before him.

"Hi," she'd said quietly. "Is this the Carson residence?"

Ty struggled to regain his composure. "Um, yeah, hi. Uh, yes, this is their house. Come on in." He stepped back to let her walk through the doorway. He couldn't believe how fast his heart was beating in his chest. She was even prettier than he had remembered from school. And there she was, standing right next to him.

She turned back to look at him. "I'm supposed to meet Mya and Jason here for dinner. You're Ty, right?"

Ty had been slightly taken aback that she knew his name. He didn't think she knew he was alive, let alone what his name was. "Um, yeah. I'm Ty. Your name is Raegan, isn't it?" She smiled shyly and nodded her head. "Well, you're at the right place, but Jason and Mya haven't made it yet. Come on into the kitchen. Mrs. Leisa and my grandmother are in there finishing dinner. Follow me." Ty tried not to show how nervous he was. His arm lightly brushed hers as he moved past her to lead her to the kitchen. He felt a sensation in his chest that he hadn't ever felt before. He took a deep breath and tried to calm himself down. *What is wrong with me? Why am I acting like an idiot! Get it together, Ty!* He scolded himself silently. He racked his brain to think of something witty to say. "I hope you're hungry. My grandma and Mrs. Leisa always cook for, like, a hundred people." It wasn't brilliant, but at least he wasn't just leading her in silence.

She chuckled from behind him. "I could be persuaded to eat," she replied.

When they arrived to the kitchen, Mrs. Carson looked up first. "Raegan! Hi! I'm so glad you came tonight!" She came over and hugged the young woman. "I see Ty let you in. I hope he was a gentleman. This is Mrs. Ernestine Casey, Ty's grandmother."

Teenie flashed a big smile at the girl. "Well, aren't you just the prettiest little thing! You can call me Teenie. What did you say your name was?"

"Raegan Nottaway."

"Well, I'm telling you, Raegan, you are just the prettiest thing I have seen in a while! Isn't she pretty, Ty?"

Ty looked, and felt, like a deer caught in headlights. Leave it to his grandmother to embarrass him in front of the one girl he actually had a crush on. "Uh, yes, ma'am." *She's breathtaking*, he wanted to say. He looked away quickly.

Raegan blushed, but smiled appreciatively. "Well, thank you both."

Jason and Mya showed up shortly after that. The dinner was nice, but Ty could hardly look at Raegan and mostly kept quiet for the rest of the evening. He was so nervous, and didn't want to look like a fool in front of her. She was polite and answered questions when she was asked, but, besides that, she did not say much either. Between Mrs. Carson, Teenie, and Mya's banter and stories, she really hadn't needed to. Jason talked a little and threw in a joke here and there. Everyone seemed to enjoy themselves pretty well. Overall, it had been a pleasant evening for all. But for Ty, it was a night he would never forget.

He stepped out of the shower and dried himself off quickly. His stomach had started growling while he was showering, and now his thoughts turned from Raegan to what was for dinner. He couldn't hear much with the shower water running, and with his mind focused on the lovely Raegan, he wasn't sure if his grandmother had made it home, or if Mrs. Carson had brought their food over yet. He pulled on his fresh set of clothes and went into the kitchen. He saw everything was just as he'd left it when he went to shower, and knew that his grandmother was not back, nor had Mrs. Carson stopped by. He then saw the note that his grandmother had left for him.

I'm at the Carson's house. There was a train accident and Annette may have been involved. If I am not back by the time you get home, please fix yourself something to eat and stay around the house until I call you. I love you. ~Grandma

So his grandmother *did* know about the train wreck. At least now he wouldn't have to lie or pretend he hadn't been where he wasn't supposed to, and fake dumb when she brought it up later. He could just act like he saw the news or something. Plus, and he sincerely hoped she wasn't, if Annette Carson was somehow involved in the accident, he was sure his grandmother would be too busy helping Mrs. Carson to ask him many questions about his game. He opened the refrigerator and pulled out some things to make a sandwich. He hoped that Annette was alright. If he knew anything, it was how much the Carson's loved their daughter. They would be devastated if anything ever happened to her.

Ty finished fixing his sandwich, and took it into the living room, where he got comfortable on the sofa. He turned on the television. Not surprisingly, most of the channels were showing coverage of the accident from that afternoon. He kept flipping channels, not wanting to relive the horror he'd witnessed firsthand on those train tracks. He finally settled on a sitcom rerun that he really didn't care to watch anyway, and munched thoughtfully on his sandwich. He decided to just chill out for a while, try to wrap his head around what had happened, and wait for his grandmother to call or came back home.

~

DT finally arrived to his sprawling home estate, located in a secluded part of Faries, closed off by a heavy wrought iron security gate. He lived on a fifteen acre lot, with beautiful old trees and a five acre pond surrounding his house. He loved his property, but often felt a longing to have someone to share it with. He was lonely, and regularly found himself reminded of the woman he had been in love with some years ago. She had gotten caught up in drugs and alcohol, and as much as he tried, he could not convince her to seek medical help for her addictions. She'd passed away nearly three years ago, but thoughts of her consumed his mind still.

They had shared lots of good times together. He loved to shower her with gifts and nights out on the town. It was actually during one of those outings that she'd gotten a taste of drugs and soon developed the habit that would ultimately take her life. Thinking back on her, which he seemed to do more and more with each passing day, usually led him straight to feelings of guilt as well. He felt responsible for her downward spiral and death because he had taken her to the places that had the drugs and the alcohol. She may never have gone that route had he not led her there.

She had managed to keep her addiction under control to a point, but then it just started to take over her whole life. He was distraught to have to watch as she changed from the happy, bright woman he'd come to know to a fiend who knew no joy beyond her addiction. She'd become sullen and vacant and only cared about getting her next fix. Over the course of their turbulent relationship after the drugs were introduced, they split up several times, but she always ended up coming back and asking for another chance. DT sincerely and passionately loved her, and always took her back. Still, she continued to disappear for days on end, binging on drugs and alcohol with people she barely knew, but he kept trying to convince her to get sober once and for all.

In one such incident, when the young woman showed up after three days of being gone, she had walked into the kitchen and announced, "I've been cheating on you, and I'm pregnant." Her declaration had shaken him deeply, because he knew that she was in no condition to have a healthy pregnancy, and he was devastated to hear how cold she was in her admission. She told him she was finished with their relationship and that she would be moving out. He pled with her to stay and get medical treatment while she was pregnant and then she could leave. After much convincing, she agreed to stay. For the duration of the pregnancy, she went to her scheduled appointments and detoxification treatments. She carried her child full term, and delivered a surprisingly healthy baby boy. Shortly after that, she'd left again, that time for good, and took her son with her. She returned to the drugs and began living in homeless shelters and with other addicts and friends.

DT sighed at the thought of the woman. He had done his best to keep up with her and send her money and clothes and things after she left that last time. For a while, he saw her every few months. But as his fledgling oil business grew and took up more of his time and energy, she'd slipped further and further away. He finally got news that she had given up her son to her mother and had passed away two years later. He was deeply saddened by the news of her death, even though he had not seen her for some time before that. He had truly loved that woman.

He was now in his bedroom, trying to get prepared to go on his trip. He picked up his phone and dialed Edward Carson's cell phone number. He activated his Bluetooth headset so he could talk while he finished the packing he had started. The phone rang several times and then the voicemail picked up. He left a brief message, telling Edward that he just wanted to check and see if there had been any news about Annie. He promised to call again the next afternoon when he settled into his hotel room.

He then called Raegan. She answered on the second ring. He told her that he would be out of town for a couple of weeks and asked her to come by and water the plants and check on things while he was gone. She had been doing this for some time, so he really didn't need to tell her much. He promised to pay her when he got back in town. She agreed and they hung up.

DT continued packing. He waited for the phone call he knew was coming. D. Baucherie was a wealthy French businessman that he knew from years ago who seemed to always know and call when he was headed out of town. In spite of DT's most valiant efforts to resist and do otherwise, D. could always convince him of their need to meet up and gamble and party in whatever city DT was staying in. This had been going on for a very long time. Had it not been for his accountant and financial advisor, Marcus, who seemed to have shown up just around the time he met D'bauch, as he was known, DT wouldn't have a penny to his name, and he knew it. Marcus kept close tabs on his finances and made sure that certain accounts remained closed and untouchable to anyone, including DT. This had saved him many times when the copious amounts of alcohol he had consumed and the thrill of winning pushed him to try to withdraw more cash from his accounts. Sadly, these weekends of unbridled revelry happened more often than he cared to think about. He was a slave to the rush he got when gambling, and suffered the effects of it as much as the woman he loved did with her drugs and alcohol. His addiction may not be killing his physical body like her addictions killed hers, but his spirit was being destroyed. Marcus was really the only other person who knew of his gambling habits and he had kept the secret. But that did not stop him from telling DT how he felt about what he was doing. DT really did want to stop, but one call from D'bauch was all it took to abandon his good intentions.

~

Raegan got up from the bed and turned on the hotel shower full blast. She let it run on high heat and stood naked in the steamy bathroom. This had become her Saturday ritual. Grimly raped her, and she tried to scald all residue of his presence from her body. She had almost become completely numb to both experiences. The blisteringly hot water no longer burned her skin, and his sick, sweaty body no longer burned her soul. Her tears had subsided, and were replaced with repulsion. She was glad the mirror was too fogged up to see herself. She didn't want to look at what gave him such twisted pleasure to see. Her beautiful curly hair was matted and tangled, and her thighs hurt from trying to squeeze them shut against his violation. She always did that too, but he always managed to pry them open.

She hated him, and she hated herself. She hated her parents for never asking her where was she going on Friday nights, or where had she been when she came home on Saturday afternoons. She hated that no one seemed to realize that this disgusting man had been molesting her since she was eleven and had now, in recent months, begun full out raping her. She hated that she wasn't brave enough to do anything about it. She hated her brother for leaving her at home with parents who barely knew she was alive.

It was shortly after her older brother, Ethan, moved out that Mr. Grimly had moved in on her. It was like he had been waiting for his chance. And with Ethan, who had always been her protector, out of the house and out of the picture, she was fair game for this man's perversion. Grimly was a college buddy of her father's and always seemed to find a way to get her alone. He would touch her inappropriately and tell her how sexy she was, even back at the tender age of eleven when all this started. Even then, she had known it was wrong, but no one seemed to notice or care what was going on. She would plead with her parents not to leave her alone with him, but they would just scold her for being rude to their friends. He'd told her that if she didn't stop whining to her parents, he would hurt them badly and tell everyone that she was doing bad things to him and not the other way around. As a young child, she had believed him and kept her mouth shut, allowing him to do whatever his dark heart led him to.

Now, she stayed in the shower until the water ran cold. She stepped out and covered her red skin with the white hotel towel. She heard her phone ringing in the other room and went to answer it. It was DT Hudson, asking her to come water his plants and check on his house while he was out of town for a couple of weeks. She agreed and hung up the phone.

In one of his many attempts to assuage her anger over his neglect, Raegan's father had bought her a high tech phone with email capabilities. She noticed that she had an email notification on her screen. She opened her mail and saw that she had an email from someone she had met in a chat room. He said he was a student at her school and the two had been communicating online for a little while. He had replied to an email she sent him.

MyDespair2000 wrote: *I'd just end it all if I were in your shoes.*

Edward didn't know where he was going when he sped out of his driveway and down the street. He just had to get away from his house and the two quietly mourning women inside. How could they seem so nonchalant? Everything seemed to have switched to slow motion and nothing seemed real. The past few hours seemed like a blur and he couldn't really connect the pieces. All he knew was that they had just found out his one and only daughter, whom he loved as much as his own life, was never coming home. He felt like he was whispering when the rest of the world was screaming at the top of their lungs. No one seemed to hear him. No one seemed to understand what he was feeling at that moment. And no words he possessed seemed big enough to voice the emptiness that had just settled in his belly. And then, there were his wife and Teenie. What was their reaction? Quiet sadness. Why had neither of them seemed to feel as destroyed as he was, knowing that Annette was gone? Why had neither of them come undone at what they just found out? Did they really expect him to just say, "Oh, well, the Lord works in mysterious ways" and keep on going? That's not what his reeling mind was saying to him right then. He knew that somewhere in this mess, God was there, but right then, he couldn't wrap his brain around that. Right now, he felt like he was dying inside. And he felt like a failure for it.

As he sped aimlessly along, bitter tears streamed down his face, blurring his vision and causing him to slow down. Even though he had come unhinged over the loss of his daughter, the spirit of logic rose up within him and told him that he didn't want to die today too. He wiped his eyes and looked around the neighborhood he'd driven into. It was a beautiful place, with quiet houses set back on the street. No one seemed to be moving around, inside or outside. He heard the sound of dogs barking, but all else was still. Not quite sure of where he was, he kept driving until he came to a place he recognized.

Unconsciously, he'd driven himself to the old diner he used to work in as a teenager. Edward had grown up in Faries, Georgia, and loved it so much that he decided to return there after college and raise his family. As a teen, he had been involved in sports, and to help pay for his uniforms and parties and things, he got a job at a little twenty-four hour diner right on the outskirts of Faries. He loved that job, and loved meeting all the people who came through. But after he returned from college, he hadn't gone back to the diner very much. He became a human resources manager for a small company and then at the oil company that DT Hudson owned, and had bought a beautiful house in a nice neighborhood across town. He started his new life, with his new bride, and never looked back. But now here he was, nearly twenty-five years later, staring his past in the face.

He parked his car and took a minute to try to compose himself before he went inside the diner. The place hadn't changed a whole lot since he had last been there. The familiar smell of hot grease and hard work penetrated his nose and his heart. He felt so at home there. He headed straight to his favorite booth in the back of the diner. He remembered his first date with Leisa had taken place in that very booth. She was such a beautiful young woman, whom he'd met and befriended in high school. They had gone to different colleges, but remained close friends throughout. When they completed college, him with a degree in Business and her with a degree in Education, they'd both moved back to Faries and decided to pursue a romantic relationship. Shortly after their first diner date, he had proposed to her. He knew, from the time they met as high school students, that Leisa Annette Piper was the woman he wanted to spend his life with.

She had been thrilled at the engagement, and happily planned a modest, but beautiful wedding. They had been attending a small church together, and looked forward to exchanging their vows there. Edward had been working as the human resources manager at a small firm, and was making decent money. Leisa was teaching at a small private school, which gave her more time to focus on planning her wedding and preparing for her marriage. They got married and bought a small house. They loved each other, and began creating a life together.

Two years later, Leisa announced that she was pregnant, and they had a daughter. Edward could still remember the day their little girl was born. She was perfect. Just a little, pink bundle of God's goodness. They had taken her to their church a few weeks later, and dedicated her to the Lord. They also recommitted their own lives to Him that day. It was one of the most wonderful days of Edward and Leisa Carson's lives.

And today, the day his little girl was killed, was the darkest day he had ever known. Sitting in that booth had taken his thoughts to where he desperately tried to keep them from going—to his wife, who he'd left to grieve by herself, and to his daughter, who was never going to smile at him again. His chest felt constricted, like an eighteen wheeler was parked on it. He could hardly breathe as he pictured his daughter's beautiful face and imagined what she must have gone through on that train that afternoon.

Stop torturing yourself! Stop thinking about her! Think about something else! He was in agony. He wanted so bad to just turn off all memories of his beloved daughter, because the pain he felt when he thought of never seeing her again was choking the very life out of him. He picked up the menu and tried to focus on the words. He knew that someone would be there soon to take his order and he didn't want them to find him sobbing uncontrollably. He wasn't really hungry, but he picked out a small meal anyway.

A waitress came and took his order. He asked for the strongest coffee they had. He had no intentions of sleeping that night. He knew the second he closed his eyes, images of his daughter would devour his mind. He just was not ready to face the reality of her not being with him anymore.

The waitress soon brought him a steaming cup of black coffee. He added one packet of sugar and took a sip. He looked around the diner, searching for something interesting enough to take his mind off what was happening to him. A woman caught his eye, and he was surprised by the butterflies that rose in his belly. He had never seen anyone like her before. She was a vision of beauty before him. He felt his heart pick up speed as she smiled shyly at him from across the room. Something was happening that he hadn't felt for a long time. He quickly averted his eyes, not wanting to stare. But when he looked over in her direction again, she was still looking at him. She nodded, ever so slightly. He smiled and nodded back. His waitress came at that moment and brought his food to him. She stood directly in his line of vision, blocking his view of the woman. He thanked the waitress, and waited until she walked away. He looked over again for the woman, but she was no longer in the booth where he'd seen her.

Then his cell phone rang. He looked down, hoping it wasn't his wife. It wasn't. It was DT. Edward sighed, and decided to ignore the call. He knew he shouldn't have, but he really didn't feel like small talk or answering any questions right then. He opened his phone and pressed the power button that turned it off completely. He didn't want to be reached tonight.

He looked around slowly, not wanting to be obvious, and scanned the rest of the diner. Suddenly, a voice behind him asked quietly, "Are you looking for me?" To his surprise, the beautiful woman had walked over while he was busy talking to his waitress and fidgeting with his phone, and now stood beside his booth. She smiled down at him, and Edward stared in awe at her loveliness. He was mesmerized. After a moment, he snapped out of it and came to himself.

"I, um, I was um…"he fumbled around for words, and nervously ran his fingers through his wavy brown hair. "Um, actually, yes, I was," he finally admitted.

"Well, here I am." Lead Astray blinked her eyes, and her long dark lashes fluttered. She smiled at Edward and stuck out her hand. "You can call me Leighda."

"How do you do, Leighda? I'm Edward." He shook her outstretched hand.

"So, Edward, do you mind if I sit down? You look like you could use some company, and I was lonely over there all by myself." She stood beside the table, waiting for Edward to respond.

arms and neck stood on end. He could hardly breathe with Lead Astray standing so close to him.

Go home! His entire being screamed those two words over and over.

"Thank you, Edward. I don't understand why your wife would not understand where you are coming from." She continued talking as they exited the diner. "If I were her, I would do whatever you wanted me to. I would be happy to have such a handsome, kind gentleman to call my own. I would never let you be unhappy. I would always leave you satisfied." She looked over at Edward, with a coy smile on her face. Her long brown hair flowed in the breeze that blew past them. She really was one of the most attractive women Edward had ever laid eyes on, and she was not so subtly coming on to him.

"Well, uh, thank you. It's not that she doesn't see where I am coming from. And it's not that we are unhappy in our marriage. People always tell us we are like newlyweds, even after twenty four years." Edward found himself backtracking, trying to let this woman know that he was not interested in her advances. But somewhere deep inside him, he was flattered and enjoying the attention. "I just want her to stop acting like she's not hurting, and like this is not such a big deal. And to not treat me like I'm weak because I *am* hurting."

Lead Astray came over and stood close to Edward, her hand brushing his and her breath sweet on his face. "You don't seem weak at all to me," she whispered suggestively. She kissed him on his cheek and let her lips slide and linger near his. "What do you want to do now?" she asked him.

Edward thought his insides were going to rip through his own flesh. Every fiber of his being shrieked bloody horror against the woman standing beside him, but he could not will his feet to move. His throat felt like a searing rake was scraping up and down it, tearing deeper with every shaky breath he took. His skin felt ice cold, and his arms were like two frozen tree trunks hanging heavily at his sides. A dense fog seemed to have settled itself over his brain, and every thought that passed through was a dark jumbled mess that he couldn't untangle.

Lead Astray stepped back and took his face in her hand. She tenderly tilted it downward until he was once again locked in her gaze. "It's alright, Edward. You don't have to feel guilty. No one can blame you for wanting a little comfort. Your only daughter just died. And your wife isn't making herself available for you. What else could anyone expect you to do besides find someone who understands? This is the darkest day you have ever faced in your life and no one will ever come close to knowing how you feel." Lead Astray's calm voice wound ribbons of lies all around Edward as he stood in a motionless daze. The words swirled and wove a tapestry of deceit above him that slowly descended and came to rest on his head and shoulders, with the corners draping themselves all the way around him and tightening like an invisible, but nonetheless deadly, boa constrictor.

"I just want someone to understand," he agreed, his hazel colored eyes still entwined with Lead Astray's. "I just want someone to be there for me. No one else knows how I feel. My baby girl is dead." The words tumbled from his mouth with ease, even though his heart pounded with total disagreement. It was like his brain and his heart had completely lost all communication. His heart was broken, and longed to be with his wife, to hold her and to comfort her and to be comforted by her, but his brain was not getting the message. He could not seem to make his mind line up with what he really wanted to do, what he knew he should do, and get him as far away from this situation as was humanly possible. Instead, he stood there like a zombie, consenting to the evil suggestions of this strange woman.

"I just want to help you, Edward. That's all. Whatever you want—whatever you need—I want to give it to you. Just let me in. It's alright. It can be our little secret, just between you and me. No one else has to know. Just come with me. Isn't that what you really want to do? For once, why don't you just do what *you* want? Don't worry about right or wrong. Is it right that you have to deal with the death of your sweet baby girl? That accident wasn't right. So why should you be required to act a certain way now? Shouldn't you be able to do what feels right as you grieve? Who's to say what's right for you in a situation like this? Shouldn't you be the one to decide what's best for you and what's going to work for you right now? What you do is no one else's business. No one else knows what's going on inside you right now. But I want to. I want to be there for you, Edward. I want to know what's going on inside you. I want to know how you feel. I want to make you feel better." Lead Astray held his face for a moment longer, and then let him go, studying him and waiting. He looked away without responding to her. Seeing that he wasn't quite ensnared in the trap she was setting, Lead Astray turned her back to him and quickly changed tactics.

"This always happens to me. I meet a great guy who has already been snatched up. I just feel like the ugly duckling who can't ever get what she wants. No one seems to ever want to be with me. All I want is a little happiness with someone. I would do whatever it took to make him happy and keep him that way. I guess I'm just not good enough." She dropped her head, making her shiny brown hair ripple, like rich chocolate waves over her shoulders, as she began crying softly.

Edward finally seemed back in some control of his faculties. He walked over to Lead Astray and gently touched her shoulder. "I'm sure that's not true, Leighda. You're *not* the ugly duckling and you *are* good enough for someone. You just have to find the right man."

Lead Astray turned and grabbed Edward, burying her face in his chest. "Why can't it be you, Edward? I've always dreamed of having someone like you!" She looked up and stared pleadingly into his eyes. "Don't you want to know what it's like to be with a woman who will do anything you say? To be with someone who will fulfill your deepest desires? Don't you want to be with a woman who can make your every fantasy come true? Please, just let me show you how that feels!"

As if she knew exactly where to aim, Lead Astray's plea penetrated the place in Edward's mind where a long fought war raged fiercest. Having her cling to him with such unashamed desperation and yearning re-ignited a spark of masculinity within him that had long ago fizzled out in his own marriage.

Looking down at her, Edward was again spellbound by the unparalleled beauty she possessed, in spite of her tear streaked face and pink flushed cheeks, both of which seemed to only further accentuate and reinforce her feminine appeal in his eyes. Being in her presence was bringing to light, in a split second, every secret struggle that Edward had worked so feverishly to keep hidden. He had never before specifically addressed the feelings that were now crashing over him with such violent force, neither in his own heart nor aloud to his wife, but right now, standing face to face with Lead Astray, sincerely considering her offer, he could not deny how real the wedge was that had come between himself and his beloved Leisa. Although he loved his wife dearly, she was one of the strongest women he knew, and she hardly ever seemed the damsel in distress being portrayed by the woman before him now. He tried to tell himself that he was glad that his wife could make it on her own, because if anything ever happened to him, he could rest assured that she would be alright without him. But the truth was, behind this logic he had programmed himself to believe, he longed to be needed—to be called upon to be the warrior and protector for his wife. It wasn't that he wanted her to come unhinged or to completely unravel in the face of every adversity. He just wanted her to be unapologetically vulnerable sometimes and to request *him*, her flesh and blood husband, to come in and rescue her.

But she didn't. His role as adored savior, riding in to save the day on his trusty white steed, had some time ago been replaced in his wife's heart by a deep reliance on Jesus Christ as her only Lord, and all she needed in times of distress. So what this other woman was doing—pining after and making a demand of him—was exactly what he desired from his wife, but couldn't seem to convey to her without feeling like a total chauvinist. He knew that Leisa loved him with every part of her being, but her lack of *needing* him had a way of making him feel like less than a man. Up until now, Edward simply pushed his feelings of inadequacy to the back of his mind, chiding himself for being too sensitive.

The most troubling issue, however—the part that Edward thought he had locked away in the darkest recesses of his mind and never intended to admit to anyone—was that this battle he fought within himself, this internal wrestling match of knowing that Leisa was righteous in making Christ number one over him but wanting to be number one all the same, made him resentful toward the Lord—not in a way to make him abandon his walk of faith outright, but enough to make him less than eager to share with his own wife in the intimacy of what should have been their mutual relationship with Him. He secretly felt as if he were losing his wife to this invisible Lover, this third party within their union. This progression of thought was irrational and completely against the plan of God, he knew, and he had worked so hard to keep those feelings of anger and jealousy toward the Lord hidden away, but now they all came boiling to the surface.

The chasm between his heart and his mind grew wider with every second he stood beside Lead Astray. The line that separated reality from fiction grew hazier by the moment. Edward felt himself being pulled further and further from what he knew in his gut to be the absolute truth, but his mind was so deeply entrenched in combat that the quiet Voice in his heart barely registered above an inaudible murmur.

Was this really him? Did he really feel this way about God and his wife's dependence on His arm alone? Something inside him whispered a frantic *No!* But Lead Astray's voice broke in and drowned out the other.

"Edward," she said softly. The sound of his name rolling off her tongue dripped with syrupy sweetness, as if the word itself had been dipped in the purest honey straight off the honeycomb. "Just give me one night. All I ask is for one night to give you what you need. One night of uninhibited passion. One night to show you what you're missing. One night and then I disappear…if that's what you want. Can you handle just one night?"

"I…I don't know," he stuttered.

Jason woke up Sunday morning feeling like *he* had been in a train wreck. His mind was in a fog, and his heart ached within him. He wanted to believe that the day before had been a really bad prank, or that he had dreamt the whole thing. But when he opened his eyes and saw that he was not at his own house in his own bed, but was lying in the Lafleur's guest room bed, he knew that it was all real, and his parents really were dead. A single tear rolled down his temple and into his hair as he lay on the pillow.

He wiped at the other tears that were welling up in his eyes. *I am not going to spend all day crying*, he vowed to himself.

He sat up slowly and stretched his stiff body. He had been mentally and physically exhausted by the time he went to bed the night before, but still surprised himself by falling asleep almost as soon as he lay down. He expected his grief to keep him awake for at least a little while, but it seemed to have had the opposite effect. He'd slept through the whole night, and could not remember waking up a single time. It seemed as if he had lain in the bed last night and hadn't moved a muscle the entire night. He slept a solid, dreamless kind of sleep that didn't really do much to renew his body or his mind. Now, as he stretched, he could hear hushed voices outside the door of the guest room, and the smell of pancakes and syrup wafted up to his nose. He found himself actually quite hungry, and went into the bathroom to wash up.

He walked out into the hallway and followed the smells and the voices into the kitchen. He was greeted by Mrs. Lafleur and Mya. "Hi, Chaz." Mya gave him a timid smile.

"Good morning, Jason. Are you hungry?" Mrs. Lafleur reached out and gently squeezed Jason's arm.

"Good morning, Mrs. Lafleur. Hi, Mya. Yes, ma'am, I am pretty hungry."

"Well, good. I'm glad to hear that. We have grits, scrambled eggs, pancakes, waffles, bacon and sausage. There is orange juice, milk and bottled water in the refrigerator." Mrs. Lafleur handed him a plate. "Help yourself, honey. Eat as much as you want. We have plenty."

Jason took the plate from her hands and walked over to the kitchen island where Mya stood beside the food. She turned and hugged him, saying, "You want me to get you some orange juice while you fix your plate?" He nodded, and she took a glass from the cabinet and went to the fridge. Jason put three fluffy pancakes on his plate and two slices of bacon. He grabbed the bottle of syrup and poured some onto his pancakes. Mya handed him the glass of juice and he went and sat down at the kitchen table. She quickly made herself a plate and joined him.

"So, this is what it's going to be like when we get married, huh?" she joked lightly with him. "Me fixing you breakfast, and us sitting together at our little table to eat. I'll be wearing my cute little Sunday morning apron, and you will have on your Sunday morning robe and jammies. It will be just like this—except my mother definitely won't be standing here with us!" Jason looked up and gave her a small smile. It was so unlike him, the eternal jokester, to let a moment like that go by without so much as a chuckle or a witty comeback. Feeling helpless and not really knowing what to do, she was trying to make him laugh and maybe take his mind off everything for a moment, but Mya could see that Jason was still trying to process what had happened the day before, so she went back to quietly eating her pancakes.

"Jason, honey, I didn't know how you would be feeling today, so I just wanted to let you know what our plans are for this morning and then you can decide what you want to do." Mya's mother stepped in. Jason looked at her and nodded. "Mya and I are going to go to church this morning, but Mr. Lafleur said that he would stay here with you if you didn't feel up to going with us. You can stay here and get some more rest. We hope you will stay at our house until other, more permanent, living arrangements can be made for you. Mr. Lafleur said he would take you to your house this afternoon to get some more clothes and your school books, and then you two can go to the police station to get your truck and bring here. You don't have to go back to school tomorrow if you aren't up to it, but whatever you want to do is ok with us. Mya can pick up your assignments if you decide not to go for a few days." She stopped for a moment. "And I know you and Mya usually go to Mr. and Mrs. Carson's house for Sunday evening dinner, but, unfortunately, they lost their daughter, Annette, yesterday as well. I don't think they will be up for dinner guests tonight, and I didn't think you would be into going anyway. So after church, we're going to stop and get something for lunch and to cook for tonight. When we get back this afternoon, we will see about getting some information as to what needs to be done for you. Do you want us to pick up anything specific for lunch or dinner?"

Jason was quiet for a few minutes. "Well, thank you for the breakfast and the invitation, but I don't think I am up for church this morning. I kind of just want to go get my truck and some stuff to bring here. Thanks for letting me stay with you guys. I think I should go to school tomorrow though. I need to get things back to as much normal as I can. And whatever you want to bring for lunch and dinner is fine with me. I don't really have anything special I want."

"I understand, and that is perfectly fine with me. I will let Mr. Lafleur know. Just get finished with your breakfast and then let him know when you are ready to go. We will be back from church around one o'clock."

~

Mya really wished Jason had decided to come to the church service that morning. It would have done his heart some good to hear hope from the Word of God. But as her mom said, it was just the first day since the accident, and they had to let him heal at his own pace, in his own way. She rode with her mother to the service in silence.

They pulled into the parking lot of the church building and headed inside. People greeted one another with smiles and hugs, but there was a tangible sense of heaviness in the building. Most everyone had heard about the train wreck and had themselves been affected directly or knew someone who was affected directly by it.

The singers took to the platform and opened the service up with praise and worship songs. After they were finished, Pastor James walked into the pulpit. He said a word of prayer, and then spoke solemnly to the congregation. He acknowledged the accident, and offered his condolences to everyone who was involved. He then changed up the usual order of the service and invited everyone to stand to their feet. They all did so. He instructed them to join hands with their neighbors, and as a congregation, they lifted their voices in prayer for the families of the victims of the tragedy the day before. After a good long while, he closed the prayer and invited those who were interested to an evening prayer meeting later that day. They would specifically pray for individuals who were involved or affected by the accident.

Mya decided to come back that evening, and planned to invite her best friend Raegan to join her. She hoped that Raegan would want to go in support of Jason as well. She made a mental note to call Raegan as soon as she got back home. For now, she would just soak in the truth of the Word of the Lord as Pastor James ministered a heartfelt message on the providence of God.

Mya fiddled absentmindedly with her hair as she dialed Raegan's number. She had just gotten home from church and was about to call Raegan to update her on what all was going on. In the midst of all the drama that went on the night before, it was early that next morning before Mya even thought to call and let Raegan know what all had happened with Jason and the Carson's. She also needed to let her know that dinner was off for that evening, and probably for a while after that night. But really, she just wanted to talk to her best friend.

The two of them had been friends for a good while. They met in elementary school and had developed a strong connection from the beginning. They were as different as night and day, but they complemented each other well. Each girl balanced out what the other lacked and it made for a great combination. Over the years, they'd had many a slumber party and gabfest, sharing some of their deepest and darkest secrets with one another. Both girls turned to each other with problems and issues that they couldn't share with anyone else, and they loved each other like sisters.

Lately, though, it seemed like the girls weren't connecting like they used to. Mya could sense that Raegan had been holding something back from her. She took little comfort in the promise they'd made years ago that said they would always open up and share everything with each other, no matter how horrible or dark whatever they shared seemed to be. And they promised to always support each other, and never judge or criticize the other for what she told. But a lot of years and experiences had passed since they made that promise, and Mya wasn't so sure it held its true value anymore—at least not in Raegan's eyes.

Mya also knew that Raegan wasn't crazy about her spending so much time with Jason recently, but she didn't think that was the only thing coming between them. Whatever it was had worked like a slow, but steady, drift, pulling them apart day by day. The two girls hadn't been spending much time together or talking much at all for several months, if not longer. Raegan seemed to be avoiding Mya, actually, and becoming increasingly sullen and isolated. And then, on the rare occasions when they did talk, Raegan seemed distant and as though her mind was going in fifteen different directions at any given time. If Mya asked her what was going on with her, she would laugh and apologize and just gloss over the question, saying that nothing was wrong and that she just had a lot on her mind at the moment. But Mya knew Raegan well enough by now to know that it wasn't just "nothing." She also knew her well enough to know that Raegan would quickly shut down if she felt trapped, or like someone was trying to force her to do or say something she didn't want to. It was as though she had this place in her mind, and like a wild animal, would retreat there when she got scared or felt threatened or as though her heart was in danger. It was a defense mechanism she had been using for years, so Mya had learned not to push, but she was growing progressively more worried about her friend.

And now she had to drop this bomb on her. The subject of Jason was a touchy one already, and adding that he would be staying with

Mya and her family was bound to cause some hard feelings on Raegan's part.

"She's got to understand that he needs me right now," Mya said aloud.

"Mya? Who are you talking to?" Raegan sounded perplexed on the other end of the line. She had picked up while Mya was lost in her thoughts and caught the tail end of what she had said.

"Raeyo! Hey! I was just talking to myself," Mya replied.

"Oh, well, you know I told you only crazy people do that," Raegan joked.

Mya chuckled. "Yeah, I know." Her tone turned serious. "Raegan, I need to talk to you though."

"What's up? You sound upset."

Mya took a deep breath. "Well, you heard about that train wreck yesterday, right?"

"Yeah, it sounded awful!"

"Well, Annette Carson was on that train. She died, Rae."

Raegan gasped on the other end of the phone. "No! Are you sure? Oh, my goodness! That's terrible! How are the Carson's?"

Mya could hear the sadness in Raegan's voice. She knew and loved Annette and the Carsons too, and this was a heavy blow for them all. "Yes, we are sure. And they aren't doing so great, as you can imagine. Teenie is over with them now. But that's not all." Mya paused, not really sure how to tell Raegan about the Harrington's or if she should even bring it up. She didn't want to seem as though her whole life revolved around Jason, but he *was* her boyfriend, and Raegan's friend too, and surely she'd want to know what happened to him. "Jason's parents were killed too, Rae. They were on their way back from a trip to Burney, and they didn't survive the crash.

Jason is staying at my house for now." Mya's voice trailed off, as she waited for a response from her friend.

"Oh, Mya! I am so sorry! Is he ok? I had no idea!" Raegan's voice cracked a little as she choked back tears. "Mya, what can I do? Do you guys need anything? Do you want me to come over? I didn't even know his parents were out of town. Is Jason alright?" Raegan's voice was full of sincerity as she tried to voice her sympathy.

Mya was somewhat shocked at Raegan's reaction. "Uh, well, he's alright, I guess. I mean, he's doing as well as can be expected. He's really sad, but he's trying to be strong. And we're all just trying to be there for him. He and my dad are at his house right now, picking up some clothes. They have to go get his truck from the police station. He left it there last night after he found out about his parents."

Raegan spoke as though she heard the surprise in Mya's voice, and knew what she was thinking. "I know he and I aren't that close, but he just lost his parents, Mya. All drama goes to the side in a situation like this. I really hate this for him. And he *is* my friend, even though we aren't the best of. So, is there anything I can do?"

"Well, there is going to be a special prayer service tonight at my church for the people and the families affected by the wreck."

While Mya spoke, Raegan's call waiting clicked in her ear. She looked at her phone and saw that it was Grimly calling on the other line. Her heart began pounding, and she lost focus of what Mya was saying.

"Do you think you can come?" Mya waited for Raegan to answer.

"I'm sorry, Mya. I have to go. I will call you back in a little while," she said and quickly hung up. She threw the phone down and left the room. She wasn't prepared to face any of that mess right then.

Mya held the phone in her hand for a moment, listening to the dial tone. What had just happened? Raegan seemed fine and then all of a sudden, she just bailed out. This was exactly what Mya had become concerned about. Something was definitely going on with Raegan and she was determined to find out what it was.

~

Even though DT Hudson III could afford to fly any airline at any time he chose, he still preferred early morning or late night flights. Over the long years he had spent building his business, he became a night owl, with many a late night spent making crucial decisions and worrying over production and cash flow issues. So now, even though those days were over, and his company was fully functioning and quite successful, his body still ran most efficiently on night energy. That was fine by him though. Unlike himself, few people *chose* to take those red eye flights so, when he did, he was often one of only a handful of people in the terminals, and he had lots of time to himself to think without interruption. He liked the quiet of the dark surrounding him as he looked out the windows of the airports and planes. During his flights and layovers, he enjoyed thinking back and remembering where he started and seeing how far he'd come. He also liked to quietly imagine all the things he'd rather be seeing and doing instead of traveling to business meetings and networking seminars.

Most people only knew him as David Tyler Hudson III, oil tycoon and wealthiest man in Faries, but there was so much more to him than that. He had the heart of an artist inside of him. It was a side that most people didn't know. Deep down, beneath the business man visage, lay a smoldering flicker of flame that dully glowed with the remnants of once consuming creativity. This flicker used to be a raging passion, a conflagration of vision and zeal, ablaze with reckless abandon and its own free will. But after his beloved Mali passed away, it was as if the joy-filled oxygen that the fire needed to survive was sucked out of DT's soul. So now, without her, this artistic side was a side that rarely came to light anymore.

DT still did things with Mali in mind though. Marcus had suggested a few years ago that he use some of the money his company made to sponsor various activities around the community, specifically for the schools in the area. DT liked the idea because, even though he hadn't known Mali's son or much about him, he knew that he was still living in the city. He felt a connection to the young man, through their mutual love of Mali, and liked to think that by helping him, he was, in some way, helping Mali. He hadn't been able to help her while she was still on the earth, but her son was a part of her, so helping him was as close to helping Mali as DT could ever get now. The guilt he felt about her was still as raw today as it was the day he found out she had died. He knew that nothing he did now could turn back the hands of time and change what had happened to her, but he still wanted to honor her memory and do what he could to make things right by her in his heart.

DT was surprised when someone sat down in the seat next to him, jolting him out of his thoughts. He looked up to see a nice-looking young man looking back at him. The man smiled and thrust out his hand. "Hello, there!" Leaning in very close, the man spoke with a thick Italian accent. "My name is Nunzi. This is going to be one great flight!" He looked directly into DT's eyes, nodding slightly. DT, whose heart had begun beating rapidly as soon as the man sat down, obediently stuck out his hand.

"Yes, it will," he said absently. He had become very warm and uncomfortable all of a sudden. There was nothing physically menacing about this other man, but DT felt uneasy with him anyway. He felt the muscles in his shoulders and neck tense up. His stomach tied itself into a tight knot and his feet began tingling. He wanted to get up and run away, but the man sat between him and the exit, and DT couldn't seem to drag his eyes away from Nunzi's. *What is wrong with me?* DT wondered. *The man just sat down and he seems like a nice enough guy. Why am I freaking out like this?*

As if he were reading DT's thoughts, the man lowered his eyes and leaned back. "I apologize, sir. In my country, we are very friendly people. I have been taught that Americans are not so, uh, comfortable with physical affection and proximity as we are, yet sometimes I forget. I do not mean to make you uneasy. I am just so happy to be here in America!" The sound of the man's voice was smooth and hypnotic. He caught DT's eye again, but this time, it was like they communicated with DT and told him to relax. DT immediately felt his body loosening up. His body temperature returned to normal and he no longer felt anxious.

He smiled back at Nunzi. "Oh, no, it's alright! I didn't mean to seem so rude! I am just so used to having nearly the entire plane to myself on these early morning flights that I was just a little surprised to have you sit down right beside me."

"Ah, yes! You fly a lot, do you, Mr. Hudson?" Nunzi nodded enthusiastically.

DT recoiled slightly. *How does he know my name?* he thought. *I didn't tell him that my name was Hudson, so how does he know?* DT instantly grew suspicious of the man again, and the feeling of panic he'd just had returned with vigor.

"You wonder how I know your name, yes?" Nunzi's voice regained its hypnotic cadence. "The, uh, flight helper told me that I would be seated next to a Mr. Hudson. I assumed that you are he, since there is no one else around. Am I incorrect?" The rhythmic lilt of his voice nearly put DT into a trance.

Well, that makes sense, DT thought. "Oh, no. You are correct. I am Mr. Hudson." *Get it together, Hudson! He's not from here and you are setting a poor example of American hospitality to this guy! What's your problem? Stop freaking out and making yourself look like a total idiot! You're making this guy feel bad when you're the one acting like a jerk!* "How about we start over?" he said finally. He stuck out his hand. Nunzi smiled and accepted his suggestion in an agreeable handshake. "My name is David Hudson. But you can call me DT. And you are?"

"Just call me Nunzi. I can tell we are going to be great friends, DT." Denunciation grinned, knowing that he had just gotten DT Hudson III right where he needed him, afraid to offend the foreigner and walking gingerly on a well-laid bed of eggshells.

It was the middle of the night when Edward finally arrived back home. He sat silently in his car for a long while. To him, the passage of time had lost all significance from the moment he knew that Annette was dead. So much had happened with him between that moment and now that he wasn't even sure what day it was as he sat in his driveway, peering up through the darkness at what used to be his dream home. And he didn't know exactly what to expect when he went in, but he knew that whatever awaited him inside that house was of no good report, so he was in no hurry to go inside to face a despondent wife and the memories of a dead daughter. He quickly shook Annette out of his mind because debilitating anguish overwhelmed his entire being with every thought of her. He quickly realized that thinking of Leisa was no better, because the guilt he was feeling right now was so great that, by itself, it was more than enough raw emotion to push him over the edge and into the depths of some bottomless pit. He wanted desperately to just turn off all his thoughts completely. If only that were possible. But it wasn't. So since it was not allowed to think about his wife or his daughter, he left his mind no choice but to wander to the one other person he was struggling with all his might to forget about. He dropped his head, and jammed his fists into his eyes, trying unsuccessfully to dam up the tears that threatened to fall.

Oh, God! He thought. *What have I done?*

~

Unaware that her husband sat miserably outside, just a stone's throw away, Leisa dejectedly lay alone in their bed. It had been nearly twenty four hours since she found out her beautiful, vibrant daughter was in Heaven. Rolling over onto her side, she reached over sadly and laid her hand in the spot where her husband's chest should have been. From the depths of her sorrow, her spirit cried out to her God.

"Father! Help me!" she begged. Her physical tears had finally stopped flowing, but her heart was still weeping nonetheless. The cavernous void that had first shown itself when she got the news about Annie, and had been slowly growing wider until she thought could not get any wider without splitting her body completely apart, in an instant seemed to double in size in the pit of her stomach. One of her best earthly friends was dead, and her life partner was nowhere around to help shoulder the burden and ease the pain.

She had spent most of the day alone. After a long night of crying and praying, she had sent Teenie home earlier that day, to tend to Ty. She thought for sure that her husband would have been back by now, but he wasn't. She didn't know where he had gone or what he had done, but she knew that the news of Annie's death had come as an unforeseen and devastating blow to him, so she tried to allow him the room to mourn on his own for a while. But after so much time had passed without hearing a single word from him, she was beginning to worry. Lying awake for the second night without her husband by her side, with feelings of hopelessness and grief she herself was fighting to keep at bay, she knew that for him to have left the way he did and still not have come back or called to let her know that he was alright, what was happening must have sent Edward to the bleakest place that existed in his heart, and she could only imagine the utter desolation he must have been facing there, especially without her there to help anchor him.

Of all his wonderful qualities as a man and a husband, without a doubt, one of the things that Leisa loved the most about Edward was how much and how well and how truly he loved their daughter. Watching them together for Annie's years on the earth was like seeing a clear picture of how God must have felt about Jesus. Leisa always joked with others that one day Edward would pop the buttons on his shirt when he spoke of his beloved Annette, because his pride in her swelled his chest a full two sizes bigger. There was nothing in the world that he wouldn't do for her, and she knew that he would have traded places with her on that train yesterday in a heart's beat.

Leisa quickly forced herself to shift her focus elsewhere, to happier times away from the train wreck, because thoughts of what had happened to Annette the day before were too horrific to bear. She went back in her mind to the day she found out she was pregnant, and began reminiscing about all the joy that her daughter had brought over the last twenty-two years. As she did, her heart was filled with warmth and comfort, and visions of her daughter's angelic face filled her mind's eye.

She could remember as clear as crystal the day she told Edward that he was going to be a father. She had never seen his face light up that way before. Tears welled up in his eyes, and he had hugged her in an embrace she hoped would last forever. He was so happy to be having a child with her that, by the evening of that same day, he had called everyone he knew to share the glad tidings. He could hardly contain himself, and his excitement was contagious. Gifts, calls and congratulations poured in from every direction. And before that week ended, Edward had already bought a stroller, crib, car seat, and booster seat.

"For when she gets older," he had replied when Leisa questioned him about it.

"She?" Leisa had said. It was still much too soon for them to know what the sex of the baby was, but from the moment she told him they were expecting, Edward had begun referring to their first-born as 'she'.

"Yes, 'she'." he said.

"And how do you know it's a girl? How do you know it's not a boy? Don't you want a strapping, handsome little Edward Duane Carson Jr. running around here?" she had teased him. But he remained firm in his stance.

"She's a she, and I know it!" he told her.

"What makes you say that, Eddie?" Leisa had been so amused by his insistence that they were having a girl. He could never give her a definitive answer as to why he believed so, but he seemed to know without a shadow of a doubt that she was carrying a little girl.

"We're going to name her Annette Piper Carson, after her mama." The night he made that announcement, Leisa wept uncontrollably. She tried to blame her tears on her rapidly changing body and raging hormones, but the truth was, she saw how much her husband already loved this unborn child that he had helped create, and she was deeply moved and honored that he would want to so readily put her name on something he held so close to his heart. So, way before they ever had the ultrasound to prove his hunch about the gender right or wrong, the baby was christened Annette Piper, Leisa's middle and maiden names.

The day they went for the ultrasound to find out the sex, Edward had stood expectantly beside the table as the nurse squirted the cold jelly onto Leisa's abdomen. He looked nonchalantly out the window as the doctor used her instrument to first locate the heartbeat and then identify the baby's genitals.

"Doc," he'd said casually, "please inform my wife that we are having a girl."

The doctor looked incredulously at him. "Mr. and Mrs. Carson, have you two been to another doctor before?"

"No, ma'am," he replied politely.

"Why do you ask? Is everything ok?" Leisa asked anxiously.

"Well, then, Mr. Carson, if you've never been to another doctor, how did you already know she was a girl?" she said, ignoring Leisa's questions and turning to Edward in amazement.

Edward had laughed triumphantly. "I was right? I knew it!" he shouted. He was excited to have been correct about the sex, but was even more enthusiastic that little Annette Piper Carson was doing just fine. The doctor went on to show them on the monitor all the things that she was looking for to gather important information. All the news she gave them was good. Edward and Leisa were walking on air when they left the doctor's office that day.

~

After several hours of sitting in the driveway, trying to muster enough courage to face the shattered remnants of what used to be his blessed and happy life, Edward finally got up the nerve to go into his house. He slowly climbed out of the car and stood beside it for a moment before slamming the door shut and heading up the front walk. When he went in the door, the house was pitch black. There was not a light on anywhere inside. Even the clocks on the kitchen appliances seemed to glow so dimly that they were barely visible.

Edward really didn't want to fool with the switches and risk rousing his wife if she was already asleep, so without turning any lights on, he instinctively maneuvered around the obstacles between himself and the hallway that led to his bedroom. His eyes eventually adjusted to the dark and he could make out a little clearer what lay before him. He reached the end of the hallway and stopped in front of his closed master bedroom door. After a moment, he pushed the door open, trying his best not to make much noise. His intent was to grab some clothes from his chest of drawers, a blanket from the linen closet in the bathroom and maybe his pillow from the bed if Leisa was not using it, and take them and try to get a little sleep on the couch in the living room.

"Eddie? Is that you?" Leisa's voice called to him from the darkness.

"Yes," he replied.

"Are you alright? Where have you been?" she asked him, before switching on the lamp on her bedside table.

"I've been out," he answered lamely.

Leisa climbed out of the bed and wrapped her arms around her husband. He just stood there with his arms at his sides. "I've been so worried about you! Why didn't you call? I thought something happened to you. And I don't think I can handle another tragedy right now. This is already too much." She stopped speaking when he mumbled something under his breath. She stepped back and studied his face. "What did you just say," she asked him.

"Nothing," he muttered.

She dropped her arms and took another step away from him. "Eddie! Tell me! What did you just say?"

"Fine," he shot back venomously. "I said, 'You're sure good at hiding it'."

"What is that supposed to mean? I'm good at hiding what?"

"Well, it was sure hard to tell that this was all 'too much' yesterday. You didn't act so broken up to me. You hardly said a word when they came and told us," Edward's voice caught in his throat, "that she is gone," he finished, his voice going flat.

"And how would you know how I acted anyway?" she retorted. "You weren't even here!"

"You're right! I *did* leave! I was going out of my mind in agony, and I just couldn't stand to stay here and watch you soldier on like a good little Christian and pretend like nothing was wrong. Like our *only daughter* wasn't dead! Like it was just fine with you that God let her die!"

"What do you want from me, Eddie? You want me to just lose all control and blame God for what is happening? Is that what you want? Do you want me to just completely fall apart? Do you want me to scream and cry and curse? Do you want me to beat my chest and rip my clothes and shake my fist at the sky? Would you feel better if I threw up my hands and gave up on everything that's left in my life? Do I have to fall on the floor and throw a fit like I have no hope? What is it? What do I have to do to make you believe that I am in agony too? Tell me, because I honestly don't know! All I *do* know is that on the worst day of my *life,* when I felt like I was suffocating, just at the time when I needed you the most, you walked out on me!" She stopped speaking and looked at Edward through the relentless tears that were now streaming down her face. "You walked away, Eddie." Her voice shook as she tried to put into words what she was going through. "You didn't pull me out of this pit I'm drowning in and resuscitate me. You didn't breathe God's life back into me. Isn't that what we are supposed to do for each other? We're each other's help. We're partners. We're supposed to be one! You are supposed to feel everything I feel. But you walked away." She could hardly get out the last words. "And you didn't even give me the chance to be there for you." She collapsed into a heap of tears and despair on the floor. Her mind reeled and began spinning out of control. All sorts of evil thoughts and images began bombarding her mind, as her husband stood silently above her. Her sadness about the loss of her daughter was quickly being replaced by anger and frustration toward her husband. She could feel the empathy she had moments before been feeling for him seeping out of her heart like helium from a pin-pricked balloon. She knew that the enemy was trying to lead her in a direction she didn't need to let herself go.

Peace, Father! Give me peace! she prayed silently. *Give me the right words to say. I won't speak another word without You guiding my tongue. Don't let me say the wrong thing right now. My emotions are running wild, but I refuse to give the enemy any foothold here. Help me, please!*

Immediately, Leisa's mind quieted. Calmness engulfed her entire body and her tears stopped flowing. Her frantic breathing slowed to its normal rhythm and her composure returned. She wiped her eyes dry and looked up at Edward. It was as if she was seeing him for the first time. He stood there like a lost and helpless little boy. But the lines in his face and the red that rimmed his eyes told a different story—a story of many years of hard life lessons learned. She could so clearly see that he was suffering. He was confused and scared and angry and sad, and the last thing he needed was for her to heap all of her emotional baggage on top of his. Suddenly, her aggravation dissolved and she was again filled with mercy and compassion toward her husband.

"You know what? This is not the time for us to pull away from each other. I need you, Eddie. We need each other. It doesn't matter what else happened. Whatever else is going on, it's alright. Our baby girl is gone, and I need you to tell me it's going to be alright. Tell me that this pain is going to stop. Tell me that we are going to live through this! Tell me! Just come down here and tell me that. Take me in your arms and tell me! I need you to hold me, Eddie. Please, hold me! Make this alright! I know you can make this alright! Can't you?"

Leisa was saying all the things that Edward had just the day before claimed he wanted to hear from her. But today her plea fell on deaf ears, coming, in his mind, a moment out of sync. Her words hung in the air for a moment and then slowly drifted to the floor beside her, like dead leaves falling from a tree in the dark of a starless autumn night. He remained silent.

It's too late, he convinced himself, his mind growing darker and stonier by the second. *What is she trying to do here? Where was all this neediness yesterday? Now she is going to try to manipulate me? I already know she doesn't need me. She's thinks she's so righteous she doesn't need anyone! I'll show her. Let Jesus rescue her now!*

Edward had already built a case against her in his mind, with Lead Astray as his star false witness, and now, no matter what she did, Leisa Carson had no defense. Lead Astray's seed of deception had already taken deep root in him, and his darling Leisa was becoming a stranger, pounding hopelessly on the door of his heart that had been dead bolted from the inside. And Lead Astray held the key.

Dreading every moment after her brain registered conscious-ness and her eyes opened, Raegan dragged herself out of bed and into the bathroom to get ready for school Monday morning. She was really beginning to hate *all* days. She definitely hated Fridays and Saturdays. Sundays were getting more unbearable by the week, and now Mondays were starting to slide into the "hellish" category too. She knew that today was going to be an especially tough day, just two days after the train accident. She hadn't called Mya back after she hung up on her the afternoon before nor did she go to the prayer meeting last night, and she really wasn't looking forward to the barrage of questions she knew was coming because of it. Just the thought of what the day held was more than enough to make her want to get back in the bed and never get back up. She already had enough of her own garbage to wade through just to make it through a normal day, so trying to take on the loads of others today seemed completely outside her realm of ability.

She hated how insensitive and selfish that made her sound, but she couldn't help feeling that way. She didn't know how to sympa-thize with others. "No one ever sympathizes with me," she muttered as she ran a wide-toothed comb through her curly hair. But it wasn't that she necessarily blamed anyone for not sympathizing with her. No one really knew they had a reason *to* sympathize with her. What bothered her was that no one seemed to care enough to dig a little deeper into a real relationship with her and find out otherwise.

Mya Lafleur was the only exception to that rule. Tears welled up in Raegan's eyes as she stood in front of the mirror, thinking about her best friend. She loved Mya like the sister she never had. And Mya loved her even more purely than that. Mya loved her from a place that she couldn't even comprehend. She didn't take from her like everyone else who claimed to love her did. Mya didn't judge her, or expect her to act a certain way based on her looks or her background. Mya didn't ask her to be anyone other than who she truly was. It had been so long since she had really been able to open up, let others in and just feel free to be herself that Raegan wasn't even sure if she knew who "she" was anymore. But even when she built up walls and pushed her away, Mya kept right on loving her. In fact, it seemed like all her shortcomings made Mya love her more!

Mya had been her friend for as long as she could remember. Everything about Mya was wonderful in her eyes. Raegan had always wished that she could be more like Mya. She loved the way Mya spoke and thought and laughed and loved and lived. Raegan wanted to be happy and confident and strong like Mya was. She admired her so much. Mya had such deep convictions about things, and lived her life without compromise, no matter how hard that sometimes became. She didn't merely exist, like Raegan did. She truly loved life and made it a point to enjoy everyday she was alive. And she was quick to share that joy with all those around her. She walked in unhindered peace and favor, and Raegan envied Mya all those wonderful things that abounded in her life.

Mya also had this way with people that Raegan didn't think she could ever master. Mya could talk to anyone and make them feel like they were the most important person in the world. That was one of her best qualities in Raegan's opinion. Mya was one of the world's most beautiful people, inside and out, but she walked in graceful humility, and no one ever seemed unreachable to her.

And although she had never told Mya this, Raegan especially loved Mya's nicknames. These were special names reserved just for Mya to call those she loved. After spending some time with someone, and developing a relationship with them, Mya would become dissatisfied with just calling them by their given name, the name that everyone else called them. So she would come up with some unique name for the person that only she was allowed to call them. It was always some cutesy word that made Mya and the person smile every time she said it, representing some special moment or sentiment understood only by those two.

Her nickname for Raegan was "Raeyo." It was a simple name, just the combination of her first name, Raegan, and her middle name, Ayo, but Raegan loved to hear Mya call her by that name. She had been calling her that since they were little girls, when their friendship thrived, before any of the bad that was now swallowing Raegan whole came into their lives. Just the way she said it expressed such love and a well-built camaraderie between the two of them. That name stood as a reminder to Raegan that no one else loved her the way Mya did, and the sound of that name alone spoke with resounding clarity the magnitude and depth of the bond they shared. They were irreplaceable in one another's lives.

Over the years, Mya and her family had been there for Raegan when very few others were. They were the family that Raegan wished she had now. They were kind to one another and engaged in each others' lives. They spent time together and chose to be close knit. The Lafleur's always tried to include Raegan in the things they did, but she didn't feel like she was good enough to be a part of them, and oftentimes, just being around them magnified how awful her own life and family were.

While circumstances were now excruciating, things hadn't always been so bad with Raegan and her family though. She used to happily live with her mother, father, and her older brother. Back then, when she was little and on into elementary school, where Raegan and Mya first met, things were actually pretty good for Raegan at home. Her father worked for DT Hudson's oil company and made a very good living. Her mother was a stay at home mom, and she took great care of Raegan and her brother Ethan. She was a hands-on mother, very involved in the lives of her family members, and because her husband was able to provide so well for the family, she, Raegan and Ethan were active in multiple hobbies and activities, very well-traveled and rarely went without anything their hearts desired.

Somewhere along the way, though, things changed drastically. The money that flowed through the household was still surging, but the affection stagnated. The Nottaway's seemed to grow further and further apart until they became four people who just happened to share the same last name and reside in the same house, rather than a tightly bonded family who lived and loved together. Each one of them had their own separate lives, and very rarely did their activities and interests overlap with the others' or bring them together. It was like the path that they had once journeyed together suddenly split into a four-pronged fork in the road and each person went their own way, leaving the others to travel alone.

Raegan's father began spending more and more time at his office, working and making more money. He justified his lack of attention to his wife and children by saying that, in order for them to keep living the way they had, he had to make sacrifices somewhere, and that eventually he would retire and become the "family man" he always wanted to be. The truth of the matter was that he was at a loss as to how he was to provide emotional stability for his family, so instead of exploring that and trying to meet those needs of his family, he just strove harder to provide financially in hopes that it would cover up whatever else was missing. But for a family that was already on the verge of a self destructive implosion, all the extra money became was fuel to the fire.

Left to cope on her own with the void her husband's lack of attention left, Raegan's mom struggled to find something to occupy her time and energy. Her children were growing up and needed her less and less with each passing year, so she began searching for stimulation elsewhere. Her husband was notorious for throwing money at every problem they faced, so she followed his lead and began spending her days and his money shopping. What started as a hobby to fill the long and lonely days that her husband worked and her children were in school quickly escalated into a full blown addiction. She began accumulating bags and bags of brand new, unworn clothing and shoes and accessories for herself and her family, as well as roomfuls of home décor and other items for the house. She had thousands of dollars worth of merchandise that still had the price tags hanging on them stored all over the house. But her obsession failed to remedy the root issues of loneliness and abandonment she was facing, and, though she tried to stop, it was all to no avail, and she just continued to slip deeper and deeper into the abyss of her caustic spending habit.

She and Raegan's father bickered about their problems off and on for years, but things turned particularly nasty right as Raegan finished elementary school and prepared to enter middle school. It got to the place where anytime her father got a bill in the mail and opened it and saw how much money was going out of his pocket toward unnecessary purchases made by his wife, he would yell and berate her for being reckless and spending all his hard earned money on things they didn't even want or need. This of course led her straight to the defense that if he would spend more time with them, then she wouldn't have to spend all his money. She tried to tell him that she didn't want to spend the money, and that money was not that important to her, but she missed him and had nothing else to do while he was gone.

He could never seem to understand why she felt as if he didn't care about her and the children and really didn't want to be with them. "That's why I work so much! I want to give my family the best of everything! I don't want them to lack anything in this world! You don't think we live in this house, or have this nice stuff, or air conditioning and electricity and gas for free do you? Where do you think all the money you are spending on shopping is coming from? How do you think we have all this?"

"We don't care about all that stuff! We care about you! All we want is you!" Raegan's mother would try to explain to him that his children needed him to be around. They were growing up without him and soon they would be gone and his chance to be with them would be lost. This always upset her father because he knew that it was true, but he had no idea how to be emotionally present and available for his wife or his children. The pressure of their expectations of him seemed too great, so he would then go back to ranting about how much money was being spent on frivolous impracticalities, and if they really felt like they had a reason to complain, then his family was just ungrateful for all that he did for them, and maybe he would just stop doing anything for them altogether. And that would just send them right back to the beginning of the argument, with lots of screaming and cursing and blaming.

It was during these times that Raegan came to depend so heavily upon her brother to protect her and provide some level of security to make up for where their parents fell short. Ethan was only six years older than she was, still very much a child himself at only fifteen, but in nine year old Raegan's eyes, he was a superhero and the smartest, bravest man on the planet. When her parents would get stirred up and things got unruly and out of control in the house, Raegan would go into her brother's room. He would gather her up into his arms, and hold her and rock her and talk to her to get her mind off what was going on around them. She loved talking to him, and he seemed to know something about everything. They talked about anything Raegan could imagine or bring up, and eventually she would fall asleep, with her head nestled against his chest, and dream about all the wonderful things that he promised awaited her outside the four walls of that house.

But a few short years later, Ethan moved out of the house and left her to fight her own battles. He didn't know it, but very soon after he left, she began to be abused and, with no one in her household to help hold it up, what was left of her already precariously teetering life came crashing down on top of her. The precious girl who was once an effervescent little being full of youthful innocence and hopeful expectancy of greatness was ripped apart and her life reduced to nothing more than a pile of rubble and stony debris. And as that young girl grew up, she began to use those same stones to build a solid wall around herself and her heart, keeping everyone else on the outside. Mya was the only one who really seemed to care to try to navigate through the wreckage to find the key to get back inside, but even *she* struggled to surmount the overgrown vines and weeds of hurt and distrust that seemed to cover the doorway into Raegan's spirit. And the more depraved Grimly's abuse became, the thicker the obstructing foliage got, and the more life it strangled out of Raegan.

Now, more than ever before, as she came to the end of her high school career and looked ahead to the possibilities of the rest of her life, did this dreary outlook hold true. There wasn't much that appealed to her these days. Nothing really held her interest or sparked any real passion in her anymore. Everyone else around her seemed to have many hobbies and interests and things to keep them happily occupied. Not so with Raegan. Everything that used to matter had drifted away some time ago. The one area of her life that had not completely faded into indifferent obscurity was her artwork. In fact, the only thing that kept her going on the days when things became intolerable, and she was ready to totally shut down, was releasing all her frustrations onto a blank canvas. She loved all media of art, and found her only solace in creating works that expressed what she couldn't put into words.

Today was no exception. She had no desire to do anything or go anywhere, especially school. But she knew that she didn't really have much choice so she promised herself that as soon as she got home from school that afternoon, she would lock herself in her room, take out her art supplies and spend the entire evening painting. With that thought tucked away in the back of her mind, she finished getting ready and headed off to face another day at school.

~

Ty loved that he lived within walking distance of his school. It meant that, first of all, since he didn't have his own vehicle, his grandmother didn't have to drop him off. The act of riding up to school, as a senior in high school, sitting beside his elderly grandmother, in their old broken down Ford pick-up would have felt like the end of the world to him. His stomach lurched at the very thought. He could just imagine what embarrassing stunts she would pull everyday if she had to take him to school, like yelling things to him about his laundry or something out the window or singing her gospel music all loud and off key with all the windows down so that all his classmates could hear. If he knew anything, it was how much his grandmother enjoyed, like most parents do with their own kids, messing with him and making him uncomfortable in front of his peers.

The second, and, in his teenage opinion, equally exciting reason that he was happy to live so near the school was the fact that he could sleep in a little later than he would have been able to if he had to ride a bus or drive himself. That extra half an hour of slumber had been his only saving grace more than once in his high school career, including the Monday after the train wreck. With all that had happened that weekend, he had not gotten much sleep, and by Monday morning when his alarm went off, his body let him know how unhappy it was when he told it to wake up. He quickly showered and dressed and walked over to the school.

Now sitting in his first class of the day, he gazed out the window as he waited for the first bell to ring and signal that the school day had officially started. Fall was one of his favorite times of year, and he studied the trees and leaves outside his classroom window. He closed his eyes and committed the shapes and hues he'd just seen into his memory and vowed to himself to figure out a way to replicate the incredible color combinations nature used in his own next art project.

Suddenly, the PA system cackled to life.

"Attention, faculty and students." There was a momentary pause as the announcer waited to give everyone a chance to settle down so that her voice could be heard by all. "I have a very important announcement to make. As most of you probably heard, there was a horrific train accident at the Faries train depot this past Saturday. Several students and faculty lost family members and friends in the tragedy. In light of that, this morning we are introducing three grief counselors to the staff here at school. While they are here especially for those individuals directly affected by this weekend's incident, this service is open to anyone who may need to talk their feelings out with someone or who needs help dealing with any other personal issues. This counseling service is free of charge and available from 7am until 6pm, every Monday through Friday until further notice. We strongly encourage anyone who feels like they need it to use this service as much as is necessary. You may come to the main office to set up a personal appointment with one of the counselors, but walk-in sessions are also permitted, contingent upon the availability of the counselors at that time. To all the students and faculty that lost any loved ones in this catastrophic event, the principal and staff offer our deepest sympathies and send our thoughts and prayers to you and your families."

Ty cringed at the reminder of what he saw that day by the train tracks. He was definitely grateful that he was not one of those whose family member had been hurt or killed, but he still got chills down his spine when he thought about how close he himself had come to death that afternoon, and was trying to keep his mind as far away from that idea as possible. But he could already see how hard that was going to be.

I better get used to hearing about it, he thought. *This thing isn't going away any time soon.*

How does the world live this life without you, Lord? Leisa asked the question over and over in her mind as she drove toward the school in silence. It was the Monday after her daughter's death and the start of a new school week. She had surprised herself that morning when she woke up and really wanted to go to school. She had expected her grief to keep her confined to her bed, wallowing in the pit of her sadness for a lot longer, but she was wrong.

In fact, it was her grief that pushed her to get out of the house that morning. She was tired of crying, and with so many pictures and reminders of Annie strewn around the house to keep the fountain of tears flowing, getting out of there for a while was an easy decision. Edward must have felt the same way because he left for his office shortly before she did.

They had spent another night apart last night. After he came home and they argued, he took his pillow and a blanket and slept on the couch. Leisa couldn't remember the last time he had done that, but she was heartbroken, that for the second night since they lost their daughter, her husband was choosing to leave her on her own. She had laid in the bed for hours, just praying that something would happen and change Edward's heart or mind and he would come back in to her. But it didn't happen that way. She must have drifted off at some point because, the next thing she knew, she was waking up and it was Monday morning.

When she opened her eyes, and rolled over, she saw his empty half of the bed, and sadness gripped her heart once more. "Oh, God," she whispered. She was getting to the place that she didn't know how she was going to make it through another day like this. She was trying so hard to keep herself encouraged and to rest and trust in the Lord. But if she was completely honest with herself, she really felt like she was falling apart. The pain of losing her daughter was almost unbearable, and then coupling that with a physically and spiritually absent husband was like pouring acid into a gaping wound. She didn't know how much more she could stand.

She finally pulled into the school parking lot and parked. She didn't really know what to expect, but she was looking forward to eight hours of other things to keep her mind off all that was going wrong in her life. Her kids were a good distraction. There was always something going on with them that could take all of her focus and place it on their needs. She hoped today would be no different. She pulled her briefcase out of her trunk and slammed it shut. She then made the short walk from her car to her classroom.

She was about forty-five minutes early, which gave her plenty of time to get set up and mentally prepared before her students began arriving. She got a set of their graded papers out of her briefcase and began stacking them according to where each child sat so that she could hand them out in order. After that, she wrote some notes on the board for them to copy for their grammar lessons that day. After a little while, students began drifting into the classroom. They stood around talking and laughing with one another before the first bell. Shortly before the bell, the announcement was made about the new grief counselors that were being made available to the students and faculty of the school.

Leisa wasn't sure how she felt about it, but then, when she thought about the lack of support she faced at her house, she decided that it was a wonderful idea. She made plans to go during her lunch break that very afternoon and meet the counselors. Talking to someone about what was happening to her couldn't hurt any more than she was already hurting, and may actually do her some real good. After the announcement was made, the bell rang and all her students sat down. She began the class by saying that she knew it had been a rough weekend for everyone, including herself, and that anyone who wanted to was free to go during her class period and talk to one of the counselors if they so chose. None of her students took her up on the offer, so she continued with her lesson plans. It proved to be an uneventful morning.

~

When Mya woke up and got dressed for school the Monday after the accident, she really didn't know what to expect from the day. She had gone to the prayer meeting last night, but Jason declined to go with her. She felt so awful for him, but knew that she couldn't make him grieve a certain way, so she didn't push him to try to change his mind. He was already in bed when she came home afterward, so she hadn't had the chance to tell him about the meeting or say goodnight.

He had told her mother that he wanted to go to school Monday so that he could get back to a sense of normalcy in his life, but Mya thought he may change his mind once Monday actually arrived. She was a little surprised when she heard him moving about in the guest room. Since she knew he was awake, she went and knocked on the door. "Good morning, Chaz. I guess you're going to go to school today, huh?" she asked, when he called out that she could open the door.

He looked up from buttoning his shirt. "Yeah, I think I can make it today."

Mya smiled at how handsome he looked with his tousled, morning hair falling around his blue eyes and his feet bare beneath his jeans. "Well, we can ride together if you want."

"That would be great. Thanks, Mya." He smiled at Mya. There was still sadness in his eyes, but she could see that he was trying to be strong. She admired him so much right then and wished with everything in herself that she could take the pain he must be feeling and send it to the moon, millions of light years away from him. He didn't deserve what was happening to him, and the thought of it made Mya's heart break.

After the two of them finished getting ready and ate breakfast, they loaded up into Mya's car and made the trip to school. They made a little small talk here and there, but most of the ride was quiet. When they pulled in to the school parking lot, they got their backpacks out of the backseat and walked hand in hand up to the front of the school. They went together to Jason's locker first, where he emptied his book bag of the books he didn't need that morning. Then he slammed the locker door shut and walked with Mya to her locker.

While they stood at her locker, talking to one another and greeting people as they walked by them, the announcement about the new grief counselors echoed through the hallway. Jason grimaced when they mentioned the accident, but when Mya asked him if he was alright, he assured her that he was fine. He even told her that he might go see the counselors one day. Mya told him that she really hoped he would. After the first bell of the day rang, she gave him a tight hug and told him that she would meet him at their usual spot for lunch, and the two of them went to their separate morning classes. Mya's only wish was that they had more classes together, so she could be there with him if he needed her. She said a quick prayer for the Lord to keep his mind and keep his heart and give him comfort throughout the morning until they could be together again.

~

By the time her lunch break arrived, Leisa was exhausted, mentally and physically. Her lack of sleep and energy-draining tears over the last few days were starting to catch up to her. By the time she arrived to the teachers lounge, all her defenses were down. She just wanted to get a cup of coffee and zone out for a little while. She was surprised to see a handsome young man who she didn't recognize sitting next to the coffee machine when she walked into the lounge.

He smiled brightly at her. "Good morning!"

She gave him a weary smile in response. ''Morning.''

"Uh-oh. Not so 'good,' huh?" The man frowned and shook his head.

"Well, it's just been a rough few days. A lot has happened and I feel like a walking robot right now. I'm here, but I'm not really *here*. So, now I just want a cup of coffee and somewhere to sit down."

The young man jumped up, and offered his seat. "Well, take a load off! I was keeping the seat and the coffee warm, just for you." He now had a sly grin on his face. He looked Leisa in the eye, and she felt a collection of butterflies flutter to life in her stomach. Blood rushed to her cheeks, and she found herself flattered and blushing at the attention of this attractive young man. He leaned over the table that held the coffee pot and grabbed a Styrofoam cup. He poured some coffee into it, and then looked back at her, "So, how do you take yours?"

"With lots of cream and sugar, thank you. I can do it myself though."

He shook his head forcefully. "No, ma'am. You sit right there and let me take care of this for you. Every woman needs to be pampered now and then." He turned and winked at her. "Especially the pretty ones! It's my pleasure." He turned back to the cup of coffee in front of him.

Once again, Leisa's cheeks flushed pink at his words. It had been a long time since Edward had said those kinds of things to her. It was nice to hear them again. And hearing them from a really good-looking man didn't hurt matters either. Leisa could feel her tiredness draining away and her spirits lifting. "Well, thank you. That's very kind of you. Especially since I don't even know who you are!" She heard herself giggle like a schoolgirl with a crush. She was surprised at herself when she saw what little effort it had taken this man to nearly sweep her off her feet. *A cup of coffee and a compliment?* she thought. *Man, I've gotten too easy!* But as soon as he turned and caught her eye again, she became too entranced with his attractively rugged face to beat herself up anymore for falling for his smooth talking.

"My name is D'molish. Pronounced like 'Polish,' like a person from Poland, not the stuff women put on their nails. Helluva name, huh?" He smiled again as he handed her the coffee. "I'm the new divisor." He grinned wickedly, showing off his perfectly straight white teeth, with his eyes still glued on Leisa's.

"Don't you mean *ad*visor?" she asked innocently.

He chuckled, "Yeah I do. But '*di*visor' works so well with 'demolish' don't you think?"

Leisa laughed too. "Yes, I guess you're right. That's cute."

"Well, you're the only one who thinks so. I use that one all the time, but it usually goes over like a lead balloon. I hope that wasn't just a pity laugh. Although I'll take whatever kind of laugh I can get from you. Your laugh is infectious. I could listen to a laugh like yours for all eternity. Anyway, you can call me Pall."

Is he for real? Leisa thought to herself. *Where did he come from? He seems way too good to be true!* "Well, that's very sweet of you to say. And no it wasn't just a pity laugh. You're funny. My name is Leisa Carson, and it's very nice to meet you, Pall."

~

Somewhere in the depths of darkness, Satan smiled at Demolish's brazenly obvious, yet cleverly veiled guise. *"Pall D'molish"? That's great! Make her lose her attraction to her husband and then, right when she's most vulnerable, DESTROY her!* he thought gleefully. *This fiend may actually pull this off!* But his mood soured and his smirk quickly turned to a scowl when his mind returned to the big picture. *At least, that's what he'd better do.*

145

~

After a few more minutes of small talk and modest flirting with Pall, Leisa finally managed to pull herself away, and went to the front office to find out more about the grief counselors and setting up sessions with them. The office secretary pointed her in the right direction and told her that there was no one in to see any of them right then, and that she could go and meet all three of them if she wanted to. Leisa agreed, thanked her and headed to the offices she pointed out.

As she walked down the hall, a swift new wave of sadness washed over her. The giggly, giddy rush of a newfound interest that she had just experienced as she talked with Pall had vanished like the smoke rising from a freshly snuffed out candle's wick. Now, she felt distressed as she thought about what she had just been doing in the lounge and the fact that another man besides her husband had turned her head. She was angry with herself for slipping so easily into such questionable territory, and fought fiercely within her mind to keep away thoughts that tried to justify what she had done as the only natural reaction to the lack of support she was facing from her own spouse. The unhappiness of discovering what kind of woman she was capable of being mingled with the sorrow of her dead child caused the tears to overflow once more, and the burden of all the feelings and emotions she felt came and settled onto her shoulders, making her nearly double over from the weight of them. She actually had to slow her pace and was only able to manage tiny little shuffle steps to reach the place where the counselors had set up shop, and then struggled to straighten herself up and wipe her eyes just so she could make out the room number written above the doorway when she got there.

But the moment she pushed open the door and staggered inside, it was like she had stepped into a different world. The tears she was crying still traced their paths down her face, but the feeling of heaviness she had just experienced on the other side of the threshold seemed to lift off her shoulders a little. She was able to stand up to her full height and saw three beautiful, shining faces in front of her. The three women looked back at her with laughter in their eyes. Just the sight of them immediately brought coolness to her burning cheeks and stillness to her troubled mind.

The lady in the middle spoke first. "Hello, there. We are glad that you came in today. Why don't you come on in and have a seat? There's no need to be afraid." She was a pretty black woman with a wildly curly hairdo. She had a lovely wide mouth, and big colorful earrings hung from her ears. She reminded Leisa of Teenie when she was younger, and that made Leisa smile and feel even more comfortable being around her. Light danced in her eyes as she looked up at Leisa.

There was no desk in the office, just several chairs, including the ones the three women sat in. One of the other two spoke up this time. "You are free to sit wherever you would like. We want you to be comfortable and able to share whatever you need to share with us. Everything you say to us stays in this room, so you can talk about anything you want."

The third chimed in, with a charming Hispanic accent, "Yes, we are thinking about adding a hammock somewhere so that people can really get comfy!" She and the other three laughed, and to Leisa it sounded like what she would imagine the twinkling of a billion stars would sound like if they made a noise. She was captivated by how the sound itself shimmered. Standing there in front of the three counselors, she felt like she was being bathed in goodness, washed clean from the grime she was just wallowing in outside their presence. She felt completely at home in that little room with them.

After a few moments of basking, she realized she was still standing up. She looked around and found the chair that was closest to them, slid it over until it was directly in front of them and sat down on it. She didn't know where to start, but even if she did, she didn't know if she had use of her voice anymore. She hadn't said a word since she walked in.

As if they knew exactly what she was thinking, the three women all leaned forward, and the black woman in the middle gently placed her hands on top of Leisa's as they set in her lap. She spoke softly, "There's no hurry here. We have all the time in the world. There is no specific direction this has to take. We will do this however works best for you. Why don't we start with you telling us your name and then we will tell you ours? And then we will talk about why exactly you are here."

Grateful for some direction, Leisa swallowed hard and found her voice. "Well, my name is Leisa Carson. I'm a twelfth grade English teacher here."

The woman holding Leisa's hands seemed to be the primary representative of the three. She spoke again. "Well, it is wonderful to meet you, Leisa Carson. You can call me Ananda."

The woman with the Hispanic accent spoke next. "And you can call me Gisella."

The third, a vibrant young woman with short blonde hair finished the introductions. "You can call me Audrey."

"It's so wonderful to meet all three of you. From the moment I walked in the door, I felt like a whole new person. I mean, everything's still the same, but different. It's like my mind cleared up and light completely engulfed my spirit. I've never been to a counseling session before. Does that always happen? I feel like I didn't even need to say anything and you all have already helped me to feel better. And you don't even know why I am in here! I can't even imagine how great I am going to feel after we actually talk!" Leisa stopped speaking and slapped her hand over her mouth. She realized that after she recovered her speaking ability, she started babbling and hadn't stopped to let them say another word. "I'm so sorry! I'm just rambling on and on! I'm doing just like my daughter Annette does!" Suddenly, the reason she was there came rushing back to her. "I mean, just like my daughter Annette *did*." She looked sadly around at the three women who still sat leaning toward her. Their eyes beckoned her to continue. "That's why I'm here. My daughter Annette is dead." She finished in a whisper. She felt so good sitting there with the women that she didn't want the mention of death to disrupt the atmosphere.

Audrey asked, "Was she killed in the train accident?"

Leisa nodded. "Yes, she was. Finding out was the worst day of my life. And things haven't gotten much better since then. On top of her dying, my husband has just completely removed himself from our marriage, and I just left the teachers' lounge where a handsome young man was trying to get my attention. The scary part is that I wasn't really resisting him. I just feel like my life has gotten so off balance since Annette died, and I am not sure how to get things back where they need to be."

"Well, we totally understand that, and we have some great news for you. We have studied under the best Psychologist in the universe, and we know exactly how to help you get things back on track. And trust us, we aren't just saying that because we work for Him. He *is* the best." A knowing glimmer flashed in Ananda's eyes, and she winked at Leisa.

Just then, the bell that signified that lunch was over rang loudly over their heads.

"Oh, no!" Leisa lamented. "We were just getting started! And now I have to get back for my afternoon classes."

Gisella smiled. "It's alright, Leisa. Like we said before, we have all the time in the world, so feel free to come in whenever you want. You can set an appointment to talk to any of us one on one if you would like. Or you can just come in and see if one of us is free."

"Oh, can we please keep doing these with all three of you here? I really like having all of you around me. I just feel so secure with all of you! I probably sound like a nutcase, don't I?" Leisa asked nervously.

"Not at all," answered Ananda. "We just want you to be yourself and to feel completely free to say whatever is on your heart. No judgments here. And we would love to do your sessions altogether. We are here to help, so whatever you need that we can provide is exactly what we are going to do, ok?"

"Well, thank you so much! I am really looking forward to talking to you ladies. I can already tell that this is going to be a great thing for me. I feel so connected to you all just from this first session."

Ananda stood up first, and the other two followed suit. When Leisa stood up, each woman hugged her. Ananda said, "We are so glad to hear you say that. We really hope that we can help you to overcome all of the issues you are facing right now. I want to ask you to do one thing before we see you next time. It's sort of a little homework assignment. We want you to think of something that was very important to your daughter while she was on the earth. What was one of her deepest convictions about the way she should live her life? We will talk about that next time we get together, ok?"

"Alright," Leisa answered, as she turned to leave the room. "It was really great to meet all of you, and I will see you next time." She waved to them and left the room.

Over the next couple of weeks, Leisa went back to visit the counselors on a nearly daily basis.

Mya and Jason walked into the police station. They scanned the room for Sgt. Williams and waved when they spotted him. He came over and greeted them.

"Hey, Jason. Hey, Mya. It's good to see you. Mr. Wilson is in the conference room. He's waiting for you." The couple thanked him and headed to the room. They opened the door and a middle aged man sat at the table.

"You must be Jason Harrington. Come on in! And who is this lovely lady?" The man looked curiously at Mya.

"Hi, Mr. Wilson. Yes, I'm Jason and this is my girlfriend, Mya." Jason shook the man's outstretched hand. Mya smiled uneasily, suddenly uncomfortable and self conscious. She stepped forward to shake the man's hand as well.

"Call me Will. We are going to be getting to know each other pretty well over the next few months, so we may as well get rid of all that formality!" Ill Will laughed heartily. He motioned for Mya and Jason to sit down in the chairs across the table from where he sat.

"Oh, I can't stay." Mya said quickly. "I just came to drop Jason off. Call me when you're done, ok, Chaz? I'll see you later." She tried to control the shudder that ran down her body when the older man looked at her. *Something is not right about this guy,* she thought. She hugged Jason and turned and left the room and the police station.

Jason and Ill Will watched as she left. Jason then sat down in the chair Will had pointed to.

"Son, I thought you said your name was Jason."

"It is."

"Then what did she just call you?"

"She called me 'Chaz'."

The man looked quizzically at Jason.

"It's the nickname she came up with for me," he explained. "She's the kind of girl who thrives on being unique. Everyone else just calls me Jase or Jason, so she wanted to have her own special nickname for me. She is the only person who calls me Chaz. She loves it that way. And people always ask her why she calls me that, so she gets to talk about it and explain what it means."

"And what *does* it mean?"

"It's a mix of the *Cha* from my middle name, Charles, and the *s* sound from Jason. Put them together, and she got 'Chaz'. She's been calling me that since the summer we met. I actually kind of like it." Jason surprised himself with how quickly and easily he was opening up to this man he hardly knew.

Ill Will leaned back in his chair, propping his feet up on the conference table and lacing his fingers behind his head. "I see. Well, that's pretty clever." He paused. "*Chaz,*" he said. "Hmmm. I kind of like it too." He closed his eyes, as if thinking about something. After a moment, he opened them and sat up. He took his feet off the table and leaned forward, looking intently at Jason.

"So, how far have you and that hot little girlfriend of yours gone? You know, she really is a pretty black girl."

Jason looked sharply at the man.

"Oh, I don't mean that offensively. I've been with some hot black chicks in my life. They're the most fun, I'd have to say." He grinned wickedly and winked at Jason.

Jason didn't know why he even responded to such a crude question, but he said, "We've only kissed. And we don't even do that very often. Mya's a strong Christian and believes that all sexual activity should be saved for after marriage."

"Man, that's a tough break. How do you feel about that? It's gotta be hard spending time with such a good looking girl and not being able to do *anything* with her. That's like my worst nightmare! I don't know how you handle it."

Jason squirmed a bit in his seat, feeling increasingly awkward, but again found himself answering, against his better judgment. "I don't know. I just try not to think about it too much, I guess. I really love her and I don't want to ruin the relationship we have. If she wants to wait, I'm willing to do that."

The older man grunted in his disapproval. "Well, better you than me, I guess. I couldn't do it. But you do know there are ways to get around that, don't you?"

"What do you mean?" Jason wasn't sure where this guy was going with all these questions. He knew this discussion was not what he had come to the station for.

The man handed Jason a business card with a web address printed on it. "My nephew, who attends the college here in Faries, put this site together. It may help you relieve some tension, if you know what I mean. It's a classy site, not some trashy woman hating site. You should go check it out sometime."

"Uh, thanks." Jason could not believe what was happening. "So, Sgt. Williams told me that you needed me to sign some paperwork or something?" He struggled to get the man back on track. He was extremely uncomfortable and wanted to get out of there as soon as possible. Here he barely knew this man and he was giving him sexual advice? Jason was totally grossed out, and confused as to how the man had gotten him so engaged in a conversation like that anyway. They had just met, and yet he felt like, whenever the man caught his eye, he had some strange mind control over him, making him powerless to stop the words from spewing from his mouth, whether he wanted to say them or not.

The man sat back and began shuffling through the papers in front of him. "Oh, right. Back to business. I have been appointed by the courts as conservator over your finances, either until you turn eighteen or twenty one. Since your eighteenth birthday is in just four months, the courts will decide whether or not to extend my conservatorship until you're twenty one or to let you handle it once you turn eighteen. But that's just a bunch of legal mumbo jumbo you don't have to worry about. Your parents had a will and left everything to you. Sgt. Williams told me that you want to stay here in Faries instead of moving back to Burney. Basically, my job is to make sure your bills are paid and that everything is taken care of financially so that you can stay here. I'm supposed to teach you about managing your money, and help you learn what you will need to know to take over your own finances when the time comes. Your parents both had substantial life insurance policies, plus they must have had a really good financial planner who helped them set up a system to take care of you should anything like this ever happen. Honestly, son, you're set for a good long while. I wish I were in your shoes."

Jason looked darkly at the man. This guy didn't seem to realize what he was saying. "You mean, you wish your parents were dead and you were left in a city all by yourself with some weirdo who didn't know when to shut up as your finance guy? Why don't we just trade lives then! I'll gladly take my old life back!" Jason surprised himself again, but this time with his biting sarcasm.

"Wow, kid. You're right. I didn't mean it like that. Sometimes I say things without thinking about how they may come out. I certainly didn't mean to make light of your parents' deaths." He cleared his throat and looked directly into Jason's eyes. Jason couldn't seem to escape his stare. "What I was trying to say is that most young people would be thrilled to have lots of money and no adults to tell them what to do with it."

"I guess." Jason said quietly.

"I mean, you're getting to live the young bachelor lifestyle that most guys only dream about. Now's your chance to live it up. No one's around to tell you what to do. All of your bills will be paid, and you get a nice house to yourself. You don't have to work unless you want to. You will be graduating school soon. When you turn eighteen, you will *really* be free! Even God couldn't blame you for having a little fun. He wants you to enjoy your life, right? What kind of God wouldn't? And if he is the God that knows everything and controls the entire universe, that means he knew about the accident and didn't stop it. He set you up to be here. He wants you to have a good time!"

Somewhere during the course of his speech, Ill Will's vile words began to make sense to Jason. The feeling of losing control of his own thoughts came back, making his mind hazy and his beliefs suddenly unclear. *God had to have known what was going to happen, and He let it. So, He must want me to be on my own and do my own thing,* Jason reasoned.

Ill Will shuffled the papers in his hands, snapping Jason out of his thoughts. He handed Jason a pen and began explaining page by page what he needed Jason to sign. Jason tried to listen and grasp what the man was saying, but it was all so foreign to him. He just waited for Will to point to a blank space and say, "Sign here." The two spent quite some time signing paperwork. When they were finally finished, Ill Will caught Jason's eye again.

"I really hope you forgive me for offending you earlier. I apologize for making such an insensitive remark."

"Yeah, I forgive you. It's fine. I know you didn't mean it that way."

"Well, good. But back to what I told you before. You're a man, and men have needs. If your girl won't do what needs to be done, you can find ways to get it taken care of. You really need to check out my nephew's site. It's better to just look than to really mess up and actually touch someone besides your girlfriend. She can't say you cheated if you never did anything with anyone else. It's just looking at pictures of pretty girls. All guys do that. I think your girlfriend would be worried if you never looked at any other women. She might wonder if you were batting for the other team!" The man chuckled.

Jason looked at the card on the table. "I don't know. I'm really not into pictures of naked girls. It's just not my style. I don't mind that Mya and I are waiting before we make our relationship physical. Mya is committed to God and I am committed to her."

"Well, look, kid, I tried all that God stuff. It didn't work for me. Having a bunch of rules and lists of things you can't do just isn't my idea of living. I'm having a great time! God seems to suck the life out of everything. And like I said, surely He wouldn't mind you having just a little fun, with all of the tragedy you have faced lately. I just thought you may want to see an alternative. And I told you, my nephew's site is classy. It's not just naked women. Most of the girls on there are clothed. It's just art. Pretty pictures of pretty girls. But if you don't mind being the guy dating the hot celibate chick, then more power to you. I just know it couldn't be me. But you do whatever floats your boat."

Jason squirmed again in his seat. "Alright. Thanks for the advice. I guess it won't hurt to just look. Especially if it's artistic. I just can't see myself looking at, you know, like, porn or whatever."

"Of course not! This is no porn site. It's just artsy pictures of beautiful women in nice clothes. I'm telling you. My nephew takes the pictures himself. He's a photographer and is paying his way through school taking pictures like this. It's really nice. Trust me."

"Alright. Are we done here?"

"We sure are. Here's *my* card. Call me if you have any questions about anything. And let me know what you think when you take a gander at that website, ok?"

"Ok. Thanks."

"It was good to meet you, Jason."

"You too, Will."

Mya was always excited about going to work out with her cheer girls, but she was especially looking forward to cheerleading practice that day. It had been nearly three weeks since the train accident, and she needed some cheer, literally and figuratively, back in her life. She was doing her very best to be available to comfort and minister to Jason and the Carson family in their time of grief, but she was starting to feel out of touch with the rest of her life. Right after the wreck, she and the rest of the squad had agreed to cancel practices for a few weeks, so they hadn't been able to really spend time together like they usually did, outside of sharing classes or passing each other in the hallways. She was actually a little surprised at how much she missed her cheer friends while they were apart. She realized how much of a family their little group had become, and joyfully anticipated their reunion that afternoon.

She was also excited to share with them the bit of news she had received the day before. The principal had called her into the office at the end of the school day and told her of some changes concerning the cheer squad that would be taking place that afternoon. They would be welcoming four new senior girls to their team. All four of them had extensive cheerleading backgrounds, so Mya was eager to add some fresh faces as well as some high levels of experience into the mix of her already fantastic group. The principal also told her that they would be introduced to the new squad sponsor.

The sponsor was like the "mother" of the squad. She was the responsible adult party when the squad was involved in any activities outside of school functions. She represented the squad to the faculty of the school as well as the outside community, and stood in to facilitate as needs arose within the group. As the captain, Mya worked closely with the sponsor to make sure that she was kept abreast on what was happening within the squad, and that the lines of communication between the cheerleaders, sponsor, and school administration remained open, making everything run smoothly. The sponsor also acted as treasurer for the group. She signed all the checks that paid for uniforms, trips and competitions. The cheerleaders paid dues yearly, and did several fundraisers throughout the year to cover most of the costs, but the sponsor volunteered to pick up any financial slack that may still remain.

Over the years that Mya has been involved with cheerleading, the team sponsor seemed to always become one of her favorite members of the squad. The sponsor was usually a woman who was a cheerleader at one point or another in her life and really understood the cheerleading world. She was able to offer insight into the issues that the squad members may face on a technical level, as well as offer support for more personal issues that may come up with the girls. She was always an enthusiastic woman who thoroughly enjoyed what she was doing. Sometimes the sponsor was one of the cheerleader's mothers, but other times, she was just a community member who volunteered to take on the responsibility. Either way, she was always available for whatever the girls may need as the school year progressed. The sponsor would accompany the team to out of town competitions and games, and she was seen by the squad as the "go-to" person for any problems they may be having. She usually attended the practices and made suggestions as to what might help improve a stunt or make a routine more exciting. The sponsor and the girls on her squad usually developed quick and lasting bonds.

So, all in all, Mya was geared up to get to practice. She was really looking forward to getting back into a daily routine, and was jazzed about meeting all the new people. She hoped that today was going to be a day of making several new friends, and taking her squad to the next level in their cheer abilities. With all that had been going on recently with Jason and the sadness that was isolating him more and more daily, and whatever it was that was making Raegan keep her at arm's length, Mya was extremely excited to have some new girls in her life that she prayed would become her good friends. She needed some people who she could just relax and spend time with, without all the hardship she had been facing in her other relationships lately.

When Mya arrived at practice, she put her bag and water bottle down near the bleachers. No one else was in the gym yet. As captain, she was responsible for getting the room ready so they could get started with practice as soon as the other cheerleaders came in. She went into the utility closet and began pulling out the floor mats to set out before the other girls showed up. She would be alone for a solid half hour, so she decided to take that time and spend it praying and loving on the Lord.

She began to hum the tune that she felt playing in her heart. It was a song that she hadn't heard before, but that she knew was a love song that her spirit wanted to sing to Jesus. Music had always been such an integral part of her life, and her time with the Lord almost always started off with some song that her spirit had written. So she just began to sing aloud to Him, and offer her heart and mind to be used for His glory. The sound of her song echoed off the walls of the gym and wrapped itself around her until she felt like she was totally surrounded by His presence, engulfed in His goodness. It was like heaven on earth.

Hearing the chatter of the other cheerleaders making their way into the gym brought Mya back down. After she had laid the mats all out, she sat down on them while she worshipped, but when she saw that her quiet time was up, she stood up to greet the girls as they came in. She felt refreshed and invigorated and ready to face whatever came her way that afternoon.

She hugged each girl tightly as she came in and tossed her jacket and bags beside Mya's, next to the bleachers. "Hey, ladies! I have missed you guys so much! I'm so glad we are all back together! Everyone come on in, say hi to each other, and then grab a spot on the mats. I have an announcement to make before we get started!"

The girls stood around hugging and greeting one another excitedly for a few minutes before they all went over and sat on the mats that Mya had set out. They quieted down and looked expectantly at her, waiting to hear the news she was going to share with them. She walked over and stood in front of the group. She took a moment to look each girl in the face and smile at her to make her feel welcomed and important. This was a practice she had employed for years, and it really seemed to work with the cheerleaders. All of the girls had the utmost respect for Mya as their captain, but they all loved her dearly as their friend as well.

"Ok, girls, I have some really cool news today! I was informed by the principal yesterday afternoon that we will be receiving four new cheerleaders to the squad this afternoon! And they are all from championship squads, so they know what they are doing! Isn't that awesome?"

All of the girls erupted into excited applause in response to Mya's statement, and began talking amongst themselves about it. Mya held up her hand to get their attention back to her. "And that's not all. We are also getting our new sponsor today! So, we have a lot to look forward to this afternoon! I'm not sure what time they will be here, but we have a lot of work to do in the meantime, so everyone get up and let's start stretching. The last thing we want to do is have these new people think we are a lazy squad and regret their decision to come join us! It's been a few weeks since we've worked out together, so let's shake the dust out of our pom-poms and get started!"

The other cheerleaders stood up and spread themselves out around the gym. Mya led them in a series of stretches, and then began teaching them a new routine. They were engrossed in practice, when they heard the doors at the back of the gym squeal open. The principal walked in, followed by four young women.

"Hello, everyone! These are the new transfer students I asked Mya to tell you about. I brought them to see where practices are held. I'll let them introduce themselves. When the new sponsor gets here, I will bring her in as well. Until then, have a great rest of your practice, ladies!" The principal nodded to all of the girls and turned and left the gym.

The original members of the squad gathered around and made a semi-circle around the new members. Mya stepped to the front.

"Hi, there! We are so excited to have you girls here!" For Mya, truer words had never been spoken. It was all she could do not to yell at the top of her lungs from the excitement she felt at that moment. She could sense that this was going to be a life-altering partnership. Her heart told her that these girls were meant to do more than cheer with her. They were somehow going to affect her in every area of her life. She wanted to turn cartwheels and do back flips. She had never felt so happy to meet someone in her life. "My name is Mya Lafleur and I am the captain of this amazing squad!" All the girls behind her started cheering and clapping.

The new girls smiled brightly. "Well, we are so glad to be here!" spoke up one of them. "We know that it is going to be an awesome year and we are looking forward to working with you guys! My name is Charlotte." Charlotte was a cute redhead, with a sprinkle of freckles running across her nose and cheeks. She had big green eyes that sparkled when she spoke.

"And my name is Nadia." Another of the new girls stepped forward for an introduction. She had long, shiny brown hair and dark brown eyes. Her skin was olive colored and she was a few inches taller than Charlotte.

"I'm Charlotte's fraternal twin sister, Bryn." Bryn had strawberry blond hair and hazel eyes. She had freckles like her sister, but they were more spread out and much lighter in color. She had a wide, toothy smile that she flashed to the group.

"I guess they saved the best for last," spoke the final girl with a mischievous grin. The other girls all laughed kindheartedly. "You all can call me Carina." Carina was the tallest of all four of the girls. She was a beautiful coffee colored girl with deep brown eyes that pierced, to the quick, whoever she looked at. Her teeth were perfectly white, and stood out against her dark skin. "We are really excited to get to know all of you, and look forward to all that's ahead for this team!" When she spoke, she looked Mya in the eyes, and Mya felt like she was speaking directly to her.

Mya felt an immediate connection with her, and felt the urge to dismiss everyone else and just sit and talk with these four girls for hours. But the sound of the doors squeaking again interrupted her thoughts. They all looked up and saw the principal lean in and wave to them. Then a petite young blond woman walked into the doorway. Mya figured she must be the new sponsor. "Hi, there!" she called out.

"Well, hello, all you gorgeous women," the woman answered loudly. "I must be in the right place because only cheerleaders are allowed to be this attractive and gather all together in one place!" The woman came over to where the girls all stood and looked around at each of them. She was pretty, and very toned, with a perfect tan that was very conspicuous in the middle of autumn, but that also made her appear even more striking.

All the original squad members giggled at the woman's comment, but the four new girls grew quiet. She looked at them momentarily, but quickly averted her attention to Mya. "You must be the captain. I can see it all over you! What's your name, darlin'?" The woman widened her already big blue eyes at Mya, and nodded eagerly, waiting for her to speak.

Mya smiled at her and nodded her head. "Yes, ma'am. I *am* the captain. My name is Mya Lafleur. Are you the new sponsor?"

"Yup, sure am! The name's Lady Canker."

"Lady? Like you're a member of some royal family or something?" One of the girls from the back of the group called out, sounding confused.

The woman's laughed filled the room. "Oh, that's rich! I wish I were part of some royal family! Yeah right! No, honey, my first name is Lady. You know, like Lady is a tramp?"

"Don't you mean Lady *and the* Tramp?" another girl called out this time.

Canker smirked and shimmied her hips a little. "When you know me, you know that this lady *is* a tramp!" Canker laughed maniacally at her own perverted wit. The girls giggled nervously in response. Mya, suddenly uncomfortable, tried to get the conversation headed in a different direction.

"Well, it's nice to meet you, Lady Canker."

"Oh, honey, you can just call me Canker. That's what all my friends call me! And I can tell that we are going to be great friends around here!"

Mya tried to push down the nauseous feeling that was rising up from the pit of her stomach. She hated to judge someone off a questionable first encounter, but she was not sure how she felt about this woman standing in front of her. But she smiled anyway, and kept talking. "Alright, Canker. We were just meeting four new members. This is Nadia, Carina, Bryn and Charlotte."

When Mya introduced the girls, Canker barely looked at them. She grunted her acknowledgment, saying, "Yeah, I know them," but didn't offer anything else. The four girls stayed silent. Mya scrambled to get things back on track.

"Um, how about we go around the room and have everyone else introduce themselves to the new members?" Looking back and forth between the four girls and Canker, she added, "I know that you probably won't remember everyone's name for a little while, but we can still tell you who is who." The original squad members all called out their names and waved. For the first time since Canker had walked through the door, the four new girls were smiling again, as they greeted each girl by name when she introduced herself.

After the formalities and introductions were over, Mya felt it would be best to just end practice and start fresh with everyone at the next session. She also wanted to talk to the new girls alone for a few minutes and try to figure out what was with their negative response to the new sponsor. She knew that she was not really at ease in her presence, and she planned to work on that, but she wanted to know why the new girls seemed to feel the same way. She knew deep down that she could trust them.

After all the other cheerleaders and Canker had left the gym, Mya stopped the new girls. "I just wanted to say that I am so glad y'all have decided to come join our squad. I just know it's going to be great!"

The girls smiled and agreed with her. "You're so right! It's going to be an awesome year. We know that this is the place we need to be. We are elated to have met you and the squad and just know this is going to turn out fantastically!" Carina spoke for the group.

Mya's manner turned solemn. "Can I ask you guys a question? I mean, I know that we just met, but I feel so close to you guys already for some reason. And I noticed something earlier and wanted to ask you all about it."

"We were just saying that we all totally feel the same way about you. You can ask us anything you want to know," Bryn said.

"Well, it's good to know that I am not just some crazy stalker girl who is in some one-sided obsession with four girls I hardly know!" Mya smiled.

"Of course not!" Nadia chuckled. "So what's your question?"

"Well, I heard Canker say that she already knew you guys. But none of you really seemed happy to see the other. What is that about? Did something happen with her before?"

Charlotte's face clouded over and she looked deep into Mya's eyes. "She used to sponsor our old team. But then she switched and began working with our rival, and just completely lost herself. You see, the four of us are servants of God, and she," Charlotte stopped for a moment. "Suffice it to say that she isn't. She is no longer one of us, and she will try to twist your mind. She is not a nice woman. Be careful, Mya. As the captain, you will have to work closely with her, but she is not a good influence. Don't be fooled by her. We've seen her work, and she can deceive you before you even realize what's happening."

Carina chimed in, "Yes, please trust us, Mya. Lady Canker has nothing worthwhile to say. She is just going to try to get you to change your mind about what you believe is right. You have to stick to your convictions."

"Wow," Mya breathed. "I had no idea! She's sounds like a piece of work. I'm glad you guys were honest with me and shared that. I was really feeling bad that I didn't get a good vibe from her, even though we just met. But now I feel like it was just my spirit disagreeing with hers. I will be kind to her, but I will definitely heed the warnings y'all just gave me. On another note, I have to say that I am not in the least surprised that you girls are Christians! That explains what I have been drawn to since the moment you girls showed up!" She looked around at each of them and then squealed excitedly, "I'm a Christian too! You guys are an answer to prayer for me! Man, just to think that it worked out like this is amazing! Four new students, who are also great cheerleaders *and* who love the Lord!? God is so good!" Mya put up her hand to high five the other girls. They laughed and high fived her. "This year is going to be even better than I thought!"

"It sure is! God has so much more in store than you even realize, girl! It's going to be awesome! We just know it!" Bryn paused and grinned as she asked, "So, where's a good church around here that we can get involved in?"

Mya was beyond thrilled to have these four new cheerleaders on the squad. When she first laid eyes on them, something had instantly stirred on the inside of her and she knew they weren't going to be just cheerleaders or even just friends. Somehow, they were going to change Mya's life drastically and permanently. All four of them were Spirit-filled believers—sisters in the Lord. They all seemed to have such kind hearts and sweet spirits. But there was something else about them; something kind of mysterious, beyond the natural. Mya couldn't put her finger on it, but they were not like any other girls she had ever met. And she had plenty of experience in that area, because any time new students came to the school, Mya was one of the first people to introduce herself to them and try to make them feel welcome.

But after being in their presence for only a moment, Mya knew there was more depth and complexity to these four girls than she had ever encountered, or probably could even understand. There was this air of intensity around all four of them that made her want to get to know them, but at the same time, when they looked at her, made her feel as though they had already known her for her whole life. She found herself instantly drawn to them from the moment they walked into practice that afternoon. It was like they had some sort of magnetism that she couldn't resist. She had gone immediately up to them when she saw them, like a moth to a flame. As soon as they exchanged their first words, a flame inside her re-ignited, and the more she talked to them, the more connected to them she felt.

Each of them had their own unique energy, deep and rich, but the concentrated force they radiated as a group was almost too much to bear. The power that surrounded them was nearly tangible. It was as if they possessed all of the character of the universe within each of them, and when they got together, the vastness and mystique of all space and time was reflected onto whoever was standing close by. It gave off the same sensation as looking directly at the sun. To a natural minded person who was experiencing his or her first encounter with these girls, it was a lot to take from four high school senior cheerleaders. But Mya couldn't seem to get enough of them.

And once she officially met them, she could hardly wait to introduce them around. The very first person she wanted them to meet was Leisa Carson. She knew that Leisa would be as ecstatic as she was to have some new women of God in their school, and would identify with how Mya felt when she was with them. There weren't many people at school who understood Mya when she began opening up about spiritual matters and her relationship with the Lord. But Leisa was different. She got it. She loved the same Jesus that Mya did, and loved to talk about Him. That was how she and Mya had become so close in the first place. They had attended the same church for a while, and knew each other as acquaintances and fellow members. But it was a voracious hunger and longing to know the Lord in a deeper way that had really solidified their bond. When Mya began seeking the face of the Lord in a new way, Leisa had taken notice and began sharing insights and revelations that she herself had found.

The two of them started talking more regularly, and the next thing they knew, they were as close as mother and daughter.

Mya was also excited for Raegan to meet them. Raegan didn't seem to have many female friends besides Mya, and Mya wanted to help her make some. She was also hoping their enthusiasm for the things of God would help get Raegan on the right track with her own salvation. She figured they may have something new to offer, where Mya had been falling short, that could get through to her and make her see things from a different perspective. She would definitely bring it up to them when they all knew each other better.

After cheer practice that afternoon, Mya asked her new friends if she could take them to meet someone. Of course they agreed, so she took the girls to Mrs. Carson's classroom. On their way, she pointed out some of the different classes and places they would become very familiar with as they got used to their new school. They all talked and laughed naturally with one another, and Mya felt at ease as though she had known these girls forever. When they reached the classroom they were headed for, she walked in ahead of them and greeted Mrs. Carson excitedly. "Hey, Mrs. Leisa!"

Leisa looked up from her desk, where she had been grading papers and smiled. She was surprised to see so many new faces standing at her door with Mya. "Hi, Mya! What's going on? Who are these lovely ladies you have with you?" She stood up and walked over to the girls.

"These are four new transfer students, who also happen to be fantastic cheerleaders and the newest members of our squad! We've become fast friends!" She turned to the girls and winked. "Right, girls?" They all smiled and nodded their agreement. Mya turned back to Leisa. "Since they are new to the school, I asked them if I could show them the ropes a little bit, and I knew you would be in here grading papers, so I decided to bring them by and introduce them to you first. This is Bryn, Nadia, Carina and Charlotte."

Each girl smiled and shook Leisa's hand as Mya called her name. She looked at the girls and told them, "And this is Mrs. Leisa Carson. She's one of the senior English teachers here. She's also a faithful member at my church. She is absolutely the best!"

Leisa smiled at Mya's kind words. "Well, thank you, Mya! I just try to do what I can. You are not so bad yourself." She nudged Mya playfully, and then looked at the girls. "It is so nice to meet all of you! It will be great to have some new young ladies here at the school!"

Mya turned excitedly to Leisa. "But I haven't even told you the best part yet!" She paused for dramatic effect. "They are all Christians too! And they want to get involved at the church! Isn't that great?"

Leisa laughed at Mya's enthusiasm. "It *is* great! It's just like the Lord to send some more warriors into our school at a time like this. With all of us together, there is no stopping us! We can evict the devil right out of here! One of us can put a thousand to flight, and two, ten thousand, so imagine what we can do! Actually, you have perfect timing. I'm so glad you brought them in here, because I really wanted to talk to you about something, Mya. Isn't that so God to have you come right on time? He's so awesome! Anyway, you know that I have been talking to the grief counselors here at the school, right?"

Mya nodded and turned to the girls. "I don't know if you guys heard about the train wreck a couple of weeks ago, but Mrs. Leisa's daughter and my boyfriend Jason's parents were victims. There were other students and faculty affected as well, so the school brought in these wonderful grief counselors, so that people who needed it would have someone to talk things through with."

Leisa nodded and continued. "Well, they have been so helpful to me throughout this whole situation. When I was talking to them the other day, they suggested that I do something special in honor of Annette. And I had an idea that I would love to get your feedback on. I'd love to hear what all of you think of it."

"Of course! Sure, you've got it," they all chimed in.

"Well, I would like to start a series of classes at the church for the young women in middle school and high school. Something Annie was really passionate about was her vow of purity until marriage. So I want to start a series called Purity with Purpose in honor of Annie's commitment, and use it to teach young women about their self worth and value with regard to sexual purity in relationships. I think Annie would have been delighted to be a part of something like that. What do you girls think? Does that sound like it could work? I mean, if we started it, would you all be interested in taking part in it? Mya? Maybe you could even help me oversee the first one, since you and I have already discussed this so much and are on the same page. And what about Raegan? Maybe she could be involved too."

"Oh, yes, ma'am! That sounds awesome! What a great idea!" The girls all agreed that the classes would be of great benefit to the young women at their church. They also felt that it would be a wonderful way to pay tribute to Annette's memory.

"That's a fantastic idea and I would be honored to help you however you need me! I know y'all never met Annie," Mya said, turning to the girls, "but she was just one of the most amazing women of God! I loved her so much!"

Tears welled up in Leisa's eyes. "So did I," she said.

"Oh, Mrs. Leisa! I didn't mean to make you cry," Mya said, hugging Leisa.

"No, Mya, it's fine! I'm just crying because sometimes I just get overwhelmed by how much I still miss her. But I know exactly where she is and that she wouldn't come back if she could. I'm just a little jealous that Jesus is getting to love on my baby girl more than I can right now!" Leisa chuckled through her tears. She and the girls continued talking for a little while, and she told them more about what she hoped to accomplish through this new program. Several times when she spoke of Annie, her eyes would well up and she couldn't help but cry a little. Mya and the others girls would reach out and touch her arm or squeeze her hand to somehow offer their understanding. They even shed some of their own tears with her. Even though they had just met, there was such a strong sense of love and companionship between the six of them at that moment, standing together and discussing such an admirable woman of faith. Finally, Leisa wiped her eyes and looked at her watch. "Girls, I'm so sorry to cut this meeting short, but I have to get going. I wanted to call Pastor James this evening and run my idea by him as well. It was so great to talk to all of you, and thank you for letting me share with you about my Annie Pie and what she means to me. I hate that you all didn't get to meet her, but I am glad that I got to meet you! You are really wonderful young ladies and I look forward to spending more time with all of you!"

"If she was anything like you, Annette was no less than amazing, and it's been awesome to hear about her." Charlotte stepped forward to speak to Leisa. She looked her in the eye. "You stay strong, Mrs. Carson. Everything is going to be alright."

Leisa was shocked at this young woman's boldness, but her words penetrated deep, traveling through Leisa's body from the crown of her head all the way to her toes. Tears once again found their way to the surface, and Leisa let them fall freely. "Thank you so much," she whispered as she hugged Charlotte tightly. She then turned and hugged the other girls.

"It was really nice to meet you, Mrs. Carson! We are really looking forward to seeing what awesome things are going to come from your idea. We will definitely talk to you soon."

As Leisa turned to gather her belongings and go home, the five girls left the room and headed out to the parking lot to find their cars and go home as well. On their way out, Mya told them a little more about Raegan and Jason and promised to introduce them all at school the following day. They agreed to meet the next morning in front of the school to pray together and to let Mya point the new students in the right directions to their classrooms. Once outside, they said their goodbyes and prepared to head their separate ways. Right before they left, Charlotte came over and looked at Mya the very same way she had looked at Leisa a few moments earlier. This time she said, "Make sure you talk to Raegan, ok?"

~

As soon as she got home, Mya called Raegan. She was ready to burst with the news about the new girls and Purity with Purpose classes. She had already personally made a commitment to purity before marriage, and, having a steady boyfriend who she loved very much, was well acquainted with the struggles and temptations that came along with that. She often talked to her mom, Mrs. Leisa and other women in the church about it. But now, if she were to get involved with this new program, she hoped she would really get to share her beliefs and the things she was learning in her own life with more girls her own age and maybe even inspire some of them and help them avoid the pitfalls of sex before marriage. And simply talking to Mrs. Leisa and hearing her ideas about the classes fired her up all the more. She was eager to tell Raegan about it so she could get involved as well. She also hoped that Raegan would be interested in meeting the new girls. She sighed impatiently as she waited for Raegan to answer her phone. Finally, Raegan picked up.

"Hello?" Raegan sounded worn out.

"Hey, Raeyo! What's up?" Mya used her nickname for Raegan, hoping to make her smile and put her in a good place to hear about Purity with Purpose and her newfound friends.

"Nothing really. I'm just kind of hanging out at my house. Alone as always. What's up with you? You sound chipper. Maybe a little more chipper than usual, if that's even possible." Raegan offered a dry laugh.

Mya giggled. "You know how I do! But I *am* so excited! I just talked to Mrs. Leisa and she had the best idea! Well, the grief counselors at school suggested the idea, but Mrs. Leisa really brought it to life!"

Raegan wanted to share in Mya's excitement, but she really wasn't in the mood right then. She had a million things on her mind, and she really felt weighed down by all the mess going on in her life and around her. But if she knew anything, it was how relentless Mya could be when she wanted to. She would get Raegan pumped up if it took all afternoon. She sighed and pressed Mya to continue, even though she wasn't really that interested to hear what she was talking about. She'd rather fake interest now and keep Mya's mind on what she had called about than to have her asking too many questions about what was really going on with her. "Oh, yeah? Well, what's this great idea she had?"

"Oh, my gosh! Wait until you hear this! It's so awesome! It's something that Mrs. Leisa and I have talked about so many times and that is really strong on my heart to share with other girls. Ok, let me start from the beginning. Mrs. Leisa has been seeing the grief counselors regularly since the accident. She said they are just really awesome women of God—now that I mention it, I really should go in and talk to them myself sometime. Anyway, she said that as she has been sharing with them about Annie, they have really helped her to replace the sadness she feels about her death with all the good memories of her that they shared while Annie was still alive. So then one of the counselors suggested that Mrs. Leisa try to think of something in Annie's life that was really important to her, and use that as the catalyst to do something to honor Annie's memory and keep a part of her alive." Mya paused, and then tried to clarify. "I mean, not alive as in she's not alive now, because she is alive in Heaven. She's more alive now that she is with Jesus than she ever was down here without Him face to face. But I just mean alive in the earthly sense, since she is no longer in the earth realm."

"I know what you meant, Mya." Raegan's response came out a little more harshly than she meant it. She checked her tone and continued. "I mean, I get what you were saying. So what did Mrs. Leisa decide to do?" She hoped that Mya was too preoccupied with this new idea to ask her what was wrong. Mya always seemed to know the difference between when she was being snappy because something was wrong and when she was just tired or not feeling really well. And she really did not feel like going into anything with her at the moment.

Speaking as if she read Raegan's mind, Mya replied, "Well, I don't know what is going on with you right now, but we will be discussing it later. Anyway, back to what I was trying to say before. The grief counselors suggested that she do something in Annie's memory that will help her see that Annie lives on in the hearts and lives of other people. So she decided to start a program at our church called Purity with Purpose that will help middle and high school girls understand the importance of saving themselves for marriage, and really show them how to do that. And she asked me to help her with the first run of it! I was flabbergasted that she would want me to be so involved. It really made my day! So, I told her that I think it's a great idea! Don't you think it's the best idea? I mean, I can't think of a better way to honor Annie's memory than taking one of the things that really made her special, and using it to help other young girls become better women. And of course I was thinking that you and I should totally be a part of the classes! I told Mrs. Leisa that I would be involved in whatever way I can. Don't you think that sounds great?" Mya waited with hope that something would click with Raegan and she would jump on the bandwagon.

"Um, I don't think so." Raegan's tone was emotionless as she answered.

Mya was shocked and disappointed with Raegan's response. "What? Raeyo, why not? What could possibly keep you from doing something like this? It's awesome! And it's for Annie! Why won't you be involved?"

"Because I'm not you! I don't belong there!" Raegan snapped angrily.

Mya felt like she had been slapped in the face. "What are you talking about? What is that supposed to mean? Of course you're not me. You're Raeyo! And you belong anywhere you want to go. What's the matter with you? Why would you say something like that?"

"Just forget it, Mya. Never mind. I just don't want to go, ok? I've had a rough day and I'm feeling a little crappy right now, and I just don't think I can be a part of those classes. Can we please just leave it at that?" Raegan wanted so bad to apologize for being such a jerk to the one person who mattered so much in her life, but she was just so lost and confused about everything that she just wanted to make everything and everyone go away. She thought about just blurting out what had been happening to her, but in the back of her mind, she was still afraid that if Mya knew that she was not a virgin and what had been happening to her, she would abandon her and not want to be her friend anymore, and the thought of that happening was too awful to entertain for a moment longer. So as much as she hated making Mya angry right then, she knew that Mya would soon get over it and they would move on. *That*, she could handle. What she couldn't handle was if she unloaded all the baggage she had been carrying for so long and Mya decided she was too much to take on and went away forever. So she kept up the snarky attitude and hoped that Mya would just leave her alone for the time being.

"Raeyo, what is up? Tell me what is going on with you." Mya felt like she had been begging Raegan to let her back into her life for ages. She was getting to the point that she was beginning to believe they would never get back to how things used to be, when life was good and their friendship was blooming.

"Mya, seriously, just forget about it. I don't want to talk about it. That's really great for you. I just don't want to be a part of it. So leave it alone. I will talk to you later." Raegan felt tears welling up in her eyes, and hung up the phone before they had the chance to roll down her cheeks. A sob caught in her throat and she buried her face in her hands as she began weeping uncontrollably.

Across town, Mya sat disbelievingly, listening to the dial tone of the deadened phone in her hand. *Oh, God! It's happened again,* she thought. *I am totally losing her. Everyday I see her slipping further and further away. I'm so scared for her! Give me wisdom, Lord! Show me what to do! Please!*

Jason was an absolute mess. It had only been a couple of weeks since his parents' deaths, but he felt as if he had aged a hundred years since that day. He walked around in a perpetual fog and dragged with him an invisible cloak of sadness that seemed to grow heavier by the day. His mind was dark and fuzzy, and he couldn't seem to find any manner of light that was strong enough to penetrate through the shadows or make it clear.

Never in his worst nightmares could he have dreamt that he would be an orphan at seventeen years old. He had always had his parents around, and just assumed that they would always *be* around. He was actually pretty close to them, and loved them dearly. Of course, like every teenager was guilty of doing, he had disappointed them at times, and at other times taken them for granted. At other moments, he felt like he wished they would just go away, or that he could move out and be on his own and do whatever he wanted to, without having them around to criticize his choices or monitor his behavior. But those feelings never lasted very long. He would always realize that he already had a great life and that his parents really weren't all that bad. And now that they actually *were* gone, and for good, he realized how unqualified and ill-equipped he was to run his own life. He realized how much he needed his parents. He missed them terribly and felt so unprepared to face the rest of his life without them.

He had stayed with the Lafleurs for a week after the accident. Within a few days of the wreck, some of his parents' friends had flown in from Burney to check on and talk to him. They had offered to make arrangements and let him come back to live with them until he graduated high school that next spring and went off to college the following fall. He considered it, but then decided that he would rather finish out his senior year with Mya in Faries. His parents' friends and the Lafleurs then took him to go see Sgt. Williams again. He helped Jason fill out some necessary paperwork to have him declared emancipated due to extenuating circumstances so that he could stay in Faries without the intervention of the Georgia state government. Because he was nearly eighteen, he was able to go forward without much ado. Plus, Sgt. Williams worked vigorously, and pulled some major strings on his behalf. So the courts had agreed to let him stay in the city on his own, and appointed Ill Will as his conservator until his situation was further assessed about six months after his eighteenth birthday. After all of the legal issues were worked out, Jason stayed for a few more days with the Lafleurs and then moved back into his own house.

Thinking back on the days following his parents' accident reminded Jason of something. He had been sitting in the living room by himself in silence for a little while, but he got up and went to the hall closet where he hung the jacket he had been wearing the first day he met Ill Will. He rummaged through the pockets until he found what he was searching for. He pulled out the two business cards Will had given him. His hands shook a little as he stood there looking down at them. He wasn't really sure what to do next.

Finally, after a few minutes of just staring at the cards, he went and got his laptop and flopped back down onto the couch in the living room. He logged his computer on to the internet, and after taking a few deep breaths, typed the web address that was printed on one of the cards into the address line. He looked around to make sure that no one was watching him, as guilt started to creep up the back of his neck. *What am I doing?* he thought to himself. *No one lives here anymore except me. I've got to stop being such a wuss! This is no big deal.*

All he wanted to think about was taking a little time to check into this webpage. As his computer pulled up the site, Jason tried to push all the other thoughts out of his head. He was just going to look around for a few minutes and see what the site was about, and then exit out of it and throw the card away. Will had said it was just an artistic site and that there was nothing to feel bad about if he looked at it. Thoughts of what Mya would say if she knew what he was about to do tried to sneak into his mind, but he quickly blocked those out too. She didn't need to know what he was doing. So instead of letting what she might say make him feel bad, Jason started to list in his mind all the reasons why what he was about to do was alright. *Like Will said, she probably already thinks that I do this. I'm sure she understands that I have to go this route because we aren't doing anything physical in our relationship and I am a teenage boy with raging hormones. She has to know that I have needs. And since she isn't ready to fulfill them, this is the next best thing. It's not like I'm cheating on her. I'm not doing anything that any other teenage guy in America hasn't done before. I am just going to look at a few pictures and then turn the computer off. It's not like I am a perfect little Christian like her who never does anything wrong. Plus, she's probably the only one who thinks there's something wrong with just looking. I'm sure even God won't mind this because it's not like I am actually doing anything with any of these girls. He should be happy that I'm not doing anything for real. I think then I'd need to feel bad. But not now. This is cool, because I am just going to take a peek and then move on.*

By the time he had thoroughly convinced himself that what was going on was acceptable, the website had come up on his screen. It prompted him to fill in some basic information about himself and then create a login name and password. He thought for a moment and then settled on "JStud." He didn't figure it mattered too much because he believed he'd only login that one time. After he got finished with all the information on the first page, an icon came up on the screen for him to click to go further into the site.

As Jason prepared to click the icon, a surge of nervous excitement ran through his body. It was a sensation he had never experienced, but really enjoyed. He clicked the screen and it flashed like a camera flash or lightening. Then a girl wearing a Catholic schoolgirl costume popped onto the screen. She was posed suggestively and seemingly beckoned for Jason to follow her. It was as if she was looking right at him, and knew him, and wanted him to come with her. He clicked the screen again and the picture changed.

With each click of his computer mouse, Jason was drawn deeper and deeper into this provocative new world he had discovered. Each picture was a little more seductive than the last, and stimulated Jason's senses in a totally different way. He continued clicking and examining each picture as it appeared on the screen. All the hairs on his body bristled with excitement and his skin tingled with every glance. He was entranced by all of the different, but equally beautiful women and the way each picture seemed to perfectly capture the curves and silhouettes of their voluptuous figures. There were girls of every type in the pictures. Some of them actually reminded him of Mya. He found himself especially enthralled by those girls – the lovely black women with tiny waists and curvaceous hips. He was quite enamored, because as attracted as he was to his girlfriend, she hadn't quite developed into this level of womanhood yet. Still, his mind started wandering and he began imagining how Mya would look in some of those poses and wearing those clothes. The more he looked at the women on the sites, the more excited he was to see Mya. Maybe he could figure out a way to convince her that taking a few pictures like these, just for him, was no big deal. After all, she claimed to love him, and she couldn't seriously expect him to be satisfied with just holding hands forever.

~

When DT returned to his office from his trip, he had a stack of messages waiting for him. The top one was a memo to contact Marcus as soon as he got back in town. It was marked *urgent* in big red letters. He sighed, wondering what Marcus needed to see him about, and dreading having to tell him about what all happened while he was away.

He was thoroughly exhausted and really wasn't in any shape to be having an important de-briefing with Marcus about what all had gone on at the office while he was gone. He decided that Marcus' urgent message would just have to wait one more day. Instead of going through his other messages and catching up on what all was left for him to look through now that he was back, DT locked his office door, went over to his comfortable suede couch and laid down. He loved having this lounging area in the corner of his office, and often stole a cat nap there during long workdays. As he lay there, waiting for sweet sleep to overtake his body, his mind drifted back to D'Bauch and Nunzi and the wild ride of a business trip they had just shared together.

After his initially rocky introduction to Nunzi, DT had spent most of the flight talking to him about the oil business and what he did for a living. Nunzi was a very willing listener, and interrupted very little. He mostly nodded and smiled. He seemed fascinated with DT's life and what type of lifestyle being an oil entrepreneur afforded DT. He did take the floor long enough to give DT a miniscule amount of information about his background. All DT was able to gather from it was that he came from a very large, but very poor Italian family. He was in America because the opportunities for success were much greater than in his little city, and he was going to try to make some money to send back to his family who were still living in his home-town. He was on his way to New Orleans to inquire about a job in the energy and mining industry that he heard about from a family friend who traveled to the United States previously. That was only his second flight, his first being from Italy to the US, and it had taken nearly every penny he had just to pay for it.

"Well, I remember days very similar to that," DT had told him. "It wasn't that many years ago that I was a poor, struggling man with a dream to run my own company. I didn't come from much, so I was pretty much on my own to get my business off the ground. I did a lot of research and spent many sleepless nights in the library, poring over books and magazines, trying to catch a break. It was a lot of hard work and sweat, but it was totally worth it. I feel blessed to have it so well now." DT surprised himself using the word 'blessed' to describe how he felt about his life, but he knew for sure that 'good luck' and 'fortune' had nothing to do with where he was today.

Nunzi just kept nodding and smiling. DT wondered if he was even comprehending what he was saying, because English was definitely not his first language, but when he asked him if he understood, Nunzi nodded his head emphatically. "Oh, yes, I understand perfectly. You are a, ah, how you say, inspiration to a poor man like myself. I want to sit at your feet and learn all that you know. I hope to one day be as you are."

DT was flattered by the young man's words. He continued speaking freely. At one point, D'Bauch disrupted their conversation with a call, as DT knew he would. D'Bauch, a stronghold in the international import-export business, was even wealthier than DT, and without a wife or children to take care of, enjoyed spending his money on riotous living. He owned his own plane, so when he found out that DT was heading out of town for whatever reason, he would drop everything and fly out to meet him. During his call, he suggested that, this time, instead of just hitting all the casinos while they were in New Orleans, they should try something new. He was getting bored with doing the same thing every time they met up, and needed a little more adventure. He knew of a few places that he wanted to show DT that would guarantee them some exciting escapades.

Because DT knew that arguing with D'Bauch was futile, and his alternative was a lonely two and a half week stay in a city he wasn't very familiar with, he agreed to meet him in the hotel bar the next evening to map out a game plan for the duration of their stay in New Orleans. The more he thought about it, the better of an idea it sounded like. He was going to be staying in a place that had lots of French speaking residents, and he really knew nothing about New Orleans. His meetings would all be day meetings, so that left him with nights to be filled with something. D'Bauch spoke fluent French and was also familiar with the city itself, so it made sense to meet up with him. He would be like a complimentary tour guide for DT. Over the years, D'Bauch had managed to gradually deposit his wild mentality and habits into DT and was always right there, ready to dredge them up the second DT got out of his hometown. DT was able to keep things under control when he was at home in Faries, but the moment he got on a plane headed for some other place, D'Bauch came calling, and all bets were off. DT became another person when he was around D'Bauch, drugging and boozing, and cavorting with strange women until all hours of the night. For anyone looking from the outside in, it was easy to see when things started going downhill for him. While Mali was alive, DT had something worthwhile to spend his money on—her. But now that she was gone, and he had found nothing or no one else as a suitable substitute in her place, he felt that he had no reason to resist D'Bauch and his *laissez faire* attitude.

Since Nunzi was sitting right beside him when he got the call, and their conversation had been going so well, DT thought it would be nice to invite him to come along and meet up with D'Bauch the following evening.

Nunzi's eyes lit up like light bulbs. "Truly? Oh, yes, DT! I think that would be a good idea! We will have a good time all together, no? And it will be good for me to meet your friend. How you say his name?"

"He goes by D'Bauch. And I think he will like meeting you too." DT thought for a moment and then said, "How about this? Since we have had such a good time getting acquainted with each other on this flight, I'd like to do something. You remind me of myself some years ago, young, ambitious and hopeful, and I would like to help give you the break that I wish someone had given me. I'll tell you what I'll do. I'm going to get you a hotel room in the hotel I will be staying in. Then tomorrow I will call the company you are looking to work for and see if there are any favors that I can call in for you. Then I would like to just put a little spending money in your hand if that's alright with you. That way, when you come out with D'bauch and me, you will be able to enjoy yourself without worrying about money."

Nunzi's eyes had filled with tears as DT spoke. "Oh, DT, you do too much! I could not accept all of this!"

DT waved him off. "It's really no trouble at all. It would be my pleasure."

Nunzi then excused himself to the restroom to try to get control of his emotions. While he was gone, DT began making calls and arrangements. He called D'Bauch back and let him know that they would be a party of three for this trip. D'Bauch agreed with gusto.

By the time Nunzi came back to his seat, the plane was preparing to touch down at the New Orleans airport. The two new friends sat back and waited for instructions on how and when to gather their belongings and head to their destination.

DT smiled thinking back on how touched Nunzi had been at his generosity that morning. He enjoyed being able to help those less fortunate than himself and got true pleasure from giving out of his own abundance. And getting a reaction like that was just the icing on the cake. From across the room, his intercom buzzed, and Cheryl's voice called out to him.

He sighed and rolled off the couch. He figured he may as well get after his to-do list because it didn't look like he would be getting any good rest anyway. He walked over to the desk and pressed the button. "Yes, Cheryl?"

"Sir, Marcus is here to see you. I told him you didn't want to be disturbed, but he insisted that it was urgent. Shall I send him in?" Cheryl sounded a little nervous, as if she didn't know what to expect in DT's reaction.

"Yes, Cheryl. Send him on in." DT walked over to the door and unlocked it. Just as he opened it, Marcus was reaching out to grab the knob. "Hello, Marcus. Come on in. Make yourself comfortable." He stepped back and motioned for Marcus to come into the room. He did, and walked over and sat down in one of the chairs facing DT's large ebony wood desk. DT came around and sat in his executive chair behind the desk.

Marcus looked at him across the desk and said calmly, "I'm glad to see you made it back safely. How was your trip? Did you enjoy yourself?"

DT looked down before he responded. Even though he was the superior, something about Marcus' intense nature made him feel like he was a child in the principal's office. For some reason, he took it hard when he felt like he had disappointed Marcus, so he always tried to downplay how bad things had gotten on his trips. But somehow, Marcus always got the truth out of him. He was never harsh or unkind with DT. He would just offer him advice and talk to him about doing better the next time. DT hated that every 'next time' ended just like the time before, with him apologizing for his recklessness and thanking Marcus for keeping things straight when he let himself get out of control. Marcus would always say the same thing, "I'm just doing my job."

DT had to admit to himself that Marcus took his responsibilities to DT and his company very seriously. He had no qualms about going above and beyond the call of his duties as accountant and financial advisor if he saw that he could help DT or someone else in need. He always seemed to be the first to know when anything was going on in the lives of any of DT's employees and made sure to relay correct information to keep DT ahead of the curve in handling these issues when they arose. He was unwaveringly loyal, and only offered DT sound advice for his decision making. He didn't judge or degrade him when he ignored the advice and messed things up, and for all the dirt he had on DT, he never gave reason for him to be concerned with his personal or professional business being spread in the streets. DT had the utmost respect for Marcus' integrity and honesty, and recognized his wisdom. And though he didn't always listen to him, he knew how lost he would be without him.

He finally gave a weak, "Yes, I had a good time."

This time, Marcus didn't pry. "Well, a lot has happened since you left town. You left right as some residents of the city received the most devastating news of their lives. The train wreck Edward tried to tell you about was worse than anyone expected." He looked straight at DT.

"What do you mean? What happened exactly?"

"Annette Carson was killed in the accident, Mr. Hudson."

DT gasped. "Oh, no! I tried to call Ed a few times and couldn't get a hold of him, but I had no idea! That's probably why I haven't been able to get in touch with him. Oh, God! He must be devastated!"

"Yes, he is. And that is part of the reason you haven't been able to reach him lately. But he is not the one you should be the most concerned about right now." Marcus kept his gaze on DT steady.

"He's not?" DT was very confused now. What could be worse than his good friend losing his only daughter in a horrible train wreck when she was on her way to visit him?

Marcus answered his question with these strong words, "No, he isn't. Someone else in your life needs your help more than Edward does right now. There is an atrocity being committed against someone you know and care about and you need to do something about it."

"How do you know about it and I don't?" DT stopped, and thought about it. How did Marcus ever know about things and he didn't? He still wasn't sure of that answer, but he knew it was true. Marcus was always more aware of things than he was.

"That's not what's important, Mr. Hudson. What's important is that you get involved *very soon*. Be warned that this is not going to be easy and this person is not going to open up to you willingly, but you must do whatever it takes to get in there and intervene on their behalf. You could be this person's only hope."

Suddenly DT's cell phone rang. He looked down at it and saw that it was Raegan Nottaway. He had told her to call him that day to see if he had come back in town yet, so that she could come and pick up her check if he was. He looked up at Marcus. "Sorry to cut this short, Marcus, but I'd better take this."

Marcus nodded and stood up. "Well, then, sir, I will leave you to it." He turned to leave and disappeared out the door.

Mya was at the end of her rope with Raegan. What started out as concern for her well-being was quickly becoming aggravation with her determination to retreat from the rest of the world. Everyday, despite Mya's continued efforts to rescue her, Raegan seemed to draw deeper and deeper into herself and pull further and further away from Mya and everyone around her. Mya was distraught as she helplessly watched her friend regress into this reclusive shell of her former vivacious self. She had never seen Raegan like this, and she was beginning to really get scared.

Raegan seemed to have lost all sense of herself, all sense of her future. Whenever Mya was able to squeeze the least bit of information out of her, it was in very short term language. She seemed to have just checked out of her own life. She was simply existing, not living. Her once rich and sparkling voice had become a monotone hum of lifeless sound.

"Lord, please give me wisdom here! Show me how to get through to her." As Mya prayed, she dialed the number to Raegan's personal line at her house. When she answered, Mya just plowed right to the point. "Raeyo, we need to talk. I don't know what is going on with you, but it's starting to scare me. And you know me better than to think I am just going to walk away from you when I know something is wrong. So I am not going to leave this alone until you tell me what's going on, and we get it worked out. It doesn't matter how long it takes, or how much you resist me, I am going to stay on you until we get this thing straightened out." She stopped and waited to see what Raegan would say.

She heard what sounded like sniffling on the other line. "Ok." It was the only word that Raegan could get out before the floodgates opened and she lost her ability to control all the pent up emotions from the last six years, and it all finally burst free. She began wailing and bawling with gut-wrenching sobs. She held the phone, but said no other words. She just wept hysterically into the receiver.

"Oh, Raeyo!" Mya exclaimed, from her end of the line, "What is it? Please, talk to me! Just hold on. Stay right where you are, ok? I'm coming over. I will be there in a minute." She hung up the phone and quickly gathered her purse and car keys. She grabbed a jacket from the hall closet and bolted to her car in the family garage. She started it up and backed gingerly down the driveway, and then made her way to Raegan's house as quickly as was possible, without breaking any traffic laws. When she got there, she jumped out of her car and rushed to the front door. When she checked the knob, she was glad to find the house unlocked. She swung open the door and went inside. She ran up the stairs and burst into Raegan's room.

What she found nearly brought her to her knees. Raegan was lying on the floor, still crying, curled up in the fetal position. Mya ran to her side, knelt down beside her, pulled her upright and held her close. She rocked Raegan like a baby, and just let her cry. She prayed silently that the Lord would cover Raegan with His peace, and that she would be able to help her with whatever she was going through.

Finally, Raegan seemed to have cried all the tears she had. She slowly sat up and wiped her face, but she wouldn't look directly at

Mya. She pulled her knees up to her chest and dropped her head. "Oh, God! Oh, God!" She just kept repeating that over and over.

"Raegan! Talk to me! What is wrong? What is going on? Please, just talk to me!" Mya's voice registered all the panic she was feeling. She felt so helpless, sitting there watching her best friend completely fall apart, and all she wanted was to help her. "Please! Just look at me. What is going on? I just want to help you. Will you let me help you?"

"I just want it to stop. I want to make it all go away."

"What? What do you want to go away? What do you want to stop? You have to talk to me or I won't know how to help you!"

"You *can't* help me. No one can. That's why I want to just end it. I just want all this hurting to be over."

Oh, God! What is she saying? Mya's alarm level shot through the roof when she heard Raegan say those words.

Pray. She heard the word as clear as day in her heart. *Out loud.*

"Lord, I just call out to you right now! I pray that your presence would come into this room right now. Satan, you and your demons have no place here. Get out *now*! In the name of Jesus, you have no right to stay here and I bind you up and cast you out now! You must go! Lord, your Word says that if we resist the devil, then he must flee. So I rebuke him in Jesus' name! I call Raegan Ayo Nottaway free in Jesus' name! No plan of the devil can prosper against her. I call it done right now. In Jesus' name, amen." As Mya prayed, she felt the peace of God settle on her mind. She stood up and looked around the room for some tissue to give to Raegan. She walked over to the desk in the corner of the room, and rummaged around for a moment. That's when she noticed Raegan's cell phone flashing.

She felt another nudge in her spirit. *Pick it up.*

She picked up the phone and pressed the button to open the mail alert that flashed on the screen. There were two recent messages. The first was a text from someone called Grimly. It said, "If you tell anyone, it's over for you." It was dated two days earlier. The second was an email from Raegan's internet friend from earlier that day.

MyDespair2000 wrote: Here's the link for that site. They have some good ways that seem pretty painless and not too messy. I haven't decided for myself. Good luck on your journey. Whatever's next has to be better than this, right? It's been nice knowing you. Maybe I will see you somewhere on the other side.

Mya nearly vomited when she read the messages. She didn't know exactly what the first one was in reference to, but she knew that the second one was suggesting that Raegan commit suicide. She turned slowly to face Raegan again. She held up the phone so that Raegan could see that she had read it. Her voice broke as she asked, "Is this what is the matter with you?"

Raegan looked up to see what Mya was talking about. When she saw that Mya held her phone, her eyes filled with tears again. She nodded her head and then covered her face with her hands. Mya tossed the phone down onto Raegan's bed and came back to sit down beside her. She gently pulled Raegan's hands away from her face and raised her chin so that she was forced to look at her.

"Tell me what is going on, Raeyo. It's ok. I promise I won't be upset. No matter what it is, it's alright."

Right then, it was as if a levy broke somewhere deep inside Raegan and six years worth of filthy, polluted, grimy gutter water came spilling out all at once. She began pouring out everything that was going on inside her. When she first started talking, it was so jumbled up that Mya couldn't understand her and had to tell her to slow down and start over. She had to stop talking for a few moments and take in a few deep breaths to calm the hiccups that she had developed from so much hard crying. When she was finally composed enough to be understood, she started again.

"It's just so horrible, Mya. I am so ashamed. I didn't know who to turn to, and I didn't know what people would think if they found out. And then I started talking to MyDespair and he just kept saying that it would just be easier to end it all. Rather than risk what everyone would say when they found out about me, I could just do something and keep anyone from ever knowing. He said he would help me. I didn't really want to hurt myself, but everything was just so bad, and I didn't think there was any other solution. Then he introduced me to another girl online, who pretty much told me the same things he did. Her screen name is Enmity. And she told me that I needed to get away from the people that I love, especially you. Otherwise, you all would just keep me from doing what I needed to do. She said that everything would be easier once I was isolated and had rid myself of all distractions. So I started making plans. I just started separating myself from the few people that I do care about, so that when everything happened, they wouldn't be so upset. I know you felt me pulling away from you. I just didn't want to hurt you or make you sad when everything worked out. And I haven't spoken to Ethan in over a month. I just stopped calling him and I ignored his calls when he called me. My parents don't really care anyway, but I stopped talking to them much too. I had decided that this was the only way to make it stop. To make *him* stop."

Mya interrupted her then. "Ok, Raegan, I know things haven't been great around here lately. But what exactly was so bad that you were ready to," Mya paused. She couldn't bring herself to say the words 'kill yourself' so she just said, "do that? What were you so worried that everyone would find out about? And who is *him*? What did you want *him* to stop doing? What has been going on that you couldn't tell me about?" Mya was sincerely clueless. In all of their time together over the years, they had been so much alike in all of their experiences, and had been through so many similar events. That made it easy to talk to each other about everything that they went through. She didn't think there was much in life that she and Raegan would feel like they had to keep from one another, so she couldn't imagine what was so horrible that it would keep Raegan from sharing it with her and instead lead her to such a drastic conclusion. She waited for her to continue.

"Well, I wanted to tell you. For so long I did. I just didn't know how. And then when I decided to go ahead with my plan, I figured there was no need to tell you. I just didn't want you to be upset or to think bad of me. So I just decided to keep it quiet and take it with me. I was planning to do it soon. I was waiting on that message from Despair to give me some ideas. But then I called DT Hudson. He had told me to call him today to find out if he was back in town from his trip. I was planning to thank him for giving me work and letting me earn my own money for the last few years and then tell him not to worry about paying me for this last time I worked for him. It was pretty much going to be my goodbye speech to him. But when I called him, the strangest thing happened. It was like he knew that something bad was going to happen. He asked me if there was anything that he could do to help me with a problem I was facing. At first I just kind of acted like everything was fine and that I didn't need any help and that there was no problem. But he wouldn't let it go. He kept asking me all these questions. I kept telling him that I was fine. I could tell that he didn't believe me. He said that he was going to find out what was wrong and get involved, whether I liked it or not. He told me that he was always around if I needed him, but if I couldn't tell him what was going on with me, then I needed to find someone who I *could* tell. He mentioned Mrs. Leisa and you. I had just gotten off the phone with him like ten minutes before you called me. Did he call you? Is that how you knew to call me and say what you said just now?"

Mya's mind flashed back to Charlotte telling her to talk to Raegan. When she said it, Mya had thought that she was just referring to telling Raegan about meeting the new girls and the Purity with Purpose idea. But now, she was beginning to see that Charlotte was leading her into something much deeper. She was learning to recognize the hand of God when she saw it, and this was definitely Him. "Actually, no. He didn't call me. And I didn't really know what was going on. I just knew I needed to talk to you—or I guess I should say that you needed to talk to me. So, go on."

"Well, after I got off the phone with him, I said in my heart, if anybody really cares whether I live or die, then they are going to have to show me quick. It was easy for Mr. Hudson to say something nice to me during a conversation that I initiated. I wanted someone to come to me this time. And then you called. It was like this whole dance was choreographed just for me. Everyone was doing all these complicated steps just to show me how much they cared. So when you called, I knew it was time to tell you about what's been happening to me." She stopped talking and took a deep breath. "But I want to ask you to promise me something. Will you promise that what I tell you won't make you change your view of me? Just hear me out, ok?" She looked at Mya with worry in her piercing gray eyes.

Mya reassured her, "I promise that I will hear you out and will not judge you for whatever you tell me."

"Ok, here goes. The reason I have been so distant and crazy lately is because I've been getting raped. Every Friday night, I go to a hotel downtown, and my dad's friend comes and rapes me. Sometimes it's just once or twice a visit. But sometimes, it's a lot more than that. He's been molesting me since Ethan moved out, when I was eleven, but now he has started full out raping me. He told me that if I ever said anything to anyone, he would hurt my family and kill me. He told me that no one would know he did it and that no one would even care. I was so scared. And then when I got some guts and told him that I was done with going through that and was going to tell someone what he had done, he said that he would just say that it was mutual and that I seduced him. And then he started sending me threatening texts everyday. I just didn't know what to do, so I didn't do anything. I just closed my mouth and let him do whatever he wanted. It didn't matter anymore. That's when I decided to just, you know, end it for good." Raegan's voice had gone flat, as she withdrew back into the defensive mode she had become so dependent on. She turned and looked at Mya. "And that's why I wouldn't go to those meetings with you. I don't belong there. I'm not pure. I'm anything but. And I don't feel like I have a purpose. But I couldn't tell you all of that because I thought you would stop being my friend. I know how important saving yourself for marriage is to you, and I figured that if you knew that I had already had sex, you would think I was a bad influence or something. I just hated the thought of losing you as my friend because of what's happened to me. I was just so ashamed."

Mya was shocked when she heard Raegan's news. But she was more heartbroken to know that she had been holding all this inside for so many years because of her fear of losing their friendship. So instead of risking the loss of the friendship, she was willing to just end her whole life. "Oh, Raeyo! I am so sorry!" She didn't know what else to say. Nothing had prepared her for this sort of situation. She put her arms around Raegan and held her tight for a long while. Finally, she let go and looked her in the eyes, "Raeyo, I had no idea that you were carrying all this for so long. I've been so caught up in my own thing that I haven't been a good friend to you. Please forgive me for that. I never would have wanted to let you bear something like this by yourself for all this time. But you have nothing to be ashamed of. You haven't done anything wrong."

"Something told me that you would say that, but then I was so scared that you would think it *was* my fault because for six years I never said anything. I just let this sick twisted freak do whatever he wanted to me, and I didn't do a thing about it. I was just so torn. You and Ethan are the only really good things I have in my life. And all this started when Ethan moved out, so I got scared when I thought about how much worse it could get if you walked away too. I just couldn't handle it."

"Well, I am telling you now that I am not going anywhere. If you will have me, I will be around forever." Mya smiled at Raegan and brushed a loose curl from her face. "You're the sister I always wanted, but never got. I don't want to go through life without you. Now that this is out, we have got to figure out what to do next. Mr. Hudson had a good idea when he suggested talking to Mrs. Leisa. She would definitely know how to help you."

Raegan looked up with apprehension on her face. "Mya I just got up the nerve to share this with you. I don't think I am ready to tell anyone else. I don't think I ever want to tell anyone else. This isn't just something you go around sharing with everyone. I just want to forget about it."

"I know you do, but it's not that easy, Rae. If you could just 'forget about it,' don't you think you would have done that already? I'm not an expert on any of this, and I really don't know what to tell you about it. But Mrs. Leisa would. And trust me, she is not going to think any less of you either. What has happened to you is not a reflection on you as the bad person. The man who has been doing this to you is the bad one. But I won't say anything to Mrs. Leisa if you don't say it's ok. I just think that will be the best thing."

"Well, I just don't know. Could you talk to her without telling her that you're talking about me? Or not tell her everything about it? I just don't want everyone to know that I've had sex with some gross old man, but then can't even seem to get the attention of a guy my own age. I just feel like such a freak and like if anyone else knows, it will somehow get out to everyone, and they will look at me like I'm some trashy sex addict or something."

"Well, I can tell you that with Mrs. Leisa, you have nothing to worry about. She knows just about everything about me and not a single word of it has gone any further than between me and her. If I tell her that it is confidential, then that's the way it will stay. And she still loves me, and I have told her some pretty unlovely stuff, so I know this will not change her love for you either. So can I please talk to her? I know she will be able to help."

"I guess." Raegan agreed, but in her heart, she still had her doubts all the way around.

"Hey, hon! What are you doing?" Mya smiled as she waited for her boyfriend's response. *Just the sound of his voice makes things better*, she thought as he answered. "Well, I really need to talk. Do you think you can come over for a little while?" She flipped her phone closed after Jason assured her he would be there shortly. She was happy to be seeing him, but her excitement was nearly extinguished when she thought about the information Raegan had just divulged to her and why she was inviting him over in the first place.

When Jason arrived and rang the doorbell, Mya quickly went to let him in. She led him to the living room and sat down with him on the couch. After a few minutes of small talk, she got right down to why she called him over. She began telling him about how she had been feeling as though something was not right with Raegan for some time, and how she had finally found out what was going on with her.

Mya looked over at Jason as she spoke. He had a curious look on his face, and was staring intently at her.

"What are you thinking about? Are you even listening?" she asked him finally.

"I really am trying to listen, but I am just so distracted by how stunning you are," he replied.

Mya smiled. "You're sweet, Chaz. But come on! Pay attention, please! This is serious."

Jason leaned over so that his face was just a few inches away from hers. "I'm very serious, Mya." He reached over and ran his fingers gently through her hair, tucking a stray piece behind her ear, and pulled her the rest of the way to him. He kissed her passionately on the mouth.

Mya was taken by surprise, but found herself melting into his kiss. She closed her eyes and leaned into it. After a few moments, he pulled away.

"Wow," she whispered, her eyes still closed and lips still puckered.

"Yeah," he said. "I know you don't really think we should do that yet, but I just couldn't help myself. You're the most beautiful girl in the world and I just wanted you to know that." As he spoke, he pulled her in for another kiss.

Mya put her hand on his chest and stopped him. She opened her eyes and looked deep into his. "Chaz! Please! That was amazing and you are so amazing, but you're gonna get me in trouble! We've got to stop while were ahead!" She chuckled. "Plus, I have cheer practice in a little while and I really need to talk to you about what's going on with Raeyo. She really needs some help and I'm not sure what to do. So focus!" She kissed him on the nose and sat back. Jason sat back too and folded his arms across his chest, glaring off into space.

"You're not upset, are you, Chaz?" Mya looked over at her boyfriend. He didn't say anything. He just kept looking straight ahead. "Chaz! Are you mad? Because I wouldn't kiss you again?"

She reached over and tried to uncross his arms and get him to look at her. "Are you seriously angry now?"

He snatched away from her touch and turned his scowl on her. "Well, yeah, Mya," he said fiercely. "I kind of am! I mean, how do you think this makes me feel?"

"What do you mean?" she asked, shocked at his sudden mood swing and dramatic reaction. She had never seen him like this.

"Well, you're always saying that you love me and that we are going to be together forever, but you never show me if that's true. We always have to do things your way, and I'm just sick of wondering where we really stand."

"What? Are you serious? I *do* love you! And I *do* want to be with you forever. That's why I want to wait before we take things to the next level. We have our whole lives to love each other and to be physical and all that. Our whole lives! But not until *after* we get married. That's my conviction. And you know that! You've known it since you met me. And I thought you understood and agreed with me. I didn't know I was just having things 'my way,' as you so eloquently put it. But *I* want something to look forward to in our marriage. I don't want to do everything there is to do now and have nothing for later." Mya stood up and walked across the room. Her head was spinning and tears were starting to sting in the corner of her eyes. *What is wrong with him?* she thought. *I've got enough to handle with this Raegan situation without adding boyfriend drama to the mix!*

"I don't need a sermon from you on holy matrimony, ok? I just wanted to show you how I feel about you. But of course you shot me down because you're too holy for everything! You can't even kiss the guy you say you want to spend the rest of your life with! How ridiculous is that? I mean, I'm the guy with the gorgeous girlfriend that I can't even kiss when I want to!" Jason nearly swore in his frustration. "It's so hard for me to hold myself back from you! I want you so bad! All the time! And there is nothing I can do about it! Do you know how hard this is for me?"

"'A *sermon*?' I can *not* believe you just said that! I am not preaching at you! I am telling you the truth and where I stand! What is going on with you? Where is all this coming from? I didn't know you were having such a hard time, but I hope you know that this isn't easy for me either! I'm the girl who is always surrounded by people but is lonely most of the time! I am the girl who loves this guy, but is having to sacrifice what her body wants to do for what her heart knows is right!" Mya's voice broke, as the tears began streaming down her face. "This life that I'm choosing to live is not easy! I have committed to live for the Lord and do what is right in His sight. The Bible says to take up your cross and follow Christ. And that almost always means going against what is cool and popular and accepted by everyone else. Do you think that's easy? It's hardly ever easy! That's why He said take up your *cross* and not your suitcase or your purse or something. Do you think I enjoy being ridiculed for what I stand for? Do you think I like having to say no when I really want to say yes? Do you think I'm happy about missing out on what everyone else is doing? This isn't just about me and you, Jason! This is about me and God! I have to do what I believe He wants of me. And sometimes that means waiting. Don't you think I would love to let myself go there with you? Sometimes I want to just let go and do exactly what my body wants to. But I can't! I love you so much that it consumes me sometimes. But that doesn't make sinning with you alright. And I won't ever let *anyone* become more important than the Lord in my life! So I'm sorry if you don't understand that, but that's how it is." While she spoke, Mya felt as though every ounce of energy was draining from her body, like someone had just pulled the plug out of some invisible drain in the bottom of her feet. Her tears showed little sign of slowing, and there was a growing emptiness in her gut that she hadn't ever felt before. She took a few more steps backward until her back hit the wall behind her, and she slid down to the floor. She waited for Jason's response.

"Well, I'm sorry, but I *don't* understand. I'm a guy! I have needs! And I thought I was important to you. I just feel like you always get to make the decisions about us and I don't have any say in the matter. I don't ever seem to get what *I* want. I don't see what's wrong with us being close if we love each other like we say we do. That's how the rest of the world works, Mya."

"Well, if you don't understand, then I don't think we can do this anymore. I can't be with someone who doesn't have the same conviction as I do. I can't be with you if you won't allow me to pursue my relationship with the Lord above all else, even if that means sacrificing some things I want right now for what I know is right. And I really don't care how it works in the rest of the world. That's not how it works in *my* life." Mya could hardly believe what she was about to say next. Her voice dropped to barely above a whisper. "You know what? I think you should go now, Jason. It's over." She pulled her knees up to her chest and dropped her head, just the same way she had seen Raegan do just a little while earlier. *Oh, God,* she thought. *What have I just done?*

When she heard Jason slam out the front door without another word, her body proved her mind wrong when she began crying a new flood tears she didn't believe she even possessed.

~

I promised myself I would never *let myself get here.* Mya scolded herself silently as she drove toward the gym. A good while after Jason stormed out of her house, she had finally stopped crying and was now trying to get herself mentally prepared as she headed to cheerleading practice. As their captain, the other girls on the squad looked to her to lead them and to always be the peppiest one of all. She couldn't walk in there with swollen, red eyes and a runny nose and expect them to overlook that and have a productive practice. So, she had dragged herself up off the floor, tried to pull herself together, washed her face, and tried to put on her best cheer smile. She knew it was probably pointless to even try, because knowing her girls and how close they had all become, they would see right through her façade.

They are going to read me like a book, she thought. *I just hope they don't ask too many questions. I don't think I am ready to talk about all this just yet.*

She pulled into the parking lot of the school, took off her sunglasses, tossed them into the center console, and took one last rueful glance at herself in the rearview mirror before grabbing her gym bag from the passenger seat and getting out of the car. She locked her car doors and braced herself for the next few hours. *I can't let my personal problems get in the way of my responsibilities right now. I have to go in here and set a good example for these girls.* She took a deep breath and smoothed down her tank top and cheer shorts before jogging inside to the gymnasium. As she ran, she said a quick prayer under her breath, asking the Lord to strengthen her heart as she worked with the girls that afternoon.

She was relieved to see the four new cheerleaders as soon as she walked in the door, and the gym was already set up for practice. Their happy faces greeted her like a breath of fresh air, and her spirit was immediately lifted by their presences. They all grinned at her as she came inside.

"Hey, Mya!" exclaimed Bryn.

"Hey, girls!" Mya dropped her bag near the bleachers and rushed over to where they stood, hugging each of the girls in a tight embrace. "I'm so glad that you guys are here!"

"We're glad to be here! We are so excited about our first practice with you and the squad. Just let us know what you want us to do, ok? We are here to serve, so whatever you need from us to help things go smoothly, just say the word!" Nadia smiled and winked at Mya as she spoke.

"Thanks so much, you guys! And thank you for getting the room set up for me! Y'all are awesome! It has been a rough day and I am kind of stressed out, but I have a responsibility to the squad to give my best. And I can already tell that having you all here will make that so much easier."

Charlotte spoke up this time. "Well, we are glad to help. After practice we can talk about whatever is going on with you and pray about it, if you want."

"That would be great. Prayer is definitely what I need. But for now, I'm just going to cast my cares over onto the Lord and let Him hold onto them. So, come on, ladies! Let's get practicing!" Mya smiled with genuine happiness at the girls and turned to face the rest of the squad that was gathering on the practice mats in the middle of the gym floor. With the four girls now standing behind her, both literally and figuratively, she felt the surge of strength she had asked the Lord to send her way. It was like they were the answer to her prayer, personified. She pushed all thoughts of Jason and the break-up out of her mind, and took a moment to let the feeling of sweet comfort wash over her like a cleansing rain.

"Alright, everyone! Let's get started! Everybody grab a partner and let's start with some stretches. We will be practicing the new routine for the game next week, as well as a few new stunts! Come on! Let's go!" Mya clapped her hands and the girls scrambled around to find partners. For the next three hours, Mya called out instructions and helped the rest of the cheerleaders prepare for their school's game the following week. Before she realized it, practice was over and she prepared to dismiss the girls.

"Great work, everyone! Keep practicing what we worked on today, and we will definitely be ready for the game. Thanks for working so hard! We are finished here, so take a break, chat, get some water and whenever you are ready, you are free to go. Have a great evening." Mya walked over and sat down on the bleachers. She pulled her own water bottle out of her bag and took a long drink. She looked around the gym at the other girls, and watched them laugh and talk with one another. All of a sudden, a feeling of heaviness came over her, and she felt like a hundred pound weight had just been placed on her shoulders. She felt a wave of sadness as thoughts of Jason once again began swirling through her mind. A shadow came across her feet as someone came and stood beside her. She slowly turned to see who it was. Lady Canker's muscular frame loomed over her. Mya instantly felt a sense of dread rush over her, knowing that this woman was bound to find out about Jason and say something horribly insensitive, inappropriate, and vulgar. Mya cringed when Canker placed her hand on her shoulder and looked down at her.

"Well, Missy, looks like you girls had a good practice. At least I hope that's what all the laughing and talking means. We don't pay for you girls to turn practices into sorority row!" She took her hand off Mya, but kept her gaze steady on Mya's face. "Oh, I'm just razzin' you, Miss Priss. Don't get your panties in a wad. You look like you've just swallowed a hornet. Who peed in your cornflakes this morning? Can't you take a little joke?"

Mya averted her gaze and silently hoped that one of the new cheerleaders would show up. Canker didn't like those girls and seemed to move along a little faster when they were around. Plus, Mya really did want to talk to them and pray with them about all this Jason stuff. Just then, right on cue, Carina walked up.

"Excuse me. I'd like to speak to Mya alone, if you don't mind." Mya was surprised at the tone in Carina's voice. She hadn't heard her sound like that before, and she certainly didn't sound like a teenage cheerleader right then. And Mya was fairly certain that Carina didn't care one ounce if Lady Canker minded or not. Carina just looked Canker square in the eye and did not back down for a moment.

"Whatever," Canker muttered under her breath as she walked over to a group of girls standing a few yards away.

The heaviness Mya had been feeling slowly began to dissipate and drain away. "Wow," she said gratefully. "It's like you read my mind or something! I was just praying that one of you guys would come over here and here you are!" She smiled up at Carina.

"Well, we can always tell when one of our sisters is in distress and I felt that you needed me just then." Carina sat down beside Mya. She looked up, scanning the girls standing around them, and spotted Nadia, Charlotte and Bryn. She motioned for them to come over. They walked over and sat on the floor in front of Mya and Carina. "And now we are all here, so let's talk. We know you have had a rough day today, so if you are ready to talk, we are ready to listen."

Sitting there with these four wonderful girls, Mya felt so at ease. She felt as though she could share her heart without fear of ridicule or judgment. It was amazing that she had only known them for such a short while because, every time she was near them, she couldn't escape the feeling that they had been part of her life forever. And right now, looking around at them looking back expectantly at her, that time seemed much longer than their seventeen years. Mya couldn't quite put her finger on why, but each one of them seemed to be much older than she was. But it wasn't physical, like their faces looked old or anything like that. It was internal—spiritual—like they held a piece of eternity within themselves. They had a quiet maturity and confidence about them that most high school girls didn't possess yet. Mya knew deep down inside that what they said was important and that the advice they gave would have lasting echoes. She was eager to share with them what had happened that afternoon with Jason and to hear what they had to say about it.

Tears welled up in her eyes as she took a deep breath and began to speak. "Well, the short version is that Chaz—I mean, Jason—and I broke up today." The words sounded so empty and juvenile coming out of her mouth, and Mya felt incredibly petty being so upset over the situation. But glancing around at the other girls' faces, etched with concern and sympathy, she felt comfortable enough share more.

Carina placed her hand on Mya's back and nodded her encouragement for Mya to continue. "So what's the long version?" she asked quietly.

The tears began sliding easily down Mya's face as she recounted the events from earlier that afternoon. As she spoke, several of the other cheerleaders came and joined the little group. Pretty soon, most of the cheerleading squad had made their way over and were listening to Mya. They had all grown to know and love her so much and knew how much she loved Jason, so they were all interested to hear what had happened.

"I mean, of course I love him and eventually want to be with him physically. But I refuse to compromise my stance on purity before marriage. Why couldn't he understand that?" Mya finished speaking and looked up. She was surprised to have so many faces looking back at her. Every person in the room was focused on her now, including Lady Canker.

"You're joking, right?" Canker spat fiercely. "You really think a teenage boy who you claim to love is just going to go along with having no physical contact whatsoever?"

Mya looked back at Canker. "I didn't say *no* physical contact!" she shot back. "I just believe that it is better to do less right now and not even tempt yourself than to rely on your being strong enough to say no in the heat of the moment." Mya's could feel her face burning in anger as she spoke. She did not want to get into this conversation with this woman. There was nothing Godly about Lady Canker, and her advice to Mya and her friends always reeked of evil intent. Mya didn't want to be rude, especially not to an adult, and the person who was responsible for keeping their squad running, but this woman sparked a righteous anger in Mya that she couldn't ignore. Canker never seemed to know when to quit.

"Well, Mrs. Goody-two-shoes, maybe that's how it works in your perfect little prissy world. But out here in the *real* world, where the rest of us live, it don't go like that!" Canker's dark eyes mocked Mya, glowing with a lusty glare.

Mya's mind spun back to her argument with Jason. He had used those same words. Had he been talking to Lady Canker? Had he heard this from her? He had never had a problem with their relationship before now. It was as though Canker had somehow wormed her way into Jason's mind with her twisted ideas and now he was starting to act and sound and think just like her. But how could that have happened?

"Well, just like I told Jason, I don't care what people are doing in the 'real' world! I am doing what I believe is pleasing to the Lord and I don't care how anyone feels about it!"

Charlotte grinned widely. "That's right, Mya! Your body is the temple of the Holy Ghost and you have to take care of yourself. Don't let anyone tell you otherwise. Saving yourself for marriage is a gift, and something to be desired!"

"Yeah, right! Who are you trying to fool with that religious junk?" Canker hurled the words toward Charlotte, but quickly turned her attention back to Mya. As she spoke, she began slowly moving forward, weaving a path among the girls, making her way closer to Mya until nothing stood between the two of them except Carina, Bryn, Charlotte and Nadia. She looked hatefully around at the four of them, then let her stare come to rest on Mya. "What's the problem, Queenie? You afraid that you are going to try something and like it and won't be able to stop? Well, you're right! Once you get a taste, you can never get enough. There is nothing in this world better than the sweet pleasure a man can give you! You will be begging for more!" She chuckled, delighted at the thought, and turned around to face the other cheerleaders. "Take it from someone who knows, ladies! To get love from a man, you have to give him what he wants. Otherwise, prepare to be alone forever, because trust me, giving it up is the only way to make him stay. You can't expect to keep a man if you don't give him what he needs!" Her back was to Mya now, but her words were aimed straight at her. "And if he can't get it from you, he *will* find somewhere else to get it!"

Bryn stood up. "That's enough, Canker! I don't think you should be talking to a group of high school girls this way. I believe it's time for you to go now!" The other three girls got up and stood next to Bryn, as Canker slowly turned around to face them again. They completely blocked her view of Mya, who sat quietly on the bleachers, tears still streaming down her face.

"I can say what I want, to who I want, when I want!" Canker's voice became a hiss. "Little Miss Princess hasn't said anything. She's the captain, remember? I don't take orders from you four twits!"

"I want you gone." Mya spoke up from where she sat.

Canker straightened up, and turned her nose in the air. "Whatever," she huffed arrogantly. "You'll see that I'm right one day. After your sweet little Jason moves on and finds out what he's been missing, he will see that he didn't really need you anyway. And then you'll be begging for my advice to get him back. Just wait and see. You'll listen to me one day! That perfect little lifestyle is going to get old really fast when you see everyone else is passing you by and actually enjoying their lives! You just *think* you want to be the so-called righteous Christian girl living for Jesus. But what good is that doing you right now? You're miserable. It seems to me that, at it's best, this whole God thing isn't making any real difference in your life. But if you really think about it and are honest with yourself, it's making you miss out on all the fun, just because God says it's a no-no. You're better than me, I guess. I couldn't do it. I mean, what kind of God would dangle something good in your face but forbid you from having it? Isn't that kind of cruel?"

"That's enough!" Bryn said again. "You heard her. It's time for you to go!"

"That's fine. You know I will be back. So I will just see you all next time! Good bye, ladies! Remember what I told you!" She tossed her blonde hair over her shoulder, smiled broadly, waved goodbye as if she hadn't a care in the world, and walked out of the gym. Mya's body relaxed and her palms stopped hurting, and looking down, she realized that she had been sitting rigidly tense, with fists clinched so tightly that her fingernails dug into her hands and nearly drew blood, since Canker had come through the door. Now that she was gone, relief flooded Mya's spirit. There was no denying that woman was pure evil.

Her four protectors were now standing facing her. Nadia spoke first. "Stand up, Mya. You need to pray."

In the weeks following the accident, it seemed that everyone wanted to re-evaluate their life's priorities. Everyone, except Edward Carson. He preferred just to pretend that everything was fine and that his life was just as it should be. He couldn't face the fact that his daughter was dead, and on top of that, he had become the sort of man who was unfaithful to his wife and who left her to fend for herself because of his own selfish desires. Even though he and Leisa were back together physically, things were still uncomfortably tense around the Carson household. He recognized that most of the issue was with him, but that revelation still didn't make him any more ready to admit to his wrongdoings and confront the iniquity he had allowed to set its hook in his heart. His thoughts and feelings had become so jumbled up that he didn't know how to act from one moment to the next. At times, he wanted to be with Leisa so they could pray and comfort one another in the Lord, but other times he just wanted to get as far away from her and her God as he could. And the shame he was feeling about his new relationship had become his constant companion over the last few weeks. He tried to shake it off, but he couldn't seem to get away from the nagging sensation in his spirit that had come to inhabit his every waking moment, nor could he escape the thoughts of Lead Astray that dominated his mind. He felt like a total fraud.

He was growing tired of feeling guilty, so he began spending more and more time away from home. He spent long hours at the office, and would then just drive around for long stretches after he got off work. He eagerly looked for any opportunity to sneak away and be with Lead Astray. The soothing sound of her voice drew him to her like the gentle babbling of a clear, alluring brook. He was intoxicated by her every word. But what he didn't discern was that just beneath her calm surface ran a swift current into an ebbing tide of wickedness, ready to snatch him and drag him far out into a deep and violent sea of lies and betrayal. He thought he was simply dangling his feet into a refreshing, swirling pool, but he had actually just stepped into the most dangerous waters that existed. And having shut out his wife from her rightful role as his life preserver, Edward didn't stand a chance of survival on his own.

In contrast, Leisa had completely forgiven Edward, for his inconsideration and disappearance, the first night he came back home, and had sincerely moved on. She continued visiting the grief counselors at the school, and with their help, was doing her best everyday to cope with Annette's death and all the sadness that came along with it in a way that demonstrated her faith in the Lord. She prayed constantly and became more involved with the young women at her school and in the church. And at home, she remained as kind and loving to Edward as she had been before the accident. Unbeknownst to her, that was eating him alive.

And even though Leisa also stumbled at first, unlike Edward, she chose not to turn to another man to meet her needs. Instead, she found a suitable support system in the grief counselors and her students. She constantly prayed for her husband and their marriage, and received encouragement from her visits with the counselors and satisfaction in her work with Purity with Purpose. She became determined to honor the memory of her daughter in every way she could, and to be a walking example of what wholly leaning on the Lord in times of trouble really meant. The sadness of not having Annette around was still very present, but she could also feel that the grace of the Lord was abounding even more in her life. She believed God's Word and trusted that this trial was working to make her a stronger woman in Christ, and that her marriage would be restored to its former glory.

During one of her first few visits with the counselors, the subject of Pall came up. She mentioned how kind he had been to her and how she appreciated having someone show her some attention. As soon as she had mentioned his name, all three of the counselors stiffened up. They asked her a few questions about him, and wanted to know what he had been doing and saying since they met.

"Well, I don't know. He's just really sweet. He always has something funny to say. And he is very free with his compliments. I just think he is a nice guy." Leisa tried to explain.

Ananda looked her in the eyes. "Leisa, please listen to me right now. You have to be very careful in this particular season of your life. Your defenses are weak, and crafty things that you would normally see from a mile away have the ability to sneak up on you and overtake you before you realize it."

Leisa looked questioningly back at her. "What do you mean?"

"Why don't you to tell us what you think. Deep down in your heart of hearts, what do you hear? And when you are around him, what kinds of thoughts run through your mind?" Audrey asked.

"Well, I usually think about how my husband used to say kind things and act like that toward me. I think that it's nice having a handsome man pay me some attention. I just wish Edward were more like Pall." As soon as the words left her mouth, Leisa was shaken by the realization and fully understood what Ananda had just said. This charming man was leading her down a path that she didn't need to go. She looked up at the other three women.

"Do you see what we mean?" Gisella asked gently. "An attack has been launched to cause you to fall. We all know that you would never have any intention of being unfaithful to your husband. But the situation with Annette has altered your frame of mind temporarily. Right now, you are more susceptible to enticement than you would be at any other time. And the enemy is subtle. He knows what will work against you and what won't. He knows your weak spots and he aims straight for them. Wouldn't it be just like him to shoot his arrows right at the target of your heart by sending someone your way to give you all of the things that your husband is withholding right now?"

"Oh, my gosh! You all are so right! I didn't even think about it that way. Look at what has been going on with me! I have been so overwhelmed with emotions in the midst of all that has been going on, that I have allowed Satan to work in my life. And I didn't even put up a fight."

Leisa was shocked at herself for missing the red flags that were all over the situation with Pall. No one could deny that she was suffering at home because of Edward's lack of interest in her, nor could they blame her because she enjoyed the attention Pall showed her when they were together. But when the counselors put Pall and her actions under the microscope to show what the motives of the relationship truly were, and she realized how she was developing feelings in her heart that were in opposition to the will of God, she was horrified. She talked a bit longer with the counselors and asked them to stand in prayer with her to be more discerning, even in her time of sorrow, and to be strong in the face of temptation in connection with Pall. From that day on, she was cordial when she was forced to be in his presence, but she made a conscious effort not to be around him any more than was absolutely necessary.

But Pall was not easily swayed. He wouldn't take no for an answer, and often changed tactics to try to persuade Leisa to give him a chance. He still pursued her, and tried on more than one occasion to get her to come out with him after work, but each time she politely declined, telling him that she was happily married and had no interest in him outside of a professional relationship. He went from kind co-worker to romantic Casanova to jilted lover and finally to downright nasty. He started out as a sweet gentleman caller, but after Leisa rejected him a few times, he began acting as though he was too heartbroken to function.

One particular day, Pall invited her out to dinner that evening. He said that he could not stop thinking about her and that she was really the only reason he enjoyed coming to work everyday. He looked her deep in her eyes and told her that he didn't think he could remain the school's advisor if he had to see her beautiful face everyday but couldn't be with her. For a split second, Leisa was tempted to say yes, just to keep him from being so pitiful. She hated the idea of hurting this young man's feelings, but then the counselors words echoed in her heart, and she quickly shut him down. She told him she was flattered by his invitation, but saving her marriage was the more important concern. He seemed genuinely surprised when his sad sack performance still did not get her to come out with him. Then he began being ugly to her and tried to guilt her into changing her mind. He threw in hateful comments about how he saw now that she was a tease and could understand why her husband would not want to spend time with her. He accused her of leading him on, then of trying to act 'holier than thou,' when he responded to her advances. He told her that she was nothing more than a trampy, miserable, and desperate housewife who'd managed to get out of the kitchen for a while, and that he never wanted her anyway. He told her that he felt sorry for her, and was only trying to make her feel better about the mess that she was. Leisa was shocked by his words, and the things he said really hurt her feelings, but they also reinforced what the counselors had said about not getting involved in wrong relationships. She could only imagine how things would be had she actually gotten physically involved with this obviously unstable man. She was grateful for the sound advice of the counselors and often told them so during her sessions.

On another day, Mya came to talk to her after school. Leisa could see that she was really having a hard time with some things, so they decided to go see the counselors together. It was a little while before a cheerleading practice, and the four new cheerleaders were in the gym waiting for practice time when Leisa and Mya passed by. They asked if they could go along, and Mya and Leisa happily agreed. So, all six of them went to see the counselors that afternoon. Once they got into the office, introductions were made all around and Mya began sharing with the entire group how frightened she was getting about Raegan. Everyone listened with their undivided attention. When she finished sharing her concerns with them, Charlotte looked her square in the eyes and told her, "Don't be afraid, Mya. Fear is the enemy of faith. You must stand in the gap for Raegan and keep her lifted up. If something is going on with her, you need to pray that the Lord would open the door for you to help her or, if you can't, that He would send someone else who can. But the main thing for you to do is pray."

Ananda, Gisella, and Audrey smiled at Charlotte. Ananda replied, "We couldn't have said it better ourselves, and we are supposed to be the professionals here!" She turned to Mya, and looked deep into her eyes as well. "Charlotte is right. All you can do for now is to pray. And we would like to join with you." She reached over and took Mya's hand. All the other women in the room joined hands as well and formed a circle. Mya began to pray for Raegan and the other women lifted up their voices in agreement. A surge of energy rolled through the room and swept over the women as they prayed. Mya felt the sweet presence of the Lord settle on them. She had never experienced anything like that before and was suddenly too overcome to speak. Tears began rolling down her cheeks as she just relaxed into the holy atmosphere that had gathered around them. After a few minutes, she finished praying for her old friend and then thanked God for the new friends that surrounded her at that moment. She asked Him for His hand of protection to cover each of them individually, and to preserve their budding relationship as a group. She concluded the prayer and looked around at each of the women.

"Wow," she said. "This is my first time in a counseling session, but I can tell you it won't be my last!" All of the ladies laughed and nodded. Then they all stood up, and hugs were exchanged all around. Everyone promised to keep the others lifted up in daily prayer. Leisa asked the counselors if it would be alright if she stayed for a while longer to talk to them after Mya and the other girls left for practice. The counsels said they were delighted to have Leisa and that she was welcome to stay as long as she wanted, so she spent the rest of that afternoon sharing, talking, crying, laughing and bonding with her new friends.

Ty lay on the couch, looking around the tiny little house he shared with his grandmother. After a few moments, he settled back and closed his eyes, letting his mind wander and picturing what his life and future might look like if he were someone else. *Someone like DT Hudson, the richest man in town*, he thought. He wondered what it must feel like to have all the money he needed and then so much more. He began to imagine what a life without limits would be like, being able to do whatever he wanted to do whenever he wanted to do it. His mind naturally drifted to his artwork, and he thought about how great it would be to go full-time into the art world. The one thing in his life that he could say he was truly passionate about was art. In fact, in his mind, his artwork was the only thing that he owned and that made him stand out from everyone else. He felt virtually invisible otherwise. He felt that, without his art, he was just traveling aimlessly through life, without making any real impact on anyone. But when he did his art, he knew that he was creating things that no one else could create. He liked the fact that his artwork was inimitable because it came from his mind and no one else in the world had the exact same mind as him. He felt truly valuable and needed when he pursued his art. There wasn't much else in life that compared to the pleasure he gleaned from being what his grandmother called an "artistic visionary". That made picturing his future simple. All he wanted to do was be an artist, using an innovative eye for color, and the resourcefulness he learned from other parts of his life, to bring beauty to others.

But the truth was, deep down, all he believed he *could* do was stay around Faries, get a minimum wage job and spend his time tagging trains and old buildings. He didn't come from the right family or background to really make anything of himself. At least, he didn't believe he did. His grandmother was always saying otherwise. She was constantly telling him that he was *already* someone great—someone important. She told him how the Lord showed her that the world was waiting on him, and that he had something to offer that couldn't be given by anyone except him. She said that he was going to reach people all over the world with his testimony. He loved his grandmother and was so grateful that she had taken him in and loved him. But he just couldn't believe it. What testimony did he have? And how could it help him surpass his current direction in life? Of course, he had his own dreams of grandeur, but he wasn't holding his breath that those dreams would come true. He didn't want to disappoint his grandmother, but what did she expect? They didn't have the money to send him to some fancy college, and without an education, he couldn't get the kind of job that he would need to make more money. All he had was his art. And no one else really even knew he was into art. He couldn't see any way to get ahead. And even if he could find something else to occupy his time, it would only be temporary. He could only stay focused on things that weren't art related for a short period before he lost interest. Nothing else held his mind and his attention the way that painting, and sculpting and spray paint tagging did. Nothing, that is, except Raegan Nottaway.

Right in the middle of his art dream, Raegan's face flashed before his mind's eye. Suddenly, it was as if she was standing right in front of him, trying to let him know, with those beautiful gray eyes, that she wanted to be included in his daydreams. In his vision, she just smiled at him, and the entire room around him seemed to brighten. She was absolutely gorgeous in his opinion, but his attraction to her wasn't purely physical. He was intrigued by her. One of the main things he admired about her was that, although she was stunning, she didn't seem to know it. Or if she did know, she didn't show it. She wasn't one of those girls who flaunted herself to be noticed by others. In fact, Raegan was the exact opposite. She seemed to shy away from attention from people who complimented her beauty. She was very guarded and didn't seem to have many close friends besides Mya Lafleur. To Ty, that made getting close to her seem like breaking into Buckingham Palace—close to impossible. But still, he had this inexplicable urge to get inside her head and find out what she was all about.

He found himself looking for her everywhere he went. It wasn't a conscious thing. He would just be looking around when he would go places, and when he thought about what exactly he was hoping to find, it was always her face that he would see in his thoughts. He hoped he would run into her when he walked down the halls at school, or when he was out and about around town. He was just always hoping to catch a glimpse of her. It was probably really self-serving to even think, and he was kind of surprised to feel this way anyway, but he was really starting to miss the Sunday dinners at the Carson's house. For one thing, his grandmother and Mrs. Carson were two of the world's best cooks and he loved getting to stuff his face every time he ate one of their meals. But, deep down, the true reason he wanted to get back to the old routine was that he was hoping Raegan would show up again, and he would have a chance to talk to her a little more. It seemed like whenever he saw her at school, she was lost in a daydream or talking to Mya or something. He could never seem to get the chance to talk to her by herself—not that he really thought he'd have the guts to approach her even if the opportunity did present itself.

The thing was, being 'cool' in those sorts of situations wasn't Ty's strong suit. He didn't know how to be smooth and talk to girls and get their interest. He was just the street kid who loved art. He didn't feel like he had a whole lot more than that to offer. He was kind of a loner, and kept to himself for the most part. At least he and Raegan had that in common. But the jury was still out on whether that was a good thing or not.

~

Edward was on a slippery slope to nowhere fast, and he knew it. But he wasn't ready to stop himself. His wife was driving him crazy with her sweet spirit and forgiving heart, and being at home, surrounded by her peace, was like shining a giant floodlight onto his own inner turmoil. So, instead of facing his demons, he ran the other direction and threw himself into his work. In the days following the wreck, he had set up several appointments to interview prospective employees from the list DT had given him, but every one of those fell through for one reason or another. By the time he actually had an interview time work out, he was down to only three applicants who were still interested in the vacant slots. Since that was the number of people he was supposed to be hiring, the three prospects were, at least for the time being, guaranteed the jobs, and all he could do was hope that they would work out and perform well in their new positions. But just as a formality, he still went ahead with the interviews.

The three men he interviewed, Malcolm, Wade, and Martin, were polite and kind gentlemen with impressive credentials. Their professional backgrounds made them natural picks for the positions being filled, and Edward was actually very happy with the way things had turned out. Their demeanors also told him right away that they would easily fit in with the culture of the company. In every other case, Edward tried as the interviewer to try to make the person he was interviewing feel at ease during the process, but with these three men, it was the other way around. As soon as he met them, they were the ones who made him feel relaxed. And on a more personal level, he saw them as the kind of men he would want to have as friends, had they met in another season of his life and if he was in a better state of being, when he was serving the Lord with gladness and his little girl was still alive. But in his current state of brokenness, they only acted as amplifiers for the guilt that screamed bloody murder in his heart and ears at his every waking moment.

Still, Edward was drawn to them like a hummingbird to the sweet nectar of a beautiful flower. He desperately wanted to flit, lightening fast, as far away from them as he could and get back to his secrets and Lead Astray, but he just couldn't resist an opportunity to be near these men. Once they were hired, he took it upon himself to personally show them around the office building and talk to them about what they could expect in the future with the company. Being around them made Edward feel more like his old self than he had felt in quite some time. With them, he found himself laughing more and thinking and talking about God as his Father in a way he hadn't since before Annette died. Something in his spirit seemed to awaken when they came around, and he thoroughly enjoyed their company, despite the guilt that gnawed at the back of his mind. It was the most peculiar thing to him, because he felt conviction with them, but never condemnation. Around them, he wanted to do right and stop leading this double life, but he didn't feel pressure. He admittedly wanted more for himself and for his life than what had been going on the last few weeks, and he was slowly starting to see that maybe spending time with these men could be the jumpstart he needed to do something about it. But there was still a fierce tug of war playing out in his spirit, with one side enjoying the clandestine pleasures of his relationship with Lead Astray, and the other side connecting to his new friends at work and begging to reconnect with the rightful people in his life, like his beautiful wife. Some days, the good side won, and he would eat lunch with them and spend his break times sitting and talking to them. Sometimes, Marcus would join in the conversations. Edward really liked Marcus, and he seemed to add a totally new dimension to the dynamic of the group. Other times, the bad side triumphed and kept him in his office all day, making secret phone calls and hiding his face from the truth.

When Edward was around his new friends, he talked easily and often about Leisa and their life and how wonderful things were with Annette before the accident. Their interest in him and his family forced him to remember some good memories that he had tucked away and covered in his mourning. He shared stories with them and enjoyed some deep, genuine, heartfelt laughs. The amazing thing was, when he talked about his wife and his daughter to Martin, or Wade or Malcolm, he felt no sadness. From the time he met Lead

Astray in the diner that afternoon to now, anytime he was with her, he had done all he could not to bring up any memories, good or bad. She convinced him that looking back on the past with his wife and daughter would only bring pain, and that he needed to stay as far away from the memories as he could. But with Martin, Malcolm and Wade, he was beginning to see that Lead Astray had told him wrong. He didn't feel pain when he shared with them about his past with his daughter. He only experienced joy and love. He looked back on the past with fondness, rather than dreading the future without his daughter, or looking at his present with bitterness or shame.

Jason whistled nervously as he walked up the driveway toward the house he had just driven up to. He felt uneasy about being there, but at the same time, there was a spark of excitement as he anticipated what he would find when he went inside. He had been pretty down since his breakup with Mya, so he was excited to get out and meet some new people. Maybe someone there could help him take his mind off how bad everything had been going lately.

He checked the slip of paper he had in his jacket pocket. Even though there were cars parked in the driveway and lining the street in front of the house, he wanted to make sure he had the right address before he rang the doorbell. He did. Earlier that week, he had gotten an email from the webmaster of the site Will had told him about, which he now frequented pretty regularly. Will's nephew ran the site and had sent him an invitation to come to a party at his house and meet some of his football teammates and some of the girls from the site. They all attended the college there in town, and Will's nephew thought it would be a good chance for Jason to make some new friends in the college world.

When he got to the door, he saw that it was already ajar, so he pushed it open and walked inside. People were milling all around, talking and laughing loudly, and no one really seemed to notice him. He timidly walked inside and shut the door behind him. He took off his jacket and threw it onto the couch that sat in the living room, right inside the entry hallway. He didn't recognize anyone, and nervously wandered into the room that seemed to be the main party area. All of the furniture had been pushed to the perimeter of the room along the walls, and there were people dancing and laughing in a group in the middle of the floor. Suddenly, a burly young man broke through the crowd with a grin on his face. He walked up to Jason and began speaking as though the two were old friends.

"What's up, dude? You must be Jason!" he bellowed. "I'm guessing so because I know everybody else here, and I was hoping you would show up!" He thrust out his hand and took Jason's. He shook it vigorously. He then wrapped his arm around Jason's shoulders and gestured toward the people at the party. "Welcome to paradise, bro! We've been waiting for you!" He laughed ebulliently and handed Jason a cup. He hardly gave Jason a moment to think before he continued on.

"Hey, man, I'm glad you got my invite. Just call me Heinous. That's what my teammates call me, because I'm *wicked* out there on the field! Right, boys?" Heinous turned his attention to a group of rowdy guys walking past them. They all turned to him and growled and hissed and barked in response. They high fived and jostled each other and kept moving, heading toward a table that held a pair of beer kegs.

Jason smirked, and looked around at the rest of the partygoers. Out of the corner of his eye, something caught his attention and made him feel a little nervous. Across the room, he noticed two young men, both with their eyes locked squarely on him. They seemed vaguely familiar, but Jason could not place them. They were not participating in the party, but just stood there, watching him closely. Heinous' voice in his ear jarred him back to the moment.

"Drink up, man! There's plenty of liquor, ladies, and fun to go around! So, just forget about all your problems and your worries." He held up his own cup toward Jason, as if making a toast. "Cheers, man! I demand that you live it up tonight!" Heinous pushed the cup Jason held up to his mouth. Jason tilted his head back and took a long gulp of the strong liquid. When he swallowed, his face turned bright red, his eyes watered and he choked and sputtered and coughed, which made Heinous laugh.

He good-naturedly slapped Jason on the back. "Looks like I got a lot of work to do with you, dude! Just stick with me though. You'll be a pro in no time!" Just then, a group of chattering girls walked by. Heinous winked at Jason, and motioned that they should follow them. Jason chuckled and shook his head. Heinous shrugged and turned and went after them. Jason, who was not an experienced drinker and was already buzzed after that one swig, felt his head start to swim. Not wanting to get sick all over himself from drinking too much on an empty stomach, and find himself labeled as an inexperienced high school chump, he figured he'd better quickly find where the food was. He stumbled over to the food table when he spotted it across the room. He grabbed a paper plate and loaded it up with snacks. He shoved a few pretzels into his mouth and grabbed his cup so he could go find a place to sit. He was startled and nearly dropped his plate when he turned around and came face to face with the two guys who had been watching him earlier.

The taller of the two spoke first, as he reached out to steady Jason and catch his plate. "Hey, what's up, man? Sorry about that.

We didn't mean to frighten you. We just wanted to talk to you. I'm Creede, and this is Bryce. You're Jason, right?"

Jason was initially a little freaked out, but as soon as Creede greeted him, he seemed to instinctively know that he had no reason to be afraid of them. The feeling of peace he felt standing next to them was in stark contrast to the jitters and sense of nervousness that he felt when he first arrived and had Heinous by his side. "Yeah, I'm Jason." He glanced around, really getting curious as to how so many people at this party knew who he was when he didn't know a single soul there. More importantly, he wanted to know why they cared. As he looked around, everything in the room became hazy before his eyes. It was as if, all of a sudden, time had halted to a crawling pace and everything in the party seemed to be moving in slow motion. He shook his head, blinking several times, hoping that he was just suffering from the effects of having had a little too much to drink, and turned his attention back to Creede and Bryce. They had not moved, nor taken their eyes off him, and they stood out, in brilliant distinction when compared to everything else, which, seeing past the two of them, still looked fuzzy to Jason and seemed to move sluggishly around the three of them.

A strong, yet kind, intensity emanated from Bryce and Creede as they stood in front of him, their eyes fixed on his. They wore the same football jackets as many of the other guys around the party, but something about these two young men was radically different from Heinous, the jovial host that had introduced himself moments ago, and his teammates. They didn't seem uncomfortable being in the midst of the chaotic frenzy of loud music and carousing, but they certainly weren't joining in with the rest of the reveling partygoers.

"So, Jason, are you having fun?" Bryce asked, looking expectantly at him. His question didn't really seem like a question at all. It sounded as if he already knew that Jason was feeling completely out of his element, and he was really only asking so that Jason would have to admit it. Bryce raised his eyebrows as he waited for Jason to respond.

Trying to maintain his composure, Jason replied coolly, "Uh, sure, I guess. Are you? I mean, you guys don't seem like a place like this would be your scene." He was not sure where this conversation with these two strange men was headed, but, even though he was no longer troubled by them, he was fairly certain he did not want to go there with them. Even so, his feet remained planted where they were and he waited for one of them to speak again.

"You're right. It's not. We hate being in places like this." Creede looked around sadly, and then returned his gaze to Jason.

"Then I don't get it. What are you two doing here?" He didn't know why he asked that question, because he knew it was just going to lead him further into the discussion he was already starting to regret getting engaged in, and he really just wanted to eat his food, have some more to drink, get a little wild and forget about all the mess that was going on in his life. And somehow, he knew that by talking to these two, he wouldn't be able to do that. He started to feel flustered that he couldn't seem to make his body do what he wanted it to. He just wanted to turn and walk away from them and get back to the party, but something in his heart prevented him from moving. *Who* are *these guys*, he thought to himself.

Creede turned serious and his voice dropped to a deep rumble that resonated in Jason's heart. "What are *you* doing here, Jason?"

"I'm having a good time! Isn't that what you do at a party?" Unable to make his break, Jason decided to try to play it cool again. He hoped that maybe the two of them would decide that they didn't want to talk to him and leave him alone.

"You're not really having a good time, are you?" Bryce spoke up. He looked around the room, and then back at Jason. "You don't belong with these people," he said matter of factly.

Jason balked at the audacity of this guy. He struggled to stay calm, because he knew deep down inside that they were right, but rebellion swelled up from his belly, and he was really aggravated to get called out like that. "Um, excuse me, but who are you to say that?" His tone grew sarcastic. "I mean, thanks for your concern, but how would you know where I belong? You don't know anything about me!" He was bothered by how rude he was acting toward these seemingly nice guys, but couldn't seem to help it. He really didn't appreciate how they spoke to him like they knew him, making judgment calls on the way he needed to behave. But something in their eyes kept him from just walking away from them.

Bryce continued on, undeterred by Jason's sharp tongue. "We know more than you think we do, Jason."

"Oh, yeah?" he snapped. "Then you ought to know that this is exactly where I want to be! This is how I always pictured college life! Parties, girls, everything! This is it for me!"

"No, Jason! You've got it all wrong! Look around. Look at where you are. *Really* look at all these people, doing things they wouldn't do if they were in their right mind. They are all acting like cowards, blindly following one another just so they can feel like they fit in somewhere, covering the truth in booze and immorality. They are all searching for one thing." Creede stopped talking for a moment, and Jason turned away from the two young men and looked around again at the people at the party.

It was as if scales began falling off his eyes, and he was able to see clearly. He didn't just see the people. It was as if he had spiritual x-ray vision—he could see their emotions as well. He saw young women, barely dressed, throwing themselves at drunken guys who clumsily groped and fondled them without any real regard for who they were. The girls were smiling and flaunting their bodies, but Jason could see the pain and worthlessness that they felt inside but desperately tried to hide. He saw the young men, drinking and laughing heartily on the outside, but he could also see the insecurity and fear that they were trying to drown out with the alcohol and loud music.

He shook his head again, trying to make his eyes focus and get those images out of his mind. He didn't like what he was seeing. He looked down at the cup in his hand, wondering what had been slipped into it, and hoping that he was just experiencing an alcohol-induced hallucination. Just then, Heinous walked into his line of vision. What Jason saw sobered him up quickly and frightened him to his core. Heinous looked back at him with bloodshot eyes and a hollow soul.

"Jason! Why don't you stop chatting with the loser brothers and come have some fun! I don't even know why these guys showed up. I know I said the whole team was invited tonight, but they are definitely not part of *my* team!" He looked darkly at Creede and Bryce. Jason felt a surge of pressure rush past him, and he could hardly stand up. Heinous returned his gaze to Jason and held him in an intense stare. "Come on, Jason. The fun is on this side. My uncle Will told me what an awesome guy you are. If you get in tight with us now, college life will be a breeze for you. But hanging out with these two is guaranteed social suicide. They have nothing to offer you. All the good stuff is right over here."

Jason had begun sweating, as a wave of nausea swept over him, but he couldn't release himself from Heinous' gaze. His mind raced and fear began creeping up his spine. The hairs on the back of his neck stood on end. He did want to fit in and have a good college life with friends and all. But there was nothing good about this guy standing in front of him. He knew that his intentions were not right. But Heinous seemed to hold the key to the future Jason longed for.

From behind him, Jason heard a strong, clear voice. "He has a choice, Heinous. You have to let him choose." Bryce then spoke to Jason. "Jason, turn around. Look at me." Heinous finally averted his eyes and Jason was able to break free from his stare. He turned to look at Bryce. "Don't be afraid. You have a choice right now. You can stay here with these people. But we are asking you to come with us. This is not the place for you, and these are not your friends." Bryce spoke sternly, but there was kindness and light in his eyes. Creede nodded. The pressure and panic Jason felt a moment ago began to subside. He straightened up and wiped his forehead.

"We are going to a coffee shop a little ways from here to meet up with a couple more of our teammates. You are more than welcome to join us. We only came here to find you and we hope you will come with us." Bryce was now speaking in a still, quiet voice, directly to Jason's spirit. He felt a wave of calm flow over him as he listened.

"Jason, I'm warning you. These boys are gonna try to 'holy' you up and nobody likes a goody-goody. Girls want a bad boy. Look around you. This is what you are looking for. Do you really want to go back to be with a girl who won't show you how she feels about you, or stay here with one of these beautiful babes who don't know the meaning of the word *no*?" Now at Jason's back, Heinous spewed iniquitous words and depraved thoughts like projectile vomit toward him. He looked hatefully at Creede and Bryce. "What's the matter, boys? Are you afraid that I am going to show him too good a time and that he won't want what you are offering? You scared that I'm gonna steal him away?" Heinous began mocking the two young men standing before Jason. Neither moved nor broke their gaze from Jason's eyes. Jason didn't move either, but his mouth went dry and his heart had begun beating wildly in his chest when Heinous started speaking again. He wasn't sure he had the strength to do what he knew he should.

Heinous quickly changed tactics and aimed his poisonous barbs directly at Jason again, growing more agitated and desperate to shake him and shatter the serenity that was gathering him in. "Oh, so you're not going to turn around now? You think you want to be one of those holy rollers, huh? Who do you think you are? You wouldn't even be here if you hadn't been on my site. You're becoming one of my best customers. All your hits will keep my site in business. You think you will fit in with these guys and their super spiritual friends? I don't think they would approve of what you've been looking at. Have you told them about that? Huh? Have you? How about you share with them what you do late at night at your house when you're all alone—which is all the time, now that your parents are dead, right?! How about you tell them about the sites you click on and the things you think about? The stuff you imagine yourself doing? I don't think these boys would be so interested in you if they knew what kind of guy you really are! Your hot little Bible-thumpin' girlfriend surely wouldn't want you back if she knew what you've become! You're one of us now, and you belong here!"

Jason felt sick to his stomach. He felt his face burning pink in embarrassment, and his forehead was moist again with perspiration. He knew that the things Heinous said were true, and he felt such shame standing before these two men. He didn't want them to know what he had been doing. It was a secret thing that no one was supposed to find out about. And now it was all out in the open. His eyes stung with the salt of his tears as Heinous' words about his dead parents pierced, like sharpened darts, deep within his heart. They wouldn't have been pleased with what he had been doing either, and he was still coming to grips with the fact that they really were gone and he was all alone. Mya's beautiful smiling face flashed before his mind's eye too, hitting him like a fist to his gut. It was as if Heinous knew everything Jason was struggling with and was using it against him.

"That's enough!" Creede turned and spoke sharply to Heinous. He looked back to Jason and spoke calmly, unaffected by Heinous' taunts. "Jason, it's completely up to you what you do right now. You can stay here with them or you can come with us. But we are leaving." When he finished speaking, he and Bryce stepped around Jason, brushed past Heinous, moving swiftly through the crowd, and walked out the front door of the house. The moment they were gone and the door closed behind them, the pressure Jason felt from before returned and grew stronger. The room seemed to dim before his eyes. It was as if all good and light left with the two young men. Jason's head began swimming again, and he felt as though he was going to pass out. He turned back toward Heinous and the rest of the people who remained at the party. Heinous looked at him with contempt and anger.

"So, what's it gonna be, kid? You one of us, or are you one of them?" Heinous looked toward the door with flashing eyes, filled with disgust. His physical appearance had changed dramatically behind Jason's back as the confrontation escalated, and his voice was now raspy with scorn. He looked less like a person and more like a rabid beast, ready to pounce on his victim.

Without responding, Jason began walking forward. His legs felt like lead weights as he staggered toward the place where he'd left his jacket. He felt as if he had no control over his own body. He wanted desperately to get out of the house, but felt like he was running through jelly. He trudged past Heinous, who reached out and grabbed his arm. He cried out in pain, and dropped the cup and plate he had been clutching, as searing heat shot upward to his shoulder from the place where Heinous' hand gripped him. He looked over at Heinous, whose red eyes seemed to be aflame now.

"If you leave now, you're gonna wish you were never born, kid. This thing is not over. I'm not going to forget it. I know who you are. I know where you are, and I will stay after you. You belong with us, and I will make sure that's where you end up." Jason tried to get out of Heinous' clutch, but it was iron clad. He whimpered in pain, feeling as though his entire arm was on fire. He tried to speak, but couldn't get any words out. Just as the room began to spin and go dark, and Jason thought for sure he was going to lose consciousness from the pain, Heinous let go. Jason nearly fell to the floor. He was so frightened now, he could hardly breathe. He wasn't sure what he was talking about, but he knew Heinous was no longer just talking about the party. This was much deeper.

He struggled to regain his balance, and stumbled to the place his jacket lay strewn across the tattered couch. He grabbed it and bolted out the door as quickly as he could. He looked around to see if Bryce and Creede were still around but they were nowhere to be seen. He walked over to his truck and leaned against it, trying to catch his breath and stop his heart from pounding. He shook his head, trying to clear his mind, with no success. His thoughts were like a jigsaw puzzle, with a million pieces scattered all over the place. He strained to put them back together.

Mya had enjoyed writing ever since she was in elementary school. Words were like toys to her; things to be manipulated and played with, and strung together to form chains of all manner of expressions, ideas, and thoughts. English and literature classes always tended to be her favorite classes in school, and she loved to read. She liked writing poetry and submitted her work to different competitions periodically throughout the school years.

Writing was her way to escape the cares of the world. When things got chaotic in the real world, Mya would retreat into her bedroom or somewhere quiet and pull out a pen and paper and let her thoughts roam free and her fingers fly. She also loved music, and so when a moment so lent itself and she felt inspired, she would pull out one of her trademark neon colored notebooks, and jot down lyrics to a new song. So far, none of these lyrics had ever made it off the pages of her notebook, but she kept them all handy, just in case an opportunity presented itself for her to share one of her original compositions with some hard-pressed Christian musician who had gotten hit with a severe case of writer's block.

As of late, Mya found herself journaling significantly more often than she had been at any other point in her life. Since the train wreck, everything in her life and the lives of so many she loved had gotten extremely complicated, and she struggled to sort them out. On the

244

pages of her journal that was meant for her eyes only, she could be completely honest about her feelings, and didn't have to worry to worry about the repercussions of anyone seeing something and misconstruing her intentions. She could say whatever she felt at that moment without concern about how she would be perceived. And she loved looking back over old entries and seeing how her thoughts or opinions of things changed over time as she grew up and gained more experiences and knowledge.

Since finding out about Raegan and her molestation, Mya had really been trying to focus on getting her moving back in the right direction. She was most concerned about being a good friend and a light to her whenever she was needed. It seemed like their friendship was recovering very well, and they were on their way to the rock solid bond they used to share with one another. She was trying to spend as much time with Raegan as possible, and rebuild some of the places that had gotten damaged and cracked in their relationship. She was really enjoying herself.

But then, the situation with Jason had thrown a wrench into things. Now instead of being able to focus on everyone else's problems, Mya was having to face some of her own. She was totally blindsided when she and Jason broke up, and was totally unprepared to face time away from him. Now that they were not together anymore, she realized how much she had come to depend on him in her daily life. It was the reminders of the little things that they used to do together, like him bringing her a bag of York peppermint patties every Monday morning before school because he knew they were her favorite candies, that would set her over the edge some days. So like she always did when things got tough, she turned to her journal and poured her heart out onto the pages. On one day that she was especially missing Jason, but determined to hold to her convictions, she wrote:

If I were to live by this world's standards, a kiss should solve all my problems right now. As absurd as that sounds, that's the message that's consistently being sent. I mean, we even teach that to our kids. Think about it. What do we say to little kids when they get an injury? "Did you hurt yourself? Let me kiss it and make it better." And watching movies these days just perpetuates the madness. I can't lie—I'm a hopeless romantic. And I love sappy, girly movies. But they all make that same point. And it's all a lie! With the way they show things, a kiss is all it takes to turn everything around. Have a fight with the one you love? Kiss. It will all go away. No discussion or solutions offered. Just kiss and it all works out. Run out of things to talk about? Kiss each other. It's just as good as verbal communication. Screw everything up in your life and relationship? Just run up to the other person and kiss them. It will all be over when your lips part. But it just doesn't work that way. And it makes me crazy, because right now, kissing is the last thing Chaz and I need to be doing, but we still have to somehow find out a way to fix this! I've been terribly unhappy without him, but unless something changes, being with him is out of the question. But the thought of him being with someone else because I won't be with him has just been consuming my thoughts lately. Ugh! I really hate feeling like this! I just want things to go back to how they used to be!

And why does everyone seem to think that life is so easy for me? Life isn't a bed of roses for me any more than for anyone else, and contrary to popular belief, I'm not always doing great. I mean, things aren't always so easy for a Christian girl. This Chaz thing BITES! Being a woman of God does not take away any of the reality of the fallen world she lives in. In fact, it seems to put a big red bulls-eye on her back and makes her a moving target for accusation. So it goes...

She felt a little better after having put her thoughts in writing, but she knew that she couldn't stay focused on how sad she was about the whole situation. And anyway, there were other much more pressing issues at hand. She rolled over and picked up her cell phone. She dialed Raegan's number and made sure that she was still planning to come to the Purity meeting with her. With the help of Leisa, they were able to convince Raegan to come to the meeting. But Mya knew that Raegan was not thrilled about going, so she was staying on her to make sure she came through on her promise. She told her that she would pick her up the following afternoon and they would ride together to Leisa's house, where the meeting would be held.

When she got off the phone, she turned her attention back to her journal and spent the next few hours writing about how she felt about everything that was going on and what she hoped would come from Raegan's attendance at the meeting. When she had thoroughly exhausted her fingers and her pen, she put her journal away and turned off the overhead light in her room. She climbed into her bed and said a quick prayer asking that Raegan would indeed come to the meeting, and that the Lord would use that time to begin the healing process and get her back from the clutches of the enemy. A short time later, she was asleep and snoring lightly.

~

Mya was so happy to have Raegan sitting in the passenger seat beside her as she drove to the Purity with Purpose meeting that next evening. She felt like her number one prayer had been answered— Raegan was actually on her way to the meeting. That was just the first step of what Mya knew was going to be an intense, yet completely worthwhile process of restoration and renewal in Raegan's life. She smiled as she looked over at her. "Don't be nervous, Raeyo. It's going to be awesome! I promise. You won't regret that you decided to come."

"God, I hope you're right. Because I am already rethinking this whole thing," Raegan replied.

"Ok, I am going to use some of the tricks I learned from the grief counselors at school. Tell me, what you are most concerned about? What's your biggest fear about tonight? What would be the worst case scenario in your opinion?"

"Um, how about that everyone there finds out about what's happened to me and they, like, stone me or something because I'm not a virgin?"

Mya struggled to keep a straight face. "Stone you, Raeyo? Really? Who *stones* people anymore? We read the Bible, not re-enact it. We don't stone people for stuff. And anyway, if the girls did find out what happened to you, why would they stone *you*? It's that pervert, Mr. Grimly, who they'd be after. Being abused is not your fault."

"'Being abused.'" Raegan repeated. "Ugh! I just hate the way that sounds. To me, it sounds so tainted and unhygienic, like I'm some old used rag and you need to handle me with a mask and rubber gloves so you don't get contaminated with anything I may have. But those words still don't come even close to how crappy I feel about myself. And I know you keep saying that the situation is not my fault, but I still feel like it is. I mean, I really haven't done anything to stop it. I just kind of let it happen. I let him do all those disgusting things to me without saying a word."

"Raeyo! That is not true. What were you supposed to do? You were a child when all this started, and an adult tricked you into believing that you were bad and that you couldn't tell anyone about it. That's not just something you can just turn off in your mind just because you get older. That is a seed that was planted and had years to get rooted in your spirit. It's like he brainwashed you to believe that you had no control over the situation, and all you could do was let him do whatever he wanted to do to you. You believed that he was going to do your family physical harm if you tried to stop what was happening, and after awhile, that just got programmed into your way of thinking. That's something that will have to be de-programmed and replaced with the truth."

Raegan laughed ruefully. "I guess, Dr. Freud. You really *have* been spending a lot of time with those grief counselors, haven't you? You're starting to sound like some psychiatrist or something. 'De-program' me? It sounds like I'm going to have to have a lobotomy or something. It's all so scientific."

"No, it's not. It's *spiritual*."

Raegan had turned sideways in her seat to look at Mya as they talked, but when Mya made the last statement, Raegan sat back as if she was truly considering her words. "Maybe you're right," she said quietly, closing her eyes. "So what do you prescribe, doc?" She opened just her left eye to look over at Mya.

Mya smiled and put on her best frantic emergency room doctor voice. "We need a two-hour Purity with Purpose meeting, filled with lots of love and hugs and prayer, STAT!"

Right about that time, they pulled into Leisa Carson's driveway. Mya turned off the car, and looked over at Raegan. "Well, are you ready?"

Raegan sighed and said, "As ready as I'm going to be. Let's do it."

The two girls climbed out of the car, and Mya went around to the passenger side to meet Raegan. They walked arm in arm to the front door and rang the bell. Leisa came to the door and welcomed them inside. She hugged each girl, and then led them into the living room. There were snacks and drinks on the coffee table and several other girls that Mya recognized from the church were already sitting around talking. When Raegan and Mya came into the room, they all jumped up and greeted and hugged them both. Even though Raegan didn't know most of the girls there, they all welcomed her with open arms. She immediately began to relax, and decided to just let her guard down that night and enjoy herself. Just a few moments after Mya and Raegan arrived, the doorbell rang again. After a few more moments, a tangible atmospheric shift occurred.

Raegan looked around and in the doorway to the living room hall stood eight of the most remarkable young women she had ever seen. It wasn't anything physical that she could put her finger on that intrigued her about any of them in particular, and each girl looked completely different from the others, but something about the group of them took her breath away momentarily. Mya turned too, and when she saw them, she jumped up and ran over and hugged four of them. She then brought the whole group of them to join the rest of the girls in the room. She seemed so happy to have them there. She looked over to Raegan and said, "These are the new cheerleaders I was telling you I wanted you to meet. This is Nadia, Charlotte, Carina, and Bryn." She then turned and looked back to them, asking, "And are these friends of yours?"

The girl she introduced as Carina spoke up. "Yup! These are some of our friends from our old school. This is," she pointed to each girl as she called their names, "Shelby, Malia, Shanna, and Emma. When they heard that we were having this meeting tonight, there was no talking them out of joining us!"

"Well, we are glad to have you!" said Mya.

"We are so excited to be here and meet everyone!" Malia spoke for the group of new girls. As she spoke, she looked straight at Raegan. Interestingly enough, rather than feel self-conscious for having this girl staring so intently at her, Raegan felt, instead, reassured.

Mya looked around the room at everyone seated with her. She had a big grin on her face. "Well, I am so glad that all of you showed up to this meeting of Purity with Purpose. Since we are still adding girls every time we gather, let's go around the room and introduce ourselves. We already know these eight, so, how about we start with Raegan and then the rest of you can tell your name and age and what grade you're in. And then we will get going with the rest of the evening!" She looked over at Raegan and nodded.

"Well, as Mya mentioned, my name is Raegan Nottaway. I'm almost seventeen years old, and I am a senior. Mya invited me a couple of times, and so I finally decided that tonight would be the night. I'm a little nervous though."

All the other girls piped up and promised her that she would have a great time and there was no reason to be nervous. One by one, the other girls went around the room and introduced themselves as well. Just as the last girl told who she was, Leisa, carrying another platter of snacks from the kitchen, came into the room and sat down with the girls. Once all of the introductions were complete, she smiled and said, "And I am Leisa Carson, and I am so very excited to have you all here tonight!"

Mya turned to her, "Well, Mrs. Leisa, we are all just glad that you have let us come and take over your house for a little while!" She then turned and looked back at the rest of the girls surrounding her. She began sharing what the intent was for that night's meeting, and how she hoped that everyone would join in the conversation. She reiterated that there were to be no judgments made for the things that people shared, and that nothing that anyone said was to leave that group. Everyone agreed and she led them in a short prayer. After that, she offered to start the discussion. "As most of you know, I recently broke up with my boyfriend of 3 years. That in itself has been hard enough, but what I am really struggling with is something that my cheerleading sponsor has said a few times. She has made repeated comments about doing what it takes to keep a man, and that if I see something I want, then God put it in front of me and that it's cruel for Him to show me something good that He won't let me have. And I know that is complete garbage, but she has also made some statements that really have gotten me to thinking. Actually, it's more like it's been consuming my every waking moment. I just keep thinking about how much I love him, and believe that we are supposed to be together, and to consider that he may find some other girl who is willing to do the things I am not just makes me sick to my stomach. I don't want to lose him over this whole chastity-abstinence-virginity thing. I mean, I believe that we are supposed to get married and that he will have the right to my body. But thoughts of sharing myself with him just to keep him around have been really heavy on my mind lately too. And even though I know that is not the way the Lord would have me do things, sometimes it just seems like the easiest route."

As Mya spoke and listened to the other girls as they validated her feelings and shared some of their own, Leisa watched her closely. She reminded her so much of Annette when she was in high school. Annie used to say some of the same things Mya had said, and faced some of the same struggles. She had been raised in church, and had always been a good kid, but sometimes the pressures of the world and her friends got to be too much. And like Mya, she had made the choice to serve the Lord for herself in her late-teenage years, but that didn't mean that things were smooth sailing after that. Things were sometimes shaky, but when it came down to it, she chose to do the right things. Annette and Mya both shared a love for their families and their faith that usually kept them in line, but the enemy seemed to have chosen the same area to strike them in—their thought life concerning dating. Leisa smiled sadly as she pictured the joy Annette would have radiated with, had she been there that day, having all of those young women in her home, honestly sharing their battles and the temptations they faced in their attempts to walk uprightly. She would have been so proud and eager to offer wisdom that she had gathered over the years. Because, just like Mya and her friends, gathered together that evening in front of Leisa, Annette was the epitome of God's beauty, and it flowed from the depths of her soul. But at times, her pain ran equally as deep. Even so, in the midst of it all, she had developed an understanding of what other women like her faced, and she got such pleasure out of helping her sisters in Christ overcome these issues, and Leisa knew right then that she had done the right thing by championing Purity with Purpose in her daughter's honor.

Suddenly, she felt the unction to share something specific with the girls. She waited until they finished the conversation they were engaged in and then cleared her throat. When she did, everyone turned and looked her way. "I want to tell you guys something that I think is really important for you to all realize. We haven't really discussed this point yet, but I really feel like the Holy Spirit is leading me to say this. I want to explain something about purity. I don't want you girls to be confused about what it means to be pure. Purity and virginity are not the same thing. You can be a virgin and not be pure, and on the flip side, you can not be a virgin and still be pure. Purity is a process. You are born a virgin, but you are not born pure. Purity is an ongoing lifestyle that you can begin at any point in your life, no matter what has happened in your past." As Leisa spoke, she looked around at each girl's face. When she got to Raegan, she saw that she was crying silently. The more Leisa said, the more the tears fell from her eyes. Leisa wondered if she had said something that offended her, so when she finished, she asked Raegan to come over to where she was. She asked her why was she crying.

Raegan said quietly, "That was for me. I didn't know that. I thought I had to be a virgin to be pure. And I am not a virgin." She dropped her head when she made the admission that she had already had sex.

It was like a light bulb came on in Leisa's brain. She had been talking to Mya for a little while about a 'friend' of hers who was in some trouble, but when Mya said that she didn't want to reveal who this person was, Leisa hadn't pushed. They talked about some things that had happened in this friend's life and how it had affected her. Leisa just assumed it was someone that Mya knew at school. For some reason, it had never occurred to her that it could be Raegan that they were talking about. But now she realized that it was Raegan that Mya was talking about the whole time. So much of what Mya had shared with her came together and made perfect sense now. Raegan was the friend that Mya didn't know how to help.

Not wanting to embarrass her, Leisa dropped her voice to a whisper. "Do you want to talk about it? We are all your friends here and will not condemn you for anything you share with us. We just want to be here to help hold you up if you want us to."

Raegan nodded bravely. "Yes, ma'am. I want to share it with you all." She turned and faced the group. She took a deep breath, got everyone's attention and started talking. She shared how the words Leisa had just spoken really hit home for her, because she was under the impression that if she wasn't a virgin, then being pure was no longer an option. She had just taken on the mindset that she was of no use to anyone anymore because she was not the clean, spotless, little Christian girl. The four new girls that Mya's cheerleading friends had brought were sitting nearest to Raegan and Leisa. When Raegan started to speak, all four of them moved in closer, and put theirs arms around her, or placed their hands on her in a show of support. She went on to share how she had been molested since she was eleven years old, and how the man had started raping her. She told them how she had not told anyone about what was going on for nearly six years, until she finally shared it with Mya the other day and was now sharing it with them. With each word she spoke, she got a little bolder, and felt lighter, as if a five ton block was slowly being lifted off her head. Her tears still flowed, and as she shared her story, others of the girls began crying too. By the time she finished telling them what she had been through, they had all gathered closer to her and reached out to show their love and concern for her.

Mya looked around the room at all the girls and said, "Let's pray for Raegan right now. The Bible says that whatever we touch and agree on together will be done for us by the Lord. So let's all lay hands on her and pray that the Lord would show her how to get out of this situation, and that the enemy would have no more place in her life." With that, they all started standing up and helping each other to their feet. Someone grabbed Raegan's hand and pulled her into the center of the room and the other girls formed a tight circle around her, and all placed their hands on her. They all began lifting up their voices to the Lord, and with every prayer, Raegan seemed to release the pain and bitterness and anger that she had held onto so tightly for so long. She cried and cried, and called out to the Lord to please help her. The girls around her began repeating over and over, "Thank you, Lord. Thank you." His presence in the room that night was undeniable.

Standing there, watching such profound healing pour out from Heaven itself, Leisa was awestruck at the way the Lord had turned the tragedy of Annie's death into a dazzling beacon, guiding other young women, just like Annette, straight into His everlasting love.

DT could not wrap his natural mind around what had just happened. As he sat in his office, holding the phone, he was completely dumbfounded. After his conversation with Raegan a moment ago, he knew for sure that there was something the matter with her, even though she denied it and would not open up to him, and he was becoming fairly certain that she was the person Marcus was referring to in their earlier conversation. Something terrible was happening to her that he was supposed to do something about. That much he knew was true. What he didn't understand was how Marcus knew what he knew—how he *always* knew what he knew. How were the two of them in the same places at the same times, yet he never saw what Marcus saw? It just didn't make sense to him.

He hung up the receiver and pressed the intercom button. When his secretary answered, he told her to send Marcus back into his office as soon as possible. DT was ready to talk. He didn't know exactly what was going to happen when he came face to face with Marcus, but he knew that it was time to come clean to him and let him in on the struggles he had been facing for the last few years. He was starting to realize for certain that if anyone could help him, it would be Marcus. He was almost positive that Marcus, with his accurate and insightful nature, knew what was going on, and even some of the sordid details, but DT knew in his heart that it was time to *tell* Marcus what was going on and get some real help. He was ready to change his course. He had spent enough time heading in the wrong direction and knew that it was only a matter of time before his bad decisions caught up to him and really began to take their toll. And he would rather things not get to that place if he could help it.

A knock at the office door interrupted his thoughts. "Door's open. Come on in.,: he called out. When Marcus walked in, DT again offered him the chair across the desk. Marcus nodded and sat down with an expectant, but kind expression on his face.

"Yes, sir?"

"Um, thanks for coming in, Marcus. I know you are probably busy keeping my finances all straight, but I'd like to talk to you about some things if that is alright. It could take a little while, but I would really like to share some things – some, um, personal things – with you, and ask for your help in some areas. Would that be ok with you?" DT was back to that "little kid confessing fault to his parent" mode.

Marcus sat forward and made direct eye contact with DT. He answered sincerely, "I'm never too busy to stop and talk to you, Mr. Hudson. Anything I can help with is what I am here for. It would be my pleasure to talk to you about anything you want. And if you don't mind, I would like to ask you some things as well. May I?" When DT nodded, Marcus continued, "Did you have a productive conversation with Miss Nottaway a moment ago?"

Had that same question come from anyone else, DT would have felt that they were overstepping their bounds and getting into his business by asking. But from Marcus, it was perfectly appropriate. After all, that conversation was the trigger for the meeting they were engaged in right then. "Well, it's hard to say. I talked to her and asked her some things, but she was very reluctant to say that anything was wrong. Is she the person you were talking about who needed my help?" DT asked the question, but knew in his heart that she was.

Marcus nodded. "Yes, sir. I can not give you all the details, as it is up to you to find out more. But yes, she is the one."

DT was again perplexed. How could Marcus have known that something was going on? And how did he seem to have orchestrated their meeting earlier so perfectly? DT had every intention to wait a whole day longer before he spoke to Marcus. So how did Marcus fix it so that he would talk to DT in time to tell him about Raegan before she called? There was no way that he knew *when* she would call, if he knew that she was going to call at all. So how had all this come together so intricately?

"The '*how*'s are not important, Mr. Hudson. It's what you do with what you now know that matters." Marcus still sat with his eyes fixed on DT. He answered like he knew exactly what DT had been thinking. Without blinking, he continued, "Now then, what is it that you would like to talk to me about?"

DT's mind was reeling. He had so many questions but didn't know where to start. He understood what Marcus had just said about not asking how, but that still didn't curb his curiosity. And now, with him answering questions that DT hadn't even voiced aloud, he was really intrigued. But he pushed all of that aside and cleared his throat. It was time to get all of his mess out on the table. He didn't want to just dump all of his personal garbage onto Marcus, but something in his eyes let DT know that he could handle whatever he said. So, DT took a deep breath and began, "Well, I know you know that my out of town business trips aren't always so productive. I'm really glad that I have you around to keep an eye on things when I get a little," he stopped, searching for the words to describe his behavior when he went on his trips. Suddenly, his phone rang. He looked at it, and saw that it was Edward Carson. He looked up apologetically at Marcus. "Marcus, I'm really sorry, but this is Ed Carson. I haven't talked to him since the accident, and I don't want to just leave him hanging. Do you mind if I take this call, and we pick this up in a little while?"

Marcus was already standing up. "No, sir, I don't mind at all. In fact, I hope that maybe the things you were about to share with me, you will be able to share with him. He is one of your close friends, and he may be able to help you. That's not to say that I don't want to help if I can. But perhaps he can give you some insight that I can not. Whenever you get the time, I will be happy to come back and talk with you though. Go ahead and get that, so you don't miss his call." With that, Marcus disappeared out the door once again.

DT would have felt guilty for calling Marcus into the office and then blowing him off to talk to someone else, but he was so sincere about not minding that DT felt better. And his suggestion of talking to Edward about his problems was a really good idea, even though DT couldn't imagine how anyone could have more insight than Marcus did after all the events of that day alone. He answered the phone and greeted Edward. He asked Edward to come into the office so that they could sit and talk a while, and Edward agreed. DT hung up the phone and moved back over onto the couch to wait for Edward to come in.

About ten minutes later, a knock came at the door. Edward pushed it open and stuck his head in. DT motioned for him to enter the room. He did, and went and stood beside the sofa. DT stood up and the two men embraced quickly. Then both sat down on the couch. DT looked over at Edward and said, "I'm really glad you called. I tried to call you while I was gone, but never got to you." He paused a moment, looking away briefly, before turning back to Edward and saying quietly, "I'm so sorry about Annette. I had no idea."

Edward swallowed hard and nodded his head, but DT could see in his face that he didn't really want to talk about it. He wanted to kick himself for even bringing it up, but he didn't know what would be proper etiquette in a situation like that. So, to avoid any further pain or embarrassment, he changed the subject and asked Edward did he mind talking to him about some personal issues he was facing. Edward, seeming grateful to have something else to think about, nodded his head and told DT to speak freely.

"Well, I just want to warn you. I'm not the good family man like you, Ed. I've messed up. I've done some things that I wish I could bleach my own mind clean of. What I want to talk about isn't pretty. I'm not proud of everything in my life and some of the things I've done. I'm not like you."

"Well, DT, the truth is, lately, I haven't been the man you may think I am." Edward looked at him sadly.

"What do you mean?" DT was surprised to hear Edward say something like that, and was even more stunned to see tears brimming in his eyes. His news would have to wait, as he could see that Edward may need to talk to him more than the other way around.

"Well, without Annette, I have just really lost myself. After the accident, I didn't think I would live through the pain I was feeling. I mean, it was becoming physical pain that I couldn't ignore. And you know Leisa. She is just the strongest woman on the planet and she was just shouldering the sadness and moving on. And the truth is, I was angry at her for that. I was angry because I felt like such a weak-ling for coming so undone when my wife was holding it together. The night we found out about Annie, I flipped out and stormed out of the house. Can you believe that? I left my wife alone because I was freaking out. I mean, I didn't know what to do, and my mind was just spinning, you know? Everything felt like it got knocked off kilter that day. Nothing made sense, and really, nothing mattered. Leisa and Teenie were at the house, but I just couldn't stay there with them. I was beside myself with every emotion you can imagine. There was rage, and fear, and sadness, and hurt. Everything. So, I just got in my car and drove. I didn't even know where I was going or why. It's all really a blur. But then, somehow, I end up at the diner where I used to work. I went inside to try to clear my head or something. And I am just sitting there, in me and Leisa's booth in the back, pretending to be ok, when really my chest feels like my heart has shattered into a million little pieces. And then I looked up, and there was the most incredible looking woman I have ever seen sitting across the room. I mean, she was breath-taking. And she was looking at me." Edward stopped talking then, and dropped his head. DT saw tears drip into his lap. He reached his hand out and touched Edward's back.

"What is it, Ed? You know you can tell me anything. It's alright. Just tell me."

Edward kept his head down, but continued speaking, "Well, as I was sitting there, torn up and messed up in the head, she came over to my table. She started talking to me, and it's like I lost what little control of myself I had left. She would look me in the eyes and I found myself telling her everything. I didn't plan to or even want to, but when I was around her, I couldn't stop myself. Then she asked me if I wanted to go for a walk. And for some idiotic reason, I said yes. So we left the diner. After that she was all over me and being just blatantly flirtatious and," Edward stopped again. He put his hands up to his face and shook his head.

DT tried to encourage him to go on. "Listen, Ed, whatever happened, it's going to be alright. But I think the only way for you to get through this is to let it out. Isn't that what you are always telling me? To 'confess my faults' so that I can be forgiven and move on? That's what's got to happen right now. I'm not going to think any less of you for whatever it is, and you aren't going to feel any better by keeping it all bottled up inside. So just say it and get it over with."

Edward let out a sob. He shook his head again, but then put his hands down. He kept his head down, but took a few deep breaths and then said, "We spent the night together."

DT tried not to let his face, voice or body language register the shock he felt at Edward's admission. He steadied his voice, asking, "You slept with this woman?"

Edward's head jerked up with a look of horror in his eyes. "NO!" he roared. "I did not sleep with her!"

"Well, then why all the tears, man? I thought you did something you were feeling guilty about. I mean, you said you spent the night with her. If you didn't sleep with her, then why are you feeling so bad?" DT did his best to lighten the mood.

Edward still looked incredulously at DT. "Don't you understand, DT? I stayed out with some random woman, away from my wife, on the night our only child died! It doesn't matter if we slept together or not. I was still so wrong! I was not there when my wife needed me the most. I was with some woman who stroked my ego and made me feel macho, instead of actually *being* macho and grieving with my wife. And it's been eating me alive." His tears overflowed onto his cheeks once more. "But you know what the worst part is? I didn't stop there. I have been sneaking around to talk to this ridiculous woman every day since that night. I have opened myself to her and closed myself off to my own wife. What kind of man does that make me, DT? A 'good family man'? No! I hardly even have a family anymore! And what I do have left I don't deserve. I don't deserve Leisa. Look at what I've done."

DT tried to reassure Edward that things weren't as bad as he thought. He began sharing with him about all the awful things he participated in when he went out of town. He told him about the women he got involved with and the drugs and alcohol and gambling. He thought hard, trying to remember some of the things Edward used to tell him when he was struggling. All of a sudden, in the midst of speaking, DT felt a nudge in his heart that he had never felt before. He knew right then that they needed to pray. He stood up and walked over to the desk and pressed the intercom button once more. He told Cheryl to call Marcus to his office again. Within a few moments, Marcus was there. But he didn't come alone. The three new hires came with him. When DT opened the door, a rush like a mighty wind swept past him as he looked at the four men standing before him.

"Mr. Hudson, don't be alarmed. I hope you don't mind, but I brought some friends of mine. We are all here to help in any way we can."

"Of course! Thanks for coming in so quickly. I don't really know what to do or say right now, but I knew that we needed someone to come and pray with us." He motioned behind him to Edward, who still sat on the couch in the corner. Edward looked up and acknowl-edged them with a nod. "You all know Edward Carson, right?"

One of the men who was with Marcus spoke up. "Yes, sir. I am Wade. And this is Martin, and that's Malcolm. Mr. Carson hired us two weeks ago, and we have all become fast friends. When Marcus told us that some things were going on, we wanted to be a part and serve however we could. We hope you don't mind the intrusion." He looked around DT and spoke to Edward. "You either, Mr. Carson. If it's alright with the both of you, we would like to stand in agreement with you for whatever you may need."

"Absolutely. Please, come on in. Sit wherever you'd like. Just make yourselves comfortable. I haven't had the pleasure of meeting you all officially, as I was out of town when Ed hired you, but I trust him and I trust Marcus, so if you are any friends of theirs, you are friends of mine. Thank you for coming with Marcus." He shook the hands of each of the men as they came into the office.

They went and sat around Edward. Wade spoke in low tones to him, and Edward seemed to perk up a little. He nodded often and even smiled a few times. After a few moments, both men looked up at the rest of the group. Edward spoke first. "I'd really like to thank all of you guys for coming to my rescue this afternoon. For the three that I have just recently met, I want you to know what a blessing you have been to me the last few weeks, just by being around, and spending time with me. I have come back to some semblance of my walk with Christ and have realized how awful I have been since my daughter passed away. I was just sharing some of that with DT, and I can feel the Lord working on my heart right now. Being in your pres-ences is just like wading into a refreshing pool. I feel like a different man when I am near you all. So, for that, I want to thank you. And to you, Marcus, thank you for standing in the gap for DT while I was flailing around out there. I can see a change in him already. And I know that you have had a major role in that. And DT, please forgive me for setting such a poor example to you after all these years of ministering to you. I hope that my selfishness and stupidity have not destroyed my witness completely."

DT jumped in. "Absolutely not! In fact, just being here right now with all of you has solidified the decision I've been wrestling with for some time now. In watching you, Ed, and you, Marcus, and the way that you both have lived your lives in front of me and served God with such joy, I have longed to share in that with you. But I have had these influences in my life that have acted as roadblocks to me. I have these people that seem to show up at the most inopportune times and I just fall into these horrible habits and traps each time I am with them. But then, when I am around you, including this very moment with Martin, Malcolm and Wade too, I have such a strong desire to live better and to do well in the eyes of God. It's just been such a struggle."

Marcus turned to DT and met his eyes. "Mr. Hudson, the choice is yours to make."

Edward felt the Lord urging him to step in. "Marcus is right, DT. I know that I have not been talking to you as much about the Lord as I used to, and after what I've told you this afternoon, I haven't shown you much by way of example either. But the truth is the same, no matter what we choose to do with it. And that truth is, we can not make it in this life without Jesus Christ. That is a lesson we can take from what I have put myself through lately. The reason I have gone so far out of my mind is because I closed my heart to Him. So maybe I *have* set the example. I've shown you what *not* to do. But the question is, what will you do? Will you join all of us and pray right now to invite Jesus into your life as Lord and Savior? He's the only way you will be able to overcome all of the problems and addictions you are facing in this life. Otherwise, you will keep going the same way you have been going. And trust me, there is absolutely no comparison between a life with Christ and anything this world can offer you. It's just taken me some time, some experiences and all of your help to remind me of that. But I am ready to give my heart back to its rightful Owner. And I'm asking you to pray with me, so that together the two of us can dedicate our lives to the Lord. Will you do it?"

DT looked around the room at all the loving eyes that were fixed on him. He had never felt so safe or so loved as he did in that exact moment. Tears filled his eyes and he nodded his head. The group erupted into joyful noise. All of the men jumped up from where they were and gathered around him. They laid their hands on him, and Edward lifted his voice to the heavens. They prayed for a long time, with DT repeating the sinner's prayer after Edward, and Edward asking for forgiveness for his wrongs and rededicating his life to Christ. When they were finished, all of them hugged each other and welcomed DT into the family of God. He felt like a new man. As they all prepared to leave, Marcus looked over at DT. He caught his eye and said, "Mr. Hudson, I am so proud of your decision today. But you have to understand that the battle is not over. It is just beginning. Be cautious of the people and influences from your past that will come in full force to try to pull you away from the choice you just made and back into your old lifestyle. You will have to choose this walk every day. It does not end with this prayer you prayed today. Guard your heart. Sever the ties that you have been entangled in that have led you astray. Stand strong. I'm here for you for whatever you may need."

Wade turned to Edward and met his gaze. "Mr. Carson, that goes for you too. Sever the ungodly ties. Give no place to the enemy and run from even the appearance of evil. We are all here for you, and will be standing behind you. Whatever you need, you can count on us." He looked around the room at the other men that stood with him. "All of us."

Marcus shared one final thought with DT before the four men walked out the door. "Mr. Hudson, you have been blessed to be a blessing. Instead of wasting your money on sinful activities and such, perhaps you can use it more productively. You have not been given all that you have to hoard for yourself. Think of all the people in your life who you could help and then let the Lord lead you to do your part. Have a wonderful afternoon." And with that, they were gone.

Ty was really starting to feel hopeless about his future. Here it was, the middle of his senior year, and he had no idea what he was going to do after he walked across the stage and accepted his diploma in the spring. And being so young didn't make matters any better. Most people, besides his grandmother and teachers, didn't even know that he was actually only going to be seventeen on his next birthday. They just assumed that he would be eighteen since he was a senior that year. But the truth was, he had skipped a grade in elementary school, so he was a year ahead for his true age group.

While Ty didn't care to spread this bit of information around to his peers for fear of being labeled a nerd or a geek, his grandmother constantly used it in her arguments in favor of him going to college. She took any opportunity she could to remind him that she "didn't raise no fool" and that he was too smart to just throw his life away by not having plans in place for after high school. She tried to get him to see that if he was smart enough to have skipped a grade back then, then he was smart enough now to consistently make good grades and get a scholarship to college. But Ty didn't see that working out. True enough, he didn't find school work difficult, or even have to exert much effort to pass his classes with decent grades, but that didn't mean that he wanted to take on more school once he graduated. If it wasn't about art, he wasn't really into it. That was the reason why he was doing so poorly in his classes lately. He was bored. None of the subjects that his teachers and other adults were so adamant about him excelling in were the classes where he got to stretch his creative muscles. He was tired of just reading books and writing papers and crunching numbers. He wanted to color and paint and sculpt and draw and cut and paste.

And although he didn't *hate* school, sitting through mind-numbing classes was becoming more and more agonizing. Such was the case as he sat in his science class one particular morning, listening to his teacher drone on about molecular devices. Just when he thought he couldn't take another second before he purposely blew up one of the Bunsen burners, there was a knock at the door of the classroom. All of the students sighed with relief. They were all happy to have any respite from the boredom of biology. Their teacher stopped speaking and walked over to the door. As soon as he opened it, a rush of cool, sweet air swept past Ty. He looked up quickly to see who was there. He saw two men that he didn't recognize walk through the door, followed by Leisa Carson. She scanned the room and then smiled when she saw him. She tapped one of the men in front of her and pointed in Ty's direction. The man looked where she pointed and caught Ty's eye. Ty felt heat run down his spine at that exact moment. He had never seen this man before, but he felt as if he already knew him after just one glance. The man averted his eyes, and he, along with the other man and Mrs. Carson, walked over to Ty's science teacher.

After speaking briefly, they all turned and looked at Ty.

"Tyler, will you please gather your belongings and go with these gentleman and Mrs. Carson? They have some things they need to discuss with you." Ty's teacher gave him the instructions, then turned to the rest of the class and resumed his lecture. Several students around him watched as he gathered his books and stood up. He wondered what these men wanted with him. He was nervous and figured he was about to get into some kind of trouble. He took some comfort in the fact that Mrs. Carson was with them, and she seemed happy. He didn't think she would be excited if he were getting in trouble. He tried to calm himself down and look nonchalant as he walked to the front of the classroom. He could feel all the eyes of his classmates following his every step.

When he got up to the front of the room, the two gentleman turned ahead of him and moved toward the door. Mrs. Carson reached out and squeezed his arm, then went after the two men. Ty followed her. When all four of them were out of the class, and the door closed behind them, the two men turned around. They both broke into wide smiles. The one who had locked eyes with Ty in the classroom stuck out his hand. "We hope we didn't frighten you in there, Tyler. There's nothing to worry about. We've only got good news to give you. I'm Devon, and this is Grayson."

Grayson stepped forward and also shook Ty's hand. Through his peripheral vision, Ty could see that the man had something in his other hand. When he stepped back from greeting Ty, Grayson held up what he had. Ty was shocked to see that it was one of his drawings. But it wasn't just any drawing. It was a drawing he had crumbled up and thrown away weeks ago.

He remembered that day so vividly. He had been sitting out in the courtyard of the school during his lunch period. He usually brought a bag lunch that his grandmother packed, but he had walked out of the house that morning and left it on the counter, so, instead of eating, he pulled out his notepad and a pencil and began sketching. He was just finishing a picture when someone came up behind him.

"Huh," grunted the person. "What's that supposed to be?" He reached over Ty's shoulder and snatched the picture. He looked at it and chuckled, then tossed it back onto the table in front of Ty. "You call that art? I wouldn't quit my day job if I were you. No one is going to want that junk. Good thing you're smart, brainiac, because there's no way your so-called art is gonna get you anywhere in this world. Better do like your mama did and start selling drugs. That's the only way you're gonna get paid!" This kid, known as Warp, had been harassing Ty for as long as he could remember. It didn't matter what Ty did, Warp was always there to try to humiliate him and try to make him feel stupid about it. Through the years, Ty tried to follow his grandmother and teachers' advice and ignore Warp's taunts, but that day, when he mentioned Ty's mother, Ty had had enough He stood up and got in Warp's face, with every intention to hurt him as much as was humanly possible. But before he could do anything, Mrs. Carson had walked up and pulled him aside. They talked for a few moments, and she tried to calm him down. She tried to reassure him of his natural talent and abilities, and he pretended to hear her and be alright. But as soon as she had walked away, he took his picture and balled it up. He stood for a few moments, seething and vowing retaliation in his heart against Warp for touching the two things in his life that meant the most, his mother and his art. When the bell finally rang, signaling the end of lunch, he'd tossed the picture into the trash, along with his classmates' half eaten sandwiches and stale chips. And he hadn't thought anymore about it until today.

"Ty? Will you follow us please?" Devon spoke kindly, breaking into Ty's thoughts. He nodded and began walking down the hall after Mrs. Carson, Devon and Grayson. He wondered where they were taking him, and was surprised when they stopped in front of the office where the grief counselors had been meeting. He had passed by this door many times since the counselors came to the school, but he never thought he needed to go in to see them. No one else knew that he had witnessed the accident firsthand, and he didn't see any reason to tell anyone now. He was more focused on trying to put together all of what was happening. He just couldn't figure out who these two strange men were, how and why they had his picture, and why they were leading him to see the grief counselors.

When they reached the office, Devon opened the door. When Ty walked inside, he felt like he had stepped into a courtroom. On the one side were three women who he assumed were the counselors, and on the other side was Pall D'molish, the new school advisor. They sat in a face-off position, and neither side really seemed happy to see the other. But when Ty, Mrs. Carson and the two men walked in, the three women's countenances softened immediately. They stood up and greeted Mrs. Carson with a hug and the two men with handshakes and nods. When they saw Ty, their faces and eyes seemed to light up, and they quickly introduced themselves and he shook each of their hands. Mrs. Carson, Grayson and Devon joined them and sat down, and Devon looked up at him. "You may sit here on this side with us, or you are free to sit over there with Pall. The choice is yours."

Ty looked over at Pall. His demeanor seemed to have soured even more when Devon, Grayson and Mrs. Carson walked in. There was a empty chair near him, as well as an empty chair near the group that had formed across the room. For a moment, Ty felt sorry for Pall sitting alone, and was tempted to go sit in the chair beside him, but then Pall looked up and caught Ty's eye, and Ty felt his chest tighten, like all the air in his lungs was being squeezed out by some giant invisible hand. A sickening feeling crept up the back of his neck and he decided to sit with Mrs. Carson and the others. When he sat down, he looked questioningly at Mrs. Carson, waiting for her to give him some signal that everything was ok.

But she wasn't the first to speak. The woman who introduced herself as Ananda was. Ty was instantly drawn to her because she reminded him of his mother and his grandmother when she was younger. The woman had a twinkle in her eye and laughter in her voice. When she spoke, Ty felt safe. "Tyler, we brought you here today to find out more about your plans for college and to talk to you about your artwork."

Grayson held up the picture. "We found this in the trashcan. It's yours, right?"

Ty nodded, still shocked that a total stranger had his drawing.

Devon spoke up. "Let us start from the beginning. Grayson and I are art buyers for a local businessman. His name is David, but most people know him as DT. Anyway, he is looking to open his own art gallery here in Faries, and he wanted to find local young artists to showcase. So, Grayson and I have been on the hunt for some new talent. Some friends of ours work for David, and told us of his sponsorship of school events and things. Naturally, we thought that one of the schools in town would be a great place to start. We were just beginning our search when we came across this beautiful picture in the garbage. We were puzzled as to why it would be in the trash, but determined to find the artist. Shortly thereafter, we ran into Mrs.

Carson, who recognized your work and pointed us in the right direction. And now, here we are."

Ty was dumbfounded. These guys were art buyers for DT Hudson III? And they were looking for talent to show in a new art gallery? Were they trying to say what he thought they were trying to say? They couldn't possibly want him—could they? He wanted to pinch himself to make sure he wasn't daydreaming again about what it must be to have DT's life. But he knew this was no dream. He didn't think he could speak without squeaking like a mouse, so he just nodded his head, hoping they would continue.

Mrs. Carson interjected excitedly. "When they asked me did I know who drew the picture, I recognized it from that day with you nearly had that fight. I didn't think you would mind if I told them who you were and encouraged them to find you. This sounds like a wonderful opportunity for you, Ty!" She grinned at him, and looked as though she were going to burst with happiness.

Ty was still at a loss as to what exactly they were trying to tell him. "So what are you all saying? What exactly do you want from me?" He just couldn't believe that they were telling him that he was going to be an artist with work in a gallery. Surely he was misunderstanding what was going on. He looked around, waiting for someone to clear things up for him.

"Here is the deal in a nutshell, Tyler. We were sent here to make you an offer. Mr. Hudson would like to commission you to do a three piece painting, based on this picture, to be shown at his gallery opening. After that, he would like to send you on a trip to Italy with another student, Raegan Nottaway, for a study abroad art program. He would then like to offer you the chance to work your way through the university of your choice, through an internship at his company."

Ty felt like he was going to pass out. He was having a hard time wrapping his mind around what he had just been told. But before he could respond, Pall spoke from the other side of the room. "Well, isn't this just precious? Giving the little street kid the chance of a lifetime? As the advisor, it's up to me to advise him on what's what. And yes, all of this sounds wonderful, but let's be realistic, people. Unlike Mrs. Carson, I like to be honest with people and give them my real view of their chances of success. She has given her blessing to this plan, but who is she to tell this young man if he is ready to take on such a big responsibility? This is not just some high school art project homework assignment. This is the real world. And I hate to rain on the parade here, but do we honestly think Tyler is good enough to impress anyone outside of his community?" A dark smirk flashed across Pall's face as he threw word daggers at both Leisa and Ty. He was subtle, but still intended to inflict real pain.

Ty suddenly felt uneasy. It seemed as though Pall was putting a voice to the concerns that were already starting to build up in his mind. He didn't think he was good enough to make it big outside of Faries, and it seemed like the only reason he was being given this chance was because DT Hudson felt the need to help some poor, needy kid. The excitement he had just been feeling was quickly shifting to aggravation and disappointment. He didn't want to be anyone's charity case, and he didn't want to get his hopes up about his art or about Raegan, just to see them dashed to the ground when reality set in. He was just about to tell the others so when Grayson spoke up.

"That's quite enough, Pall. Ty, don't listen to that." He turned to Mrs. Carson and addressed her as well. "You either, Leisa." He turned back to Ty. "This guy is supposed to be an advisor, a helper and colleague, but he is advising you to pass up your dream and a chance to fulfill your destiny, instead of accepting and walking into a brand new future. I hope that you see that he is just trying to keep you back from God's best, and that his heart is not for you. This is just a job for him, and he doesn't really care one way or the other how you turn out. But still, all we can do is present the option. It's up to you to make the decision. None of us can make it for you. But we will be behind you the entire way. Don't let fear and doubt set in and stop you from pursuing the vision that God has set in your heart. You are one of a kind, and this is no accident. Those dreams you've had in your spirit were put there by the God of creation before you were even born. So don't listen to anyone or anything that would try to steer you away from that."

"Oh, so now God is behind all this? I thought David Hudson was. Make up your mind, *Grayson*, was it? I'm just trying to keep the kid's head out of the clouds. This is the real world, and without the right background, money and connections, he won't last a second." Pall sneered at Grayson. He looked over at Ty. "Listen, kid. I'm not telling you that this isn't a sweet deal. I'm just wondering what is this Hudson guy going to want in return. This seems like an awful lot to offer with no strings attached. What's it going to cost you, because we all know everything costs something."

"That's the beauty of this offer, Ty. It's a free gift to you. Mr. Hudson wants to bless you. All he asks in return is that you develop the artistic talent that he already sees is there. He's willing to pay the price. He doesn't need anything from you. He just wants to get something *to* you. But the decision is yours." Devon's voice was strong and sincere.

All of this was sounding so familiar to Ty. He had heard all of these same words before. But it wasn't about DT Hudson. He was beginning to see a parallel between what was happening here and what his grandmother and Mrs. Leisa were always talking to him about. This sounded a lot like what they said about Jesus and how He just wanted to bless Ty and see him succeed, and all He asked in return was that Ty accept what was already on the inside of him—the knowledge that Jesus is the Christ, and the only begotten Son of God Himself. It wasn't a lot to ask in return for such amazing benefits, and accepting both of these gifts would change his entire life forever.

"We really want this for you, Tyler. Please choose it." Devon spoke again, catching Ty's eye. Somehow Ty knew that he was not just talking about Mr. Hudson's offer. He was talking about the other thoughts Ty held in his heart at that moment.

Suddenly the door swung open, and Teenie's voice filled the room. "Don't you know it's the goodness of God that brings men to repentance, baby?" She stepped into the room and walked over to Ty, who quickly stood up. She took his face in her hands and said, "Leisa called me with the news of what they were going to tell you today. This is exactly what I was telling you about what the Lord has for you. Don't you see it? This is His hand. He will do whatever it takes to get to you. He wants you bad. He has a plan so much bigger than you could possibly know yet, and all you have to do is accept it. This is it! This is your moment, baby! Will you?"

Tears welled up in Ty's eyes when he saw the love reflected in his grandmother's. "Yes, ma'am. Will you pray with me?"

"Sweet Jesus!" she whispered, as she pulled him into a tight embrace. "You know I will." The others in the room, except for Pall, stood up and gathered around them as she and Ty said the sinner's prayer together. When they finished, a cheer rose up from the group to the heavens.

Pall, looking disgusted, stood up and walked to the door. "This is, by *no* means, over," he muttered. He walked out the door and slammed it shut behind him. No one in the room seemed to notice him or care. Teenie and Leisa embraced, both crying tears of joy at Ty's conversion.

"I can die happy, satisfied and fulfilled right now." Teenie quietly said, and Leisa looked over at her, horrified. "But I've got too much to watch my baby do to go anywhere just yet," she reassured her, nudging her playfully and nodding toward Ty.

Then Grayson spoke up. "So, hold on a moment. Does all this mean that you are accepting Mr. Hudson's offer as well?"

Ty turned to look at him with a grin, then looked around at all the eager faces surrounding him, waiting for his answer. "Are you kidding me? There is a whole world out there waiting for me. You better believe I'm accepting! When do I get started?"

Devon walked over and put his arm around Ty's shoulders. "Right now, my friend. Welcome to the beginning of the rest of your life! It's going to be quite a ride!"

Mya put her arm around Raegan's shoulders as the two girls left Leisa Carson's house that evening. "Raeyo, I'm so proud of you! And I am so glad that you chose to come to the meeting, but to share your story with everyone was the bravest thing I've ever witnessed. I know that whole situation was hard for you, but you made it through! I've never experienced anything like what just happened. How do you feel?"

Raegan put her arm around Mya's waist and looked over at her. "I feel like my whole face is swollen and I will never have another tear to cry in my lifetime, but I really feel great! I feel lighter than air right now! I honestly haven't felt this good in *years*. You were so right about me coming to this meeting." She stopped walking and turned to Mya, her eyes glistening with tears again. "I guess I was wrong about the tears," she said, laughing and pointing to her eyes. "But I just have to say 'thank you', Mya. I've never had anyone else in my life besides Ethan to care about me so much. It's been so hard for me since he moved out, and I have just kind of let myself completely shut down. But you kept pushing. Even when I was mean and hateful and told you to mind your own business, you were always there for me, and you never stopped trying. You didn't know what I was going through, but you still cared. And I am so grateful to have you in my life. I love you so much! I don't have the words to tell you just how much you really mean to me. I just feel so blessed to be your friend." She reached her other arm around and hugged Mya tightly.

When Raegan finally released Mya from her grip, Mya stepped back with a tearful smile on her face. "Wow! That's the nicest thing anyone has ever said to me! I'm honored to have you as my friend. I'm not doing anything special. I just want to share the same love that Christ gives me with other people. That's all. And I love you more than you probably even have a clue of. I know the Lord brought us together for a purpose, and I am just having a blast finding out what that purpose is. That's what life is all about—finding God's purpose and then daily pursuing the fulfillment of it." She took a breath and then started with a more serious tone. "And listen, Raegan. Ever since you shared with me what has been going on, something has been really strong in my heart. I don't believe in accidents or coincidences. I believe that everything that happens has a reason and that whatever it is, good or bad, God can take it and use it for His plan. So, even though the first reason this person came into our lives was to bring Jason the horrible news about his parents, I believe that the Lord wants to use our connection with Sgt. Williams to bring a different message—a *good* message. I think we need to give him a call and tell him what has been happening to you. I think he may be the way for you to get all this mess to stop. If you tell him what has been happening to you, then he can do whatever he needs to and have that Grimly perv arrested. It's time for him to pay the price for what he has been doing to you. And Sgt. Williams may be the key! So will you let me call him? Or can we both go talk to him? You know I will be right by your side the whole time." She reached out and took Raegan's hand. "Please, Raeyo. It's time to end this season of your life and start a brand new one. I mean, look at yourself right now. You didn't think you could come to a Purity meeting, or share what has been happening to you with anyone, but you did it today. And look how great that went, and how awesome you feel right now! Don't you want to keep that momentum going and take the next step? Don't you think it's time to put an end to all this once and for all so that you can move on with your life, fresh and clean?"

Raegan took a deep breath and looked into Mya's pleading eyes. Her own welled up with tears again, but this time, there was fierce determination mingled with them. She squeezed Mya's hand. "Do you promise to go through it with me? You're the only one I've got."

"Are you kidding? Did you already forget all your supporters and friends in that room just now? Me, Mrs. Leisa, Bryn, Carina, Charlotte, Nadia? And then the awesome new girls too! Shanna, and Shelby, and Emma, and Malia? They really seemed to like you. And everyone else in there too. We all have your back! We will be there for you the whole time. All of us! You don't have to go through any of this by yourself. You never had to." Mya took a moment to consider if that would be the right time to bring up Raegan's salvation. With the way everything else was working out, and as receptive as Raegan had been to it all, it seemed to be the opportune moment to say something. She waited for a few more seconds to see if she felt peace about it, and when she felt like she did, she took the plunge. "Raeyo, you have never had to deal with anything on your own. I know you feel like your family hasn't been there for you, and other people haven't been there for you, but there is Someone who has always been there. Other people, including me, will let you down. As much as I don't want to, and will try my hardest not to, it's going to happen. For the rest of your life, there will always be someone to hurt you or leave you or disappoint you. But there is Someone who will never leave you nor forsake you, and you can depend completely on Him. I know I have talked to you about this before, but I think you may have a better understanding now after what we just experienced back in the meeting. That was all about Jesus. Can you see that now? He wants to heal you. He wants to totally restore everything that has been lost in your life. He wants to take all the pain in your life and replace it with his love. I have seen that so much recently with all this breakup drama. With all the holes that not being with Jason have left in my heart, Jesus has been constantly showing me that *He* wants to fill them. He doesn't want anything or anyone to take His place in our lives. He doesn't want us to depend on anyone else for our happiness or comfort or strength. He wants to be the center of our lives. He wants us to trust Him with every aspect of our lives. Jesus loves you so much more than even I do. As hard as that is for either of us to fathom, it's true. He knows the deepest, darkest parts of you, and still He loves you and wants to come in and reside in your heart. But he's such a gentleman that He will never force His way in. He wants you to ask Him. He just wants you to invite Him to come in and light up all the dark places in your life. He wants to go through everything you go through in this life. It's not going to be an easy road, but it's one you don't have to travel alone. He wants to be with you. That's what this has always been about. He died for us so that we wouldn't have to be separated from Him anymore, by our sin or by death. He paid the price for our redemption. His salvation is a free gift to us from Him, but we have to receive it. So Raeyo, my question is, will you please accept His gift?" Mya was crying now, begging Raegan to choose eternal life. Every fiber of her being wanted to hear Raegan say yes.

"I just don't know, Mya. I mean, I understand everything that you are saying. And I believe it's true. But this is all so much all at one time. Please don't be upset, but I just don't think I am ready to make that leap yet. Just pray for me. I don't know what's stopping me, but I just don't think I can do it right now. I need some time. Is that alright?" Raegan hated to do this to Mya, but at that moment she just couldn't say yes with conviction. She wanted to accept what Mya was telling her, but she didn't want to do it on an emotional whim. She wanted it to be real. She wanted to mean it from the depths of her soul. "You have to understand. I want to say yes. I want to accept Christ and become a Christian and live a better life. But today, right now, I would just be doing it to make you happy. And I want to make *Him* happy by *meaning* it. I am going to do it. I just need to be in the right frame of mind when I do."

"I understand that. I just don't want you to wait too long. The enemy already has his eye on you, and if your heart is really ready to make this change, you've got to know that he's going to turn up the heat. It's going to feel like it's getting worse before it gets better. But you can't believe his lies. All the hardships and heartache we face in this lifetime are miniscule when compared to the glory that is to come if we are children of God. But salvation is not just about the afterlife. Jesus wants us to have abundant life while we are on the earth as well. But that's only after you accept Him. Until then, you are out from under his promises. And that makes you fair game for Satan. He's going to do anything he can to get you to reject the Word of the Lord and to reject salvation. He's already been doing it, but he is going to unleash even more fury should you decide to get saved. He doesn't want anyone else to come to the knowledge of God's saving grace. And that is what is going to happen when you accept Jesus as your Lord. People are going to see you and hear your testimony and they are going to turn to Christ too. And that makes Satan mad. He's not going to take it lying down. And I'm not trying to scare you into or out of anything. I just want you to understand how important this decision is. It will have lasting ripples in this life and the one to come. So, I will definitely be praying for you, and when you are ready, I will gladly pray with you to accept Christ as your Savior. Nothing in this world would give me more joy!"

"Thank you, Mya. I appreciate that more than you know. And I mean what I said. I am going to do it. Just as soon as I get it together. So, do you think we can call and talk to Sgt. Williams today? I would really like to get that out of the way. That will be one less thing on my mind. I just feel like there is so much that I have to get straightened out."

"Sure, we can call him today. But don't let the enemy use that mindset as a hindrance either. You can't fix yourself. Don't try to wait until you have everything "worked out" before you come to Jesus. That doesn't make any more sense than, when you have a cold, coming to the doctor after it's developed into pneumonia, almost killing you, and then when he asks you why you waited so long to come see him, you say, 'I was sick, so I didn't want you to see me that way.' That's what a doctor is there for, to help you get well when you're ill. You don't make yourself well and then go see the doctor. Jesus is the ultimate Physician, so we should come to Him when we are our sickest and let Him heal us."

Raegan nodded thoughtfully. "Yeah, that makes sense."

Mya jumped in. "But you know what? You are right. I don't need to be trying to force you to make a decision that your heart isn't in line with. It takes your heart *and* your mouth for salvation, so when your heart is ready, I will be glad to guide your mouth in what to say. You know my beliefs, and I don't want to bully you into anything, so the choice is yours to make whenever you are ready. As far as Sgt. Williams goes, we can call him right now if you would like. I have his number in my phone."

Raegan agreed and the two girls got into Mya's vehicle. She dialed Sgt. Williams phone number and, when he answered, told him that she had someone who needed to talk to him and probably press charges. He told her to come in with her friend the next morning and he would be happy to help get them whatever help they needed. After she got off the phone with Sgt. Williams, she drove Raegan home and dropped her off. She reiterated how proud of her she was, and how after they talked to Sgt. Williams the next morning, Raegan would feel like a brand new person. She told her that she was praying for her and that all was well, and she would see her the next day.

Raegan went into her house and headed straight for her bedroom. When she got there, she got undressed and put on some pajama bottoms and a t-shirt. She went into her bathroom and washed her face. She then ran a comb through her hair and quickly twisted it into loose braid. She went back into her room, took her cell phone out of her purse and climbed into her bed. She dialed DT Hudson's phone number, and leaned back onto her pillows, making herself comfortable while she waited for him to answer. When he did, she greeted him warmly and asked him if he had a little while to talk to her.

"Of course, Raegan. I meant what I said when I said that I am going to be here for you if you need me. So, what's up? What do you want to talk about?" DT was glad to hear from Raegan, and even happier to hear a little sparkle in her voice. That had been missing for some time, so he was interested to hear what had been going on with her since he last talked to her. It had to be good news, because he could actually hear a smile in her voice when she greeted him.

"Well, that's sort of why I called. I wanted to say thank you for what you did before."

"What did I do before?" DT was genuinely touched that this young woman had called to express her gratitude, but he wasn't quite sure what she was thanking him for. He hadn't felt like he made any headway with her during their last conversation, so he wasn't really expecting this sort of reaction from her now.

"I called you and you asked me all those questions and told me that you were going to get involved in my life and help me and do whatever you could for me. That was exactly what I needed at that time. And I don't know how you knew I needed it, but I'm glad you did. And I'm glad you suggested that I talk to Mya about what has been going on with me. I had been trying to deal with something all by myself, and because of that issue, I pushed everyone away, especially Mya, even though she's been a great friend and tried to talk to me a million different times, and I just wouldn't open up. But then I talked to you and you said what you said, and then almost as soon as we hung up, Mya called. And I did like you said. I told her what was happening and she talked to Mrs. Leisa and, long story short, they are helping me get through a very tough situation that I haven't been able to get myself out of for years. And I have you to thank for encouraging me to talk to them. I didn't feel like anybody cared about me, and you proved me wrong. So I wanted to say thank you."

DT smiled broadly at Raegan's kind words. Just then, Marcus' words came back to him about using his money in a productive, rather than destructive, way. He was reminded of an idea, and said to her, "Wow, Raegan. When we got off the phone that day, I really didn't think I had gotten through to you, and that I had just made a total fool of myself for what I did, but now I see that I wasn't just crazy for thinking I needed to say what I said. I didn't know where it was all leading, but I am so glad to hear that it somehow made a difference and things are working out for you. I don't feel like I deserve any sort of accolades or thanks for what I did. All I did was try to help and it was my pleasure. Thank *you* for calling to share that with me." He waited for a moment, and tried to get straight in his head what he was going to say next. "I know what it's like to struggle with something that you don't want the whole world to know. I know what it's like to keep secrets that eat away at your soul. So I am glad to hear that you were able to finally shed some light on whatever secret you were trying to keep so that it can be dealt with and put away. There is no better feeling in the world than to be able to share your whole self with people because you don't have anything to hide. It's going to be a wonderful thing to feel that freedom in your life. So, to help you celebrate this new chapter in your life, I'd like to do something for you. I want to offer you an internship at my company this summer. But it's going to have to be later in the summer, because, if you will accept, I would like to first send you and another student from your school, a young man named Ty Casey whose work I was introduced to by some new employees of mine, on a study abroad art trip to Italy for six weeks. Then you will have an open position at my company when you return for the remainder of the summer, but only until September. By then, I should have everything finalized for the art gallery that I am opening, where I'd like to commission you to be one of my premiere artists. So this trip to Italy isn't just a vacation for you. I will be expecting some great work when you get back. And I'm sure the teachers at the Institute for the Arts will have some high expectations too, when you are a freshman there in the fall. I was able to pull a few strings and get your acceptance confirmed early. That is the school you applied for, right?" He asked her, in a teasingly innocent tone.

Raegan was totally speechless on the other end. She could hardly believe what she was hearing. An art trip to Italy? With *Ty*? An internship? Original art in an art gallery? It was like she had just walked in on someone else's life and overheard a conversation between Mr. Hudson and the luckiest person in the world. This wasn't the sort of thing that happened to her. She was the girl that all the bad things always happened to, and no one seemed to be able to do anything good for her. And now here was this man offering to give her all of her heart's desires, just because he wanted to and was able to, if only she'd accept. Immediately, Mya's words about Jesus and his gift of salvation and abundant life came rushing back to her mind. She remembered how Mya said that everything led back to Jesus, and that everything good that happened was just another morsel He left to give us a glimpse of what was to come. She could see that right now in this situation. She could see that as wonderful as this gift that DT offered was, it was nothing compared to what Jesus wanted to do in her life.

DT interrupted her thoughts. "Listen, I know that I am putting you on the spot, Raegan. I want you to know that there are no strings attached to this offer. I just want to help. I have been talking to my really good friend and some really special employees of mine lately, and I have decided to give my heart to Christ. I see that He gave freely of Himself for my sake, and while I could never repay Him for that gift, I'd like to do what I can for the people He puts in my path on this earth. I hope that you will consider my offer, but even more than that, I hope that you will accept His. You are a wonderful young woman, and I know that He has an incredible plan for your life, and if I can help that purpose to come forth in any way, that is my only goal. Take some time to consider what I proposed and then get back to me."

"Mr. Hudson, you just don't know what this means to me. I haven't had anything this good happen to me in such a long time! It's like you peeked into my dreams, picked out the best parts and then told me you were going to make them come true. I don't even know what to say! So, before I say anything else, let me just say thank you so much for even offering me such a thing. It means so much to me that you would even care to hire me, let alone do all that you just said. I also want to say that I will definitely consider the other things you said. Mya has been talking to me about my salvation as well, and I know it's all the truth. I just need to be in the right mindset when I do accept Christ. I'd like to talk to you more about your decision when I can think clearly. You blew my mind with all that you just said to me! Would you be ok with sharing with me how you feel and what really made you finally decide to say yes to becoming a Christian?"

"Raegan, it would be my honor to share my story with you. And I hope you wouldn't mind sharing a little of yours with me." DT answered kindly.

Raegan smiled on the other end. "I'd really like that, Mr. Hudson. Again, thank you so much, and I will talk to you soon."

"I'm looking forward to it. Goodbye, Raegan."

"Jason! Come on in, son. Have a seat." Ill Will looked with concern at Jason and motioned for him to come inside his office. When Jason came through the doorway, Ill Will shut the door behind him. He then turned and came around Jason, patting him on the shoulder as he passed, and sat in the desk chair across from him. Before Jason could say a word, Will began speaking.

"Listen, son. I heard about what happened this weekend." At the mere mention of the ill-fated party, Jason's cheeks burned in embarrassment and humiliation all over again. He had hoped that he could just forget about that night and never revisit it. But not with this busybody of a man. He just *had* to bring it up again.

"What do you know about it?" he asked. Then he thought better of starting *that* conversation. "Never mind," he mumbled.

"Well, I know that I want to apologize for my nephew. When he gets to drinking, he can get a little, um," Will paused for a moment. "*Overzealous*," he finished, diplomatically. "I heard that he said some rather harsh things to you, and I don't want you to feel as though, in his altered state, he was a true representation of my family! We are much better than that." While he was speaking, Will had again gathered Jason in an intense gaze, just as he had the first time they met. He seemed to be speaking to Jason's inner self, and Jason felt as though he was slipping into some sort of trance. "We are much

292

kinder than that. He just really wanted you to have a good time at his gathering, and meet some new people. We heard about your breakup with Mya, and I know that's got to be hard on you. That's why I told him to invite you in the first place. I hope I wasn't out of line." Will stopped speaking and looked expectantly at Jason, waiting for his response.

Jason shook his head vigorously. His eyes were locked on Will's. "Oh, no, sir!" Jason heard himself speaking, but it was like what came out weren't his own words. He began saying things that he himself didn't even believe, but like some sort of out of body experience, it was as if he was on the outside watching himself have this conversation with no ability to do anything about what he heard himself saying. "I appreciate the thought. It wasn't all that bad anyway."

"Oh, well, I am glad to hear that. I'd hate for you to have been miserable at what I was told was to be the greatest party of the year!" He chuckled to himself. "Heinous is very confident in his party-throwing abilities. But he was quite distraught after you left that night. From what I heard, it was a total disaster. Apparently he didn't relay the night's events properly to me though, if you say it 'wasn't that bad'. Why don't you give me your side of the story?"

Not wanting to relive the horror of that night, and not ready to share with anyone what had happened at the coffeehouse afterward, Jason tried to change the subject. "It was no big deal. I was just still a little upset about the whole Mya situation and I think I may have overreacted a bit. I'm sure Heinous was just trying to show me a good time. I'm just still all over the place with losing my parents and then losing Mya too. I just don't think I was ready to hit the party scene yet."

As he spoke, his mind drifted back to that night, and to the young men he had spoken to at the coffee shop after he'd gotten out of the party. Outside, beside his truck, he'd finally managed to compose himself and had driven until he found the place and made his way inside. It was an encounter he would not soon forget.

Will cleared his throat loudly. Jason snapped back to attention. He had been so deep in his own thoughts that he forgot he was still sitting in Will's office.

"Well, as I said a moment ago, I know how hard the break-up with Mya must be on you. Especially now, with everything else you have going on. But you know what? I always say, everything happens for a reason. I know it's hard to fathom right now, but maybe this was the best thing that could have happened. I mean, if she's not the girl for you, then wouldn't you rather know that now, instead of investing a lot of time and energy in a doomed relationship? I don't mean to sound harsh. I just think you're young. You have your whole life ahead of you, and if she's not the one, then someone better is out there. You can be free now to sow your oats. Play the field. Date around. There's no need to be tied down yet."

Jason's head had started pounding almost as soon as Will began speaking, and a migraine was developing behind his left ear. Will's words really bothered him, and he knew that he wouldn't be able to just sit and listen to him talk badly about Mya. This all reminded him even more of the coffee shop guys from that night after the party. They had mentioned some things about what to do when his head started swimming like this, and when he felt as though someone was making him lose control of his own thoughts. He tried desperately to bring back to his memory all of what they had told him. They'd all had such a great conversation that night. He hadn't felt that good since before his parents died. But, sitting in that little office, Will's voice seemed to drown out their words, and he couldn't unscramble the jumble of notions swirling about in his mind. Confusion gripped his intellect and he couldn't separate his own thoughts from the words that Will was speaking. He knew that there was something that the guys at the coffee shop had told him that he needed to remember about Will specifically. But no matter how hard he strained, he couldn't recall what it was. His mind was lost in Will's stare. Whatever those young men had wanted him to keep in mind was fading fast.

Suddenly, there was a knock at the door. It opened and a young man stuck his head in. Jason turned around and found the young man looking directly at him. He smiled and winked at Jason. He then became stone-faced and said to Will, in an almost mechanical voice, "Excuse me for interrupting, but I was sent to remind you to go see your supervisor this afternoon. He has some issue with your plans, and needs to talk to you." And then, just as quickly as he appeared, he disappeared back out the door. His disruption gave Jason just enough time to break free from Will's gaze and words and think back to that night after the party when he went and talked to the young men at the coffeehouse. He racked his brain, and for a few moments had some clarity. He was starting to remember what they had been telling him.

When he arrived to the coffee shop that night, still shaken and breathing irregularly, the group of football players stood up. Each one embraced him as though they knew him. At any other time, he would have felt uneasy with this much physical affection from strange men that he didn't know, but he was so frightened from what he had just experienced back at the house with Heinous that the hugs were a welcome relief. When they all had a chance to greet him, they all stepped back and looked intently at him.

Creede started speaking first. "Jason, we are glad that you came. You don't need to be afraid anymore."

Immediately, Jason felt safe. At the sound of Creede's words, all the fear that had built up inside of him vanished in an instant. He felt as if he were standing inside of a helium filled balloon. He felt lighter than air, and found himself looking down just to make sure that he wasn't floating away. *Who* are *these guys*, he asked himself again, marveling at what power they exuded.

As if answering his question, one of the two young men that hadn't been at the party stepped forward. "I'm Felix. And this is Ben," he finished, pointing to the second guy. "We've heard a lot about you, Jason, and we'd really like to be your friends." The sincerity in Ben's words was palpable.

In the back of his mind, Jason was shocked at how comfortable he was with these guys he didn't know, even though they talked to him and acted like they already knew him. He wasn't against close relationships or anything, but he didn't really have men in his life who were so free with their feelings and expressions of their caring. "I'd like that," he said to them, and really meant it from his heart. He didn't know if they would approve of the things that he had been doing lately, but he really felt like they wouldn't abandon him just because he didn't have everything together at the moment.

Ben spoke this time. "Well, let's sit down and talk. Would you like some coffee?"

Jason nodded his head. He figured a bit of coffee may do him some good and counteract the alcohol in his system. He hadn't had that much to drink, but he knew that every little bit made a difference, especially in someone like him, who wasn't much of a drinker anyway. Ben called over one of the waiters and ordered coffee for everyone. Then they all sat down and made themselves comfortable. Then they all returned their gazes to Jason. Again, in any other situation, he would have been nervous having all those eyes fixed on him, but with these guys, he felt completely relaxed.

Bryce got the conversation started with a question. "So, Jason, what happened after we left the party?" He had the same tone in his voice that Jason had heard when he first spoke to him when they met at the party. It was as if he already knew the answer, but was just giving Jason the chance to say it aloud and really process it for himself.

Jason shuddered when he thought about what had just happened. "Well, long story short, Heinous scared the mess out of me."

"Yeah? How so?" Felix pressed.

"Well, he grabbed me and looked at me with these crazy eyes. I mean, I know he was drunk, but it was more than that. There was something, like, *otherworldly* about him. And he kept saying that he was going to be after me, and if I left the party, I would regret it. He just kept saying things about how I belonged with them and that he was going to make sure that was where I ended up."

"Who do you think the 'them' was that he kept talking about?" asked Ben.

"That's the thing. I don't know. But I do know he wasn't talking about the people at the party. There was something much deeper in what he was saying. I'm just not sure what it was."

"I think you're right, Jason. You see, we've known Heinous for a very long time and we've seen him do this many times before. He is ruthless when it comes to getting what he wants. He gets his eye on someone he thinks will be good for his team, and he will stop at nothing to get them. He will manipulate, intimidate, dominate and whatever else it takes to get his way." Creede looked solemnly at Jason.

Then Bryce asked the question that Jason was hoping wouldn't come up in the conversation. "Well, how did you get in contact with him in the first place?"

Jason struggled to find words that wouldn't make him sound too bad. "His uncle is the conservator of my finances since my parents died."

"Oh, and he told you about Heinous' party tonight?" There again was that knowing tone Bryce was so fond of using.

Jason hung his head. "No. He didn't invite me. Heinous runs a website that I've visited a couple of times and he sent me an email inviting me to the party."

Bryce kept digging. "Oh. Well, what kind of website does he run?"

Even though Bryce's tone wasn't accusatory in the least, Jason felt like he had shrunk down to only a few inches tall. He did not want to tell these guys what kind of site he had been looking at. He didn't want them to know that he had gotten interested in pornography. They were obviously strong men with high morals, and if they knew what kind of perverted junk he was looking at, surely they would decide he wasn't worth their time or energy. And he realized right then that he desperately wanted them to be his friends. He had never felt so connected to anyone in such a few short moments of meeting them. Heinous' degrading words came flying back to his mind with blinding clarity, ringing like a clanging cymbal inside his head: "Who do you think you are...You think you will fit in with these guys and their super spiritual friends? I don't think they would approve of what you've been looking at. Have you told them about that…I don't think these boys would be so interested in you if they knew what kind of guy you really are!" He couldn't pick up his head, or find his voice to admit to what kind of website he had been visiting.

"Jason, it's alright. Look at us. No matter what has happened, or what Heinous has said to you, you don't need to be ashamed. We're not going to walk away from you just because you may have made some missteps. What kind of site was it?" Creede reached over and patted Jason on the back.

With everything that was in him, Jason fought back the tears that were playing around the corners of his eyes. "It's a pornography site," he said quietly. He looked up at the four young men around him. None of them had moved or changed their expression. His whole body relaxed with relief. It felt as if a heavy weight had been lifted off him. He was glad to have been able to tell someone about what he had been doing, and even more grateful that his disclosure hadn't sent his new friends packing. He waited for one of them to respond.

"And how long have you been looking at this pornography site?" Ben asked him.

"Just a few weeks. I started after I met Will. He gave me a card with the site address on it. He told me that if Mya wouldn't, you know, do stuff with me, then no one could blame me for just looking at girls online. For some reason, I believed him and started looking."

"And how has that been working for you? Do you feel like looking at that site has met your needs and made things easier in your relationship with Mya?" Felix asked.

"Actually, no, not at all. Since I started looking at the website, I've been having all these really strong urges and sexual thoughts toward Mya. And then when I tried to get a little closer to her, we ended up fighting and breaking up. That's how I wound up at Heinous' party tonight. He invited me because he thought it would take my mind off Mya to meet some new girls."

"Well, from what we hear, your troubles really got started when Will came into your life. He does not sound like someone you should take advice from or spend a whole lot of time with. Jason, it is so important to be careful of who you allow to speak into your life. You can't let just anyone advise you on how to live. If they are telling you to do things that you would be embarrassed to do out in a public place, but is alright in the dark somewhere, you don't need to listen to them. This Will character seems like he does not have your best interest at heart. He may be the conservator over your finances for now, but that doesn't mean he has to be conservator over your life. Don't let him lead you down the wrong path. Stay away from people who try to manipulate you or control how you think. If they want to change your mind, it should be by showing you what the benefits of following them are. They shouldn't brainwash you or try to control your thoughts."

"Felix is right, Jason. Please be careful who you listen to. If someone just tells you something that you don't believe or that doesn't give you a sense of calm in your heart, think twice before you heed their voice. Everyone is not for your good. There are those in this world whose only goal is to steal, kill and destroy. So, be careful. We know that your parents aren't here anymore, but there have to be people in your life right now who love you and who are interested only in your well-being. Stick with those people. And now you can include the four of us in that group." Creede beamed at Jason as he spoke.

Jason smiled briefly, but then became sad again. "Well, I had a great support system behind me, but I think I may have messed that up when I upset Mya and we broke up. Her family has been so great to me, but now that she and I are no longer dating, I don't know how that's going to work anymore. And my teacher, Mrs. Carson was the same way. But she is much closer to Mya than she is me, and I think she will take Mya's side now."

Bryce jumped in. "Well, I wouldn't be so sure of that. There are no sides here. I'm positive that if these people loved you when you were with Mya, they will love you still. You just have to keep an open attitude with all of them. And that includes Mya. You can't think that any of this is easy for her either. I'm sure she is struggling as well with concerns for how things are going to work out. Just because your relationship has changed right now doesn't mean that she doesn't still care for you and hope for your best. You just have to give this situation time. You may be surprised at how things turn out in the end."

Thoughts of Mya flooded Jason's heart once again. The words his new friends spoke to him reminded him of words that she had shared with him so many times before, when she tried to minister to him about life and his need for salvation. "The important thing to remember is that the only one you can always depend on in any situation is Jesus Christ. He is the one Person who will never leave you, nor forsake you. When everything around you seems to be like quicksand, you can always call out to Him and He will be there to save you. He wants to be in a relationship with you and He wants you to be able to face all the temptations that will come your way. He wants you to be victorious in this life. Without Him, you will fall every time. Being a child of God won't stop you from being attacked by the enemy while you are on the earth, but it will provide you the means to overcome any and every negative thing that comes against you—body, mind and soul. So you need to make the choice of whether you want to face this life without Christ or if you are ready to make Him the Lord of your life. It's up to you, but I am ready to stand with you if you want to take a stand for Him and accept His sacrifice as the price for your salvation."

As much as Jason was enjoying talking to Ben and the other guys, when they began talking, and he was reminded of Mya's words about Jesus and eternity and getting saved, he got uncomfortable. Just like he did when she talked about Him, Jason felt a prick in his heart, but he just wasn't ready to make a commitment to be a follower of Jesus. "Well, thank you guys for listening. I'll definitely keep that in mind. It's getting late though. I think I better head home."

They asked if they could exchange phone numbers before he left. He agreed and put each of their numbers into his cell phone. They left him with this warning, "Don't be fooled, Jason. Your true enemy is a subtle opponent. He won't attack you wearing a scaly red suit with horns and a pitchfork. He will come to you dressed for success, and will only give you glimpses of the parts of his plan that look good to you. And his main battlefield isn't physical. It's your mind."

"JASON!" Will nearly shouted his name, and sounded if he had been calling him for quite some time.

Jason looked up awkwardly, wondering how many times Will had called his name. "Uh, yes, sir?"

"Well, I am glad you are back with me, son! I was beginning to wonder if I needed to call someone to come and give you CPR or something! You just completely zoned out. I hope you weren't still thinking about that little party incident. What do you say we just leave that one behind and move forward?" He locked his eyes on Jason's again. "I wanted to talk to you about something else though. I know that you have really been dealing with a lot here in the last few weeks. And it really seems to be taking it's toll on you. I'm just concerned for you, son, and I'd like to offer some advice to try to help." Will exuded sympathy, but something felt less than honorable about his true intentions. Even so, with his eyes relentlessly focused on Jason's, Jason, like a mindless android, just kept nodding and absorbing every word he spoke.

"Yes, sir."

"I just think you need to take some time for yourself. You just need to take a little while and figure out what it is that you want out of life. It seems to me like you've had a lot of people telling you what you should do, and telling you that it's time for you to make a decision about your life and your future. And they are right. It *is* time for you to make some decisions. But you can't let other people live your life for you. You just need to get away from all the people that are putting so many thoughts in your head. You need to just clear your mind, and sort through all the opinions that people are throwing your way as to where you should go from here. I mean, am I right? Do you feel like it's hard for you to hear yourself think because of all the other voices in your head?"

Jason kept nodding. "Yes, sir. I feel like I don't know what I want to do with my life. Everyone keeps telling me what they think is best. But I don't know what is best."

"You see? That's what I am talking about. You should be able to plan your own future. Captain your own ship, if you will. It's just not right that everyone is trying to tell you what to do. They don't know what you have been through or how you feel."

"Right. I just want everyone to shut up for a little while. Just let me figure it out!"

"I totally understand. Let me ask you something. Have you considered going back to Burney? I know that after everything that happened with your folks, it's got to be hard being here alone. And I just think the change of scenery may be just what you need. Are there any friends you still have in Burney that you might be able to go stay with for a while? What about an old girlfriend or something whose family you were close to that may be willing to take you in?"

Suddenly, Kendall Greenley's face flashed across Jason's mind. Kendall was a girl in Burney that he had dated before he moved to Faries and met Mya. She was the all-American girl, and they'd had a good relationship and remained friends, even after they broke up. He hadn't thought about her much lately, but at Will's suggestion, he thought it might be a good idea to give her a call. Maybe a trip out to see her would be good for him. He didn't have anything keeping him in Faries, now that his parents were dead and his relationship with Mya had fallen apart.

"I can see that someone just popped into your mind when I said that. Listen, I don't want to be another one of those voices telling you what you should do, but it just seems to me that you need the break. So I am just going to give a little friendly advice and say, go for it if you want to. I've made sure that all your financials are in order, and can get you set up with the money for a plane ticket or whatever other accommodations you may need, and you can be well on your way. Don't you have some sort of break coming up soon?"

"Yes, sir, I actually do. We will be getting out for Thanksgiving break soon. Some of my parents' friends back in Burney have already said that I can come and stay with them while we are out of school. So I think that I will do just what you said. You're right. I do need the break. I need to get away from here for a while and clear my head. Thanks for the suggestion. Can I call you in a few days and have you help me set this trip up? I don't really know what all I would need to do." Jason was getting more excited at the idea of a trip back to his hometown. But what really got his blood pumping was the notion that he would be able to see Kendall. She was a lot more like him than Mya was, and he was sure that she would be up for some adventures without preaching to him about why everything he wanted to do was wrong in the eyes of God. His heart started racing, and he could hardly stay in his seat. He was starting to anticipate this visit like a starving dog would a juicy steak.

"Absolutely! Just give me a call when you are ready, and we will get you all taken care of. I'm glad you like the idea, Jason. I think this is going to be the trip of a lifetime for you."

"Thanks, Will! I really appreciate your help." Somehow during the course of the afternoon, Jason had gone from dreading any time he had to spend talking to Will to wanting to leap across the table and hug him. He had allowed himself to be carried to the exact spot the young men at the coffee shop had warned him about going. But he was blissfully unaware that he had, with that one poorly thought out decision, become embroiled in the fight of his life, and had just placed his heart in the center of the bulls-eye.

Ill Will smirked. "You bet, son! It is no trouble at all."

~

Jason was driving toward his house from his meeting with Will when his phone rang. He knew from the ringtone that it was Mya, and he was shocked that she was calling him. He picked up, answering casually, "Hello?"

Mya's heart caught in her throat at the sound of Jason's voice. "Um, hi, Jason." It took every ounce of mental strength she possessed not to let her usual *Chaz* slip out. "I just wanted to talk to you. Do you have a moment?" She tried to keep her voice from shaking. She had not been this nervous to speak to him since their first official meeting. In fact, she wasn't this nervous even then!

"Sure. What's up?" Jason kept his voice as level as possible. It was strange to hear Mya call him 'Jason' after all this time, and he was intrigued by the fact that she had called him and wondered what she wanted, but he also had Kendall on his mind. He really wanted to get Mya off the phone as quick as possible because he wanted to get back to daydreaming about seeing Kendall without any guilt, and the thoughts he was entertaining would certainly not be appropriate while he was speaking with his ex.

Mya cleared her throat and tried to calm herself down a little before she spoke again. She took a few deep breaths and then said,

"Well, I just wanted to call you and tell you that I miss you. I mean, I miss your friendship. I hate that we broke up the way we did, but I think it hurts worse that we aren't really even friends anymore." She stopped to see if he would say anything, and when he didn't, she pressed on. "I just wanted to let you know that our relationship was real to me. And it doesn't stop just because we aren't dating anymore. I love you, and I always will. That hasn't changed. You still have a piece of my heart, and I still think about you and pray for you all the time. It's just that I don't think I can do the things you want me to and be ok with myself. I want to be with you, but I'm just not ready to take things to the next level. And if that means that we can't be together, then as much as it tears me apart inside, that's just how it's going to have to be. But as I said before, I hope that us not dating doesn't mean that we can't be friends. I really want you in my life."

Jason chose his words carefully. "Well, that's cool, I guess. I just don't know, though, Mya. I don't know if I'm ready to step back into all of that. I just need some time to figure some things out, ok?" His mind was still on Kendall. He knew that she wouldn't have nearly as many stipulations on a relationship with him. And he was getting a little tired of Mya's "Little Miss Perfect" routine. Still, he didn't want to hurt her. He couldn't deny that his love for her was real and still lingered in his heart.

"Of course! Yeah, sure, I understand." Mya replied, forcing a cheerful tone into her voice. "I'm not trying to push you into anything you are not ready for. I just wanted you to know how I feel. Um, on a different note, my parents told me to invite you to join us for Thanksgiving dinner, if you'd like."

"Oh, well, um, tell them I said thanks, but I won't be able to make it. I decided to go back to Burney during Thanksgiving break. So I won't be in town. But let them know I appreciate the invitation." Jason hoped Mya would end the conversation soon. He didn't want to answer too many questions about his plans. And he was pretty sure she didn't want to know what he was expecting out of this trip anyway. He was relieved by her reply.

"I see. Well, that's cool. It will be good for you to go back and see some of your old friends and your loved ones out there. I hope you have a really great trip. I'll be praying for you. I guess I'll talk to you later. Bye, Jason."

"See you around."

After his experience with Wade, Malcolm, Martin, Marcus and DT, Edward Carson felt like a new man. He was renewed and invigorated and felt as though his spirit had been lifted to a height he had never known was available. The weight of the guilt he had been feeling since his daughter's death and his encounters with Lead Astray had been lifted and he was happy to leave all that in the past. In the place of his shame, he felt a sense of devotion and adoration for his wife that was steadily swelling up inside his heart, and surpassed any physical sensation he had ever experienced. He found himself elated at the very thought of going home to her, willfully sharing his heart, and joyfully receiving hers.

He wanted to hold her, and pray with her and love her the way He knew the Lord would have Him do. He wanted to show his affection as the natural expression of the unfailing love of a spiritual God. He wanted to be like the lover that he read about in the Bible. He wanted his wife to know that she was the most precious and valuable thing he had. The revelation of all this struck him like a bolt of lightning, and electrified to blinding brightness what he had always known was the truth—that he treasured his wife and no one else could ever take her place. His new friends at the office had just peeled away the layers of cunning trickery that Lead Astray had so painstakingly wrapped him in to reveal what still lay inside.

As he drove home from work that day, Edward opened his heart to the Lord and made a very specific request. "Lord, please protect my wife's ears. Please protect her tongue. Please protect my ears and my tongue. Let us not say anything to one another except what you want us to. And let us not hear anything except your truth. Knit our hearts together and bind us once more with the three fold cord that can not be broken. Thank you, Lord. In Jesus' name I pray, amen." His heart fluttered when he pulled into his driveway. Even though he had been living and crossing paths with his wife for this entire season, he hadn't felt connected to her since Annette passed away. But as he prepared to go inside the house, he felt like a teenage boy going on his first date. His palms began sweating, his mouth went dry, and he actually found himself checking to make sure he smelled alright. That part made him laugh. It was a genuine, belly laugh, and another reminder of all he had been missing out on since he ejected himself from his own marriage. He was looking forward to getting reacquainted with his wife and the love they shared, and to rediscover all the wonderful things that made his life on this earth have meaning.

Edward was also starting to notice the vibrancy of the world around him. Everywhere he turned now gave his senses a thrill ride of color and brilliance. For a while, he had been trying so hard to keep his secrets hidden away that he could no longer focus on the beauty of God's creation. It had come to the point that when he looked around, it wasn't to enjoy the scenery. It was to make sure that no one he knew was around to see what he was doing or where he was going or who he was with. His paranoia had taken the place of his curiosity and enjoyment of nature. He didn't have a chance to stop and smell the daisies because he was trying to make sure that he didn't smell of another woman's perfume. He didn't have the time to spot a majestic eagle that flew overhead because he had to make it to his rendezvous spots on time. He had missed out on so much of what God had already so generously given for him to enjoy his life by trying to experience something that didn't belong to him.

No more! He vowed to himself. *That part of my life is over! I'm forgiven and set free!* After he met and hired the three new employees for DT's company and spent some time with them, it was like a light switch in his spirit had been flipped back into the 'on' position and he came to his senses. He was mortified when he thought of what he had been doing behind his wife's back. And while his visits with Lead Astray had never turned sexually physical, they were definitely not purely platonic. But he had confessed his indiscretions with his new friends at work, and they had set him straight and prayed with him for restored commitment within his own marriage, and for him to exercise his ability to evict Lead Astray and their improper relationship out of his life for good.

So now, he was ready. He had removed all traces of Lead Astray from his life and was excited to make a fresh start with his darling, Mrs. Leisa Annette Piper Carson. He walked into the house and looked around for his wife. She was in the kitchen, sweeping the floor and he was nearly overwhelmed by how stunning she looked at that very moment, with her dark brown hair pulled back, and her face slightly flushed. *Lord, I'd forgotten how beautiful my own wife is! Forgive me for taking her for granted. And may she forgive me as well.* She hadn't noticed him come into the house, so he quickly ducked around the corner before she saw him. He decided to quietly sneak up behind her. He tiptoed around, and when her back was to him, he put his hands out and slipped his arms around her waist.

He nuzzled his face in her hair and kissed her neck. She squealed in surprise, but quickly dissolved into delighted giggles. She turned to face him, and looked deep into his eyes. Tears glistened in her blue-green eyes, making them sparkle like the sun reflecting off the ocean's surface.

"Hi," was all she could whisper before the tears started flowing down her cheeks.

Edward tightened his grip around her and whispered back, his mouth gently brushing against her ear, "Hi." She laid her head onto the space between his shoulder and his neck, wrapped her arms around him and wept. He felt her body relax against his, and he held her for a long time. When she finally pulled away from him and looked up into his face, he asked her, "Can we talk?"

She nodded her head, and took his hand. They walked into the living room together and sat side by side on the couch. She still clutched his hand, and stroked it gently. They sat in silence for a few moments, and then she spoke. "I've missed you."

All of a sudden, the sadness and pain of the last few months and being away from the one person who knew how to hold things together hit Edward like a bullet to the chest. He began sobbing as he slid to his knees on the floor in front of his wife. He took her face in his hands and looked her in the eyes. "I am *so* sorry, Leisa. I was not the husband I promised you I would always do my best to be. I left you when I should have stayed by your side. I let my own grief cloud the fact that you were hurting too. I gave the enemy free reign in my heart. And I hurt you in the process. I was so terribly wrong and I want to know if you will please forgive me."

Leisa's tears began flowing again. She covered his hands with her own. "My love, don't you know that I have already forgiven you? All I wanted was for you to come back to me. The past doesn't matter. All that matters is where we go from here, and that we go together." She leaned forward until her forehead was pressed against his. "I have never stopped praying for you. I know that this has been the hardest thing you have ever had to face. I just want to be there to help hold up your arms while you fight. I don't want you to pretend that it's all ok and you don't feel any pain. It's alright to hurt. Of course you will hurt. We just can't let the pain pull us away from the truth. And the truth is that in everything that happens in our lives, both good and bad, Jesus Christ is still our Lord. He is still on the throne and He still has our best interest at the forefront of his mind. We just have to trust him. And we have to trust each other." She sat up and took his hands into her lap. "So will you trust Us?"

Still kneeling in front of her, he squeezed her hands and nodded his head. "With my very life."

"Good answer!" she said playfully, through her tears. She reached down and brushed the tears from his face. "How about we seal this with a prayer?"

"My thoughts exactly." The two stood up and joined hands. Edward began, "Our Father, who art in heaven, hallowed be your name. Your kingdom come, your will be done, in earth, in us, in our lives, today and everyday, just as it is in heaven. We come before you tonight in humility and gratitude, knowing that only because of the blood of your precious Son Jesus, can we come boldly before your throne of grace. Thank you for free access to your presence. Lord, I ask you to forgive me and cleanse me from all my unrighteousness. I am so sorry for taking this wonderful woman that you sent into my life for granted. I know that I have not been the husband you ordained me to be, nor the husband she has needed me to be.

313

For that, I am truly sorry. Please remove the guilt and shame of my mistakes and send them as far as the east is from the west, so that, together, we can move forward, new creatures, in newness of life. Lord, I ask that you would rekindle the flame that burns within Leisa and me for one another. Help us, Lord, to rebuild the relationship I nearly destroyed. Give her the strength, Lord, to continue on as you would have her to do, and help me to be a better man. Thank you for putting such a precious and rare gift into my life. May I walk worthy of the call to be her husband. Lord, give us daily opportunities to show forth our love for one another, and to honor the memory of our Annie, the beautiful woman you called home to be with you. May our sorrow and mourning be turned to gladness and dancing, for your glory. May we always present our lives as living sacrifices, well pleasing in your sight. In Jesus' name. Amen."

Almost as soon as Edward closed his prayer, the telephone rang, startling the two momentarily. Leisa kissed his hands, then turned and walked over to the phone and answered. Edward noticed her expression change, registering surprise and confusion. "Sure, hold on a second." She pressed a button on the cradle of the phone that sent the call to speakerphone. "Ok, we are both here." She motioned for Edward to come closer so that he could be included in the conversation.

"Hello, Mr. Carson. As I was telling your wife, my name is Emery Tyne and I am a nurse at the trauma center. I'm calling because I have some interesting news to share. I asked to be put on speakerphone so that you and your wife could both hear all the details at once."

"Of course. Go ahead." Edward spoke into the phone. He reached over and pulled Leisa closer to his side. He draped his arm around her shoulder and she put her arm around his waist. Neither of them knew what to expect from this phone call.

"Alright. Well, first of all, let me say that I am so sorry to hear about the loss of your daughter. That is actually what I am calling about. I feel like I have been around the world in eighty days trying to get in touch with you, so let me start from the very beginning. All of what I'm about to say started with the train wreck. We saw many, many people come through the center that day and for many days following. It was a really difficult situation, because many of the people who came in were not from Faries and did not have their identification information readily available. So, we had to do a lot of digging just to figure out who most of them were and to be able to contact their friends and families to let them know about what had happened to them. Anyway, we had several patients who were critically injured and were unable to provide any help in telling us who they were or where they had come from. Well, I have been assigned to one such patient since the day of the accident. Along with another nurse named Adabel, I have been taking care of him in the ICU. Adabel is a relief nurse who steps in when she is needed. Anyway, this young man has been in a coma since they flew him in." Emery paused to catch her breath, and Leisa found herself grinning from ear to ear. Hearing this young woman talk was like hearing Annie speak. She thought about how Annie used to tell a story and would just talk a mile a minute, only pausing long enough to suck down another big gulp of air and start again. Emery was relaying her story the same way. "Anyway, the good news is that the young man came out of his coma the other night. Unfortunately, I wasn't there. It was during Adabel's part of the shift. But he woke up and was able to give Adabel some information, which she then passed on to me. She told me to contact a lady she knew named Ernestine Casey, and *she* gave me your information, so now I am talking to you!" she finished breathlessly.

"Ok. Well, what did you need to contact us for?" Edward asked politely, though clearly still confused.

Emery started up again. "Right!" she continued. "So, I thought to myself that this was a roundabout way to help someone, but I called Teenie anyway. When I told her who I was and why I was calling, she nearly flipped her lid! She's a spunky old girl!" Emery chuckled. "But she told me that I had to call and talk to you two. So here I am. Does the name 'Caden Braime' ring a bell to either of you?"

Leisa and Edward looked at each other. Edward shook his head. Leisa closed her eyes and ran through a mental list of the names she recognized. The one Emery mentioned sounded familiar, but she couldn't put a face with it. She told Emery as much.

"Well, he said that he was on his way to visit his girlfriend's family. His girlfriend's name is Annette Carson. That's your daughter right?" As soon as she said the words, Leisa's mind cleared and she remembered where she'd heard the name. It was during one of her conversations with Annie. She told her that she had been on a few dates with a wonderful freelance journalist named Caden Braime. She confirmed that information and her daughter's name to Emery. "Well, here is the thing, Mr. and Mrs. Carson. Caden is doing extremely well now that he is awake. All of his vitals are normal and he is showing no signs of brain damage or any other permanent injuries. His leg is broken, and he has a couple of cracked ribs, but those will heal just fine. He will be ready to leave the hospital in a few days. I have been talking to him a lot since he came to, and have really gotten a sense of the kind of woman your daughter was. He really loved her. In fact, he told me last night that he was going to talk to you two about asking for Annette's hand in marriage in the near future. Just by the way he talks about her, I just know that she was an incredible person and a committed woman of God. I admire her and I've never even met her. It was so difficult to tell him she died in the wreck. I don't mean to drag this out. I just wanted to be sure that you knew all that before I say what I am about to say next." She took a deep breath. "As I mentioned, Caden will be able to leave the hospital soon, but he is not fit for long distance travel yet. He is from New York, and doesn't know anyone here in Faries. So, Adabel and Teenie suggested that I ask you two if you would be willing to let him come and stay with you while he is recovering. It will be several weeks at least, and I understand if you don't want to take on that kind of burden, but I thought I would at least ask."

Edward and Leisa stared at each other in amazement. They had just asked the Lord for an opportunity to present itself as a token of their recommitment to one another and also to honor their beloved daughter. And right on cue, here was one, dropped into their lap. Neither hesitated, and they said in unison, "Of course!"

The relief in Emery's voice was evident. "Oh, my gosh! Really? Oh, that's incredible! Thank you guys so much! He's going to be so happy to hear this! I will call you back in a few days and get everything set up. Right now, I have some really good news to deliver to a really great man!" She stopped for a moment. "Wait a minute! I've just asked you to take in a strange man that you don't know without any real information. How about this? Why don't you guys come up to the center tomorrow and come meet him and talk to him a little. Then we can all iron out the details together. How does that sound?"

The Carson's agreed and set up a time to go up to the trauma center and meet Caden and Emery. They said their goodbyes and hung up.

"Can you believe this? Annette's boyfriend? I can't wait to meet him and see what kind of man our little girl was bringing home. I see God all over this, don't you?" Leisa asked her husband, smiling and shaking her head in disbelief.

"All over." he replied. "Well, you better call Teenie. You know she is probably bursting at the seams waiting to hear your reaction to this news!"

"You're probably right. But, wow! A son-in-law! Tomorrow we are going to meet the man who could have been our son-in-law! We lost our daughter, but then the Lord brought a son into our lives. He's amazing, isn't He?" She walked over and put her arms around her husband. "He restores everything the enemy steals from us. And it's always better than we could ever anticipate. I'm so excited! About everything! You and me, Caden, Emery. Just *everything*! We serve a great, big God, don't we, Eddie?"

Edward leaned down and kissed Leisa tenderly on her forehead. "Yes, we do, baby. We serve a great, big God."

His hollow chest heaving, Satan roamed to and fro, like a hungry lion seeking to devour the first prey he laid his eyes upon. *Do these people think this thing is over? It's never over!* he mused within himself. *I'm just getting started. They haven't seen anything yet!* Although a few demons had again failed miserably in their missions, the devil tucked away his echoing irritation to use against them for a later time. Right now, he needed to reorganize. It was time to regroup, rearrange his strategy and put in order a new plan of attack. Not easily discouraged, he didn't back down at all from the challenges that stood before him. Failure had never slowed him down before, and this time was no exception. He had an extra special assignment to dole out today. It could be the single most important task of this battle for the souls of the inhabitants of the earth. His success depended entirely upon the taskmaster he set over this mission. And he knew exactly who to send.

"Come!" he bellowed. Immediately, the space was filled with the underlings of the underworld. Satan took his place in front of the horde. He faced them and raised his arms high and wide in a sweeping gesture that encompassed them all.

"Today, we begin anew! We must move ahead! This world is mine and I *will* control it! I AM the lord and these people will not stop my kingdom from reigning upon the earth! And once I conquer this world, I will ascend and triumph in the heavens, and they will be mine as well! And then I will be sovereign over this entire universe! Are you ready to rule with me?"

"Yes, lord! We will rule and reign with you!" the legions ranted and chanted their agreement to his misplaced desires. They clamored and clawed for the chance to show forth their adulation and exaltation of the god of the earth. They pushed and shoved and cried and hissed. They bowed and waved. The noise of it all resounded in the ears of the devil like the swell of a well trained orchestra at the climactic height of a well written composition.

Satan scanned the crowd until his eyes landed on the one he was searching for. "Ah, Baal Berith, there you are. Come forward, my friend! Today is your day! I have a work that only you can perform. I think about your past works and it sends the most delicious chills down my spine. No one else can deceive the Christians the way you can. And, like always, it's those so-called believers who are giving me the most headache. Of course, the non-believers are like putty in my hands. Therefore, my main focus must be those infuriating radicals! That is where you come in. It's time for us to strike them the hardest! Can you handle the task?"

Baal Berith stepped forward, and bowed his knee to the floor before Satan. "Yes, my lord. Your will is my command."

~

Unfettered by the loaded threats of the enemy of mankind, the melodic voice of the Lord rang out strong and clear through eternity. He spoke to His angels, His messengers of light. "You all have made Me proud! But our work is not yet complete. There is much left to do. The fiery darts of the devil have not been extinguished yet. You must continue to take the message of My love to My people. I AM their Light in the dark places. I AM their Way out of no way. I AM the Lord that made the smith that blows the coals in the fire, but no weapon that he forms against them will prosper. I AM the God that keeps them in perfect peace when their minds are stayed on Me. I AM their Strong Tower, and they can run to Me and be safe. I AM the Lord that has given them power over all the power of the enemy and nothing shall by any means harm them. Tell them! Share the message of hope that lies in My Word. Encourage them. Strengthen their battle-wearied hearts. Remind them that their troubles won't last always, and this too shall pass. Open the eyes of their understanding to My Truth—My love for them is unfailing, My grace is sufficient for them, and My strength is made perfect in their weakness. I AM the Lord their God who reigns upon the throne. Go forth!"

About the Author

Keiah Ellis is a passionate, young author from Shreveport, Louisiana. She is thrilled about the completion of her first novel, which she envisions to be the first in a series. Aside from her love of writing, she is a self-proclaimed foodie whose favorite pastimes include cooking, eating, entertaining, and spending time with her family and friends. She loves music, and sings in the Praise and Worship ministry with her dad at their church. She has a heart for teenage girls, and has a vision to start her own women's ministry in the very near future. At 25 years old, she is the younger of two sisters, and currently lives with her parents, who recently celebrated 30 years of marriage. She loves God with all her being, and strives daily to be a light in darkness, bringing glory to her Lord and Savior, Jesus Christ, with every opportunity she is presented!

Breinigsville, PA USA
12 April 2010
235946BV00003B/2/P